SHADOW PARTISAN

A Novella By NADJA TESICH

New Rivers Abroad

NEW RIVERS PRESS

Library of Congress Catalog Card Number: 88-62982
ISBN 0-89823-108-6
Front Cover Painting, "Red Horses," by S. Gall (from a private collection)
Author Photograph by Nat Boxer
Typesetting and Design by Peregrine Publications, Inc.
Edited by Vivian Vie Balfour

The author would like to thank the MacDowell Colony where she started this book and Yaddo where she finished it. And Dean, as always.

Shadow Partisan was published with the aid of grants from the First Bank System Foundation and the Arts Development Fund of the United Arts Council (with support from the McKnight Foundation).

New Rivers Press books are distributed by
The Talman Company
150-5th Avenue
New York, NY 10011

Shadow Partisan has been published in a first edition of 3000 copies by New Rivers Press (C. W. Truesdale, Editor/Publisher), 1602 Selby Ave., St. Paul, MN 55104.

FOR STEFAN, STOJAN, MOTHER;

and for all my families

CHAPTER ONE

G ERMAN SOLDIERS came once in the middle of the night in that little house where we lived that winter four of us in one room, the old couple sleeping in the kitchen next to the stove. Soldiers carried everything out, blankets, sheets, pillows, everything mother rescued from the other time before. A tall blond man, a giant in a helmet snatches my blanket, my blue one the one I always had, I snatch it back then he points his gun at me but grandma was faster. She falls to her knees and begs and begs in German. *"Pardon her foolishness, she's only a child, 'kinde,'" she says, "you must have one too, look she is as blond as you."* She begs slow and fast at the same time. He looks at me, the gun still at my chest. *"God will pay you back, let her go please, may you come back to your mother some day. God will hear, spare her please."* He lowered his gun and I lived to tell stories thanks to her, my grandma.

She spoke many languages, all sorts, some funny, some fast, but couldn't read or write at all, even counted on fingers and signed her name with a cross. I tried teaching her later but it was too late. She knew many things unknown to others, how to stop a cough with plants, how to cure nervousness with teas and find food in the bushes by the creek. Nobody knew this except her, nobody on the entire street. She went in the morning and gathered nettles in her apron, then washed and cooked them for us to eat with some salt or anything

1

else, if there was anything. This was to help me grow since there wasn't much food around, mostly bread and potatoes and even that not as much as you wanted some days. This was in the very beginning, right after, then later there was more. Things changed. We even had eggs once a week.

Grandma also thought and lectured to everyone — grown-ups that is — that kids should be punished only when they really, really deserved it and then only the bottom and nothing else. Don't hit the head, don't pull the hair, don't hurt the child, they are God's angels here on earth, God speaks to them directly, better than the rest of us sinners! Did mother listen? Not at all. She pulled on my hair so hard it gave me headaches, my head already hurt from that other time when the house fell. But once grandma saw her just as she was doing it and gave her a huge, red slap on the cheek. It made such a nice sound, it really did. Mother just stood there, head low in shame. This was only her second slap. I learn about the first one as grandma lectures and mother looks at the floor. I don't really learn all of it immediately, just a bit, but then it gets repeated until it has a story. The first time mother got slapped happened like this:

I am only eight months when she threw me across the room to the floor. She, angry at my father for some reason, says, very mean, eyes flashing: "Take this baggage with you. I came without it, it's yours." (That's me, the baggage.) Grandma picked me up from the floor, rocked and rocked me till I fell asleep then she went up to my mother, my father standing by, and slapped her such a good one she almost fell, just like the other one. Good for grandma!

I don't remember any of this although I see it just the same as if I had. It takes place in the summer and it's all very silent except for the slap and my cry when I hit the floor. FEMALE BLOND FIRST BORN GIRL, NO GOOD. If only one of these had been different, then maybe everything else would have been different, too, nicer. Bratso, the male and dark, was nursed until he was two and a half while me she stopped early, became ill, had no milk. Their worlds continued together, mine was somewhere else.

The real reason why she threw me across the floor like that when

I was eight months was because father took all the money saved for the payment on furniture and dishes, and gave it all to his own dad, a red-faced peasant who then went to spend it on gypsies and music and didn't sober up for three days, he had such a good time in a tavern not far from our street.

"I was angry at him, not you, can you imagine what that meant, no money left, the furniture and dishes bought on credit."

Fine, sure, I think, but why pick on me to throw across the room. You could have chosen a pot or a pan or a shoe. I am sure there had to be a reason why we—me and the anger—were connected so. Was it because I looked like him, blond, frail? Maybe yes, maybe no.

German soldiers passed by the house many times, then many different kinds of soldiers as well. But just this one time when the soldiers passed, they had red stars on their caps, a red flag in front. A few rode on horses, most walked, many had bandages around their heads like me, clothes mostly rags, not a uniform in sight. I recognize them by these signs to be O.K. and start waving. They wave back, smile at me; they are ours.

Mother gives me a nasty look as I grin. "This is the end," she says. "It really is. Your father will never be back and you grin like a fool. This is the end." The end of what, I wonder but say nothing.

CHAPTER TWO

"D EATH TO FASCISM!" teacher says, entering the class.

"FREEDOM FOR THE PEOPLE!" we scream back, fists clenched.

Marx and Lenin and our own heroes look at us from the walls. My first grade, the first year after the revolution.

"Do any of you remember the bombings?" she says. "Do you remember the enemy? You shouldn't forget that!"

Nobody wants to say yes or no. Silence in class as she wants us to tell, be sure not to forget. *She will pick on me now, my hair short, barely six months since it started growing back again after the wound healed. She'll ask me to tell, to show my scar near the left temple where the hair covers it, almost.*

"Anna, what's the matter?"

"Can I go to the bathroom please? I don't feel good."

She signals me to leave then I hear her say to the class:

"Anna was wounded in the war, that's why she gets headaches so much. They tried to destroy us, even the children. Don't forget!"

The story of how I was rescued from the ruins is told over and over again at home, my mother in the center, me to the side, other women listen, drink coffee and cry.

It was a sunny day like this one, she says now looking at other women, she had just finished having some coffee with Dara, dead since, may she rest in peace, they had just finished their coffee and started examining the grounds, when she sees this horrible thing on the edge of the cup, this black thing in the grounds, like a knife splitting the house in half. The other woman sees that omen in the cup too and says to mother "it doesn't look good." Mother spits in the cup three times then throws it out of the window, "may it happen elsewhere, Lord be praised, may it pass over." Then the other woman leaves and mother goes in the bedroom to check on Bratso, her baby, her sweet, her male child lying in bed all nice and pink.

"That kid never gave me any trouble from the start," she says to the women interrupting the story about the omen in the cup.

"I don't know how you survived, my good woman, six kilos at birth, why he was as big as my own at six months."

"Yes, he was big all right, but it didn't matter at all. And then a male child likes his mother the best. Why, I could just put my hand on his back and he would stretch and fall asleep like that. And my milk just flowed and flowed."

Mother says this as if to herself, me, the girl child listening in the corner.

"So, I just went in there to check him when the airplanes arrived. They seemed different than usual, more of them, very low, the whole sky. I just had enough time to jump in the bed and cover him with my body, then the house collapsed." Then comes the part where she gives Bratso to another woman, and starts looking for me. That part of the house is no longer there, gone, crumbled, where the kitchen used to be. Everything is red from the dust, people yell and scream, a second raid is coming. They shout to her to go and hide. "Anna is dead anyway, save yourself for that other child." But she didn't listen to them and started digging and digging through the rubble calling my name.

"Yes," says one woman, "I remember that."

"You wailed like for a dead person. We heard you all the way down the street. 'ANNA, MY DARLING, DON'T LEAVE ME NOW!'"

At this point all of them cry, everyone except me. I had been there, there is no way to cry about it. It is one of my nightmares except that it happened.

Mother digs and digs with her hands, brick by brick. At one point a brick falls and hits her on the head, or maybe it was something else. She sees blood on her dress, blood on the ground, and says to herself: "Maybe I am dead already and this isn't me," but continues to dig anyway calling my name. That's how she found my shoe and knew then she was on the right track, then my leg appeared, then the rest. We were still alive, grandma and me, under the iron bed, under a large cement beam which fell only seconds later and would have crushed us, prevented escape had it happened before.

Women cross themselves and cry some more. "God exists," they say, "that's the sheer proof of it. He wanted them to live and they survived under that beam, that's why. Lord save us always!"

That is why the icon survived and the Christ in the glass jar given to grandma long ago by the sailor she loved. This jar went across the room back and forth several times when the bomb fell, several times it hit the wall and remained intact, not a scratch on it. "You can see for yourself." Mother brings out the jar with the crucifix. They touch it, cross themselves, and cry some more. They can never figure out how Christ got up into the jar, there are no seams at all, too narrow at the top.

Stories about my rescue do strange things to my stomach, something in them is wrong but has no name, not yet. Maybe it is the way women cross themselves and say, very low: "She gave you life for the second time, she really did," then raise their heads up and look at me expecting tears but I don't cry. Nobody says: "Well, kid, how was it when the house fell and there was no air, no light?" I volunteer a couple of times but mother stops me fast:

"What do you know? If *only* I didn't come in time . . ."

When the house fell, or just before it, I am playing hide and seek with Boris. We are both five. We play and sleep together in a large brown bed whenever Sara goes away and cannot return after the police curfew.

When the airplanes arrive, it's not for the first time. They come daily and people run around a lot, then go and hide in basements or the countryside. We never do this because mother will not go and hide since others have gotten buried in the basements, shot in the countryside. We just sit there and wait for it to pass. Mother even opens the windows so they won't get broken if the bombs fall nearby.

The sound of the planes is very near now, a big roar, sirens scream at the same time. There are hundreds of them, big scary bugs, almost touching the rooftops. Boris and I get frightened and hide under the iron bed but he gets nervous and runs out, leaving me alone. Then, grandma crawls under the bed just as the house falls, her arms around me.

We descend through the darkness, no air, no light, pebbles in my mouth, we move with walls and bricks. You can't see or hear or scream. You are gripped very tight all around the ribs, under the feet, over the head. Only the skin is still you, and your thoughts. A small voice in me says, very quiet: "Am I dying now, or soon, is this death?"

"Grandma touched my neck to see if I am still alive, to see that I'm not dead," I say to my mother and the women drinking coffee.

"What do you know, kid, about death and dying?"

"She DID touch me. Go and ask her and you'll see. Grandma tell them, did you?"

"She is smarter than you think. Children are angels, God's gifts, God speaks to them directly. Sure, I touched her with this finger here to see if there was any life in her neck."

There! I knew she touched me, and I knew I was going to die soon except I didn't.

Buried, under the bed, I stop remembering at some point, or fall asleep or something like that, then a sharp pain and a very blue sky. My dress is red in front, head hurts a lot. German soldiers are asleep on the ground, one without legs. A big black fly sits on top of his nose; he has a green helmet on. Somebody says, "She is wounded, that little girl is wounded." That must be me, in the red dress. They pull me toward the basement, I trip and fall over the dead German, then another explosion somewhere else, then quiet. Our house looks funny, split in half. My clothes, toys, dishes, things are among the bricks. We sleep with Sara and Boris in the other half of the house for three more nights since there is nowhere else to go. Everything was bombed around us, other houses fell, not all, but many. We eat nothing but the strawberry jam mother dug out. After three days, we move to another place where mother begged them to let us in and they did, leaving us their bedroom, grandma and I in one bed, mother and Bratso in the other. It is very cold and we stuff the windows with pillows mother rescued from the other house. It doesn't really help and we sit in beds and shiver all the time. There grandma discovered that my head stank, yellow stuff dripped on my neck. In the hospital, set up in somebody's house, four men hold me, one for each limb. Two of them are German, two ours, neighbors I think. One of them gives me brandy to drink, forces me to swallow, then their doctor cuts into my head. I scream and yell until I forget. I scream against her, my mother who is there watching all this, as they cut my head. I say:

"Why did you bring me here to the enemy?"

"Why are you letting the enemy torture me, why?"

"Why don't you make them stop?"

Mother tells this part of the story mostly to show how patriotic and smart I was at five and how well I screamed against enemy soldiers who thank God understood nothing. They would have killed me had they known the names I called them. Mother's stories change, always get bigger, my curses become different, more daring each time. I even spit at them as the years pass. Yet, she never said: "Anna was hurt, she suffered, they tortured her" because that's what that was. It's always: "What suffering I had to endure, my dear woman, watching her on that table with her legs apart." Or still: "Children can kill you with worry," she repeats, "and will never be grateful for anything you do."

My hair is shaved off, a large bandage covers everything then somebody gives me a cap. I have to see Dr. Giovanni every few days, sometimes at night, the street completely dark. A

*German soldier, enormous with a steel helmet, accompan-
ies us every time. I think he will kill me each time and get
prepared for it. He pounds on his chest and says his name
is August like the month, what a strange name to have, I think.
My wound heals slowly but my hair will not grow for a long time.*

Mother was wounded too when the bricks hit her on the head
but she only put some brandy on it and it healed right away
without anybody's help. That's because she has "good blood" and
is tough in general and I am not. Bratso's skin was infected too,
right behind the ear, from dirt and dust. Mother worried and
worried that that ear might fall off. She washed and dried that
ear all the time, prayed and prayed. There was no chance of it
falling off really, it was only a scratch. I was the only one seriously
wounded, (even *my* doctor says that), operated on, even
have the certificate in my name for war damage, but if you listen
very carefully you'll notice, impossible not to, that that ear was more
important to my mother than my head. She says, washing and drying the ear, "What will happen to my child?" I am not called "child,"
a soft word in our language, just Anna always.

Mother says that before all this happened, before the operation,
I was a feisty, active girl, a blabber mouth, even invited neighbors
to my first birthday, I could speak so well and so much. Now, that
is not me, definitely not, although the picture of that person is in
the back of my head, just a small blur. I am a thin blond girl with
big eyes, very shy they say, don't talk to anyone ever for a long time
after the bombing. When the airplanes fly over the house, any plane,
even now in peace time, I hide under the table and howl, then grandma
hugs me and cries a bit. I wake up at night, do not know where I
am, arms and legs thrash against the wall, then I sit up in bed and
start my work:

"What are you doing, Anna?" they ask.

"Just digging, digging," my answer.

I dig for a long time after the war, then I stop, and the fear of
the airplanes stops and I start talking again.

I do not speak yet when mother takes me to school, one week

before the start. The principal asks simple things:

"How old are you?"

"What is your name?"

"How much is five and five?"

"What is this season called?"

I know the answers but can't open my mouth.

"What is wrong?" he wants to know.

"Is she shy?"

Then the two of them whisper and he looks at me, sad.

"She is not the only one, we have others," he says, and pats my head. "It will pass in time, it really will."

And it did.

When I am well again, as well as I can get, I often think like this: It is quite possible that that other child, the one who played with Boris, had much candy, wore organdy dresses, and talked a lot—that she really died for good and the new girl took her place. It sort of fits. Me, the new me, was born at the same time as the country, right after the revolution. I like to believe it. I like it a lot.

Even the fortune teller, a young gypsy with a kid, even she said when mother asked her to look at my palm.

"Good Lord! Look at that, madame! Her life line stops around five, then continues again. Look at that! God damn!"

So there! It fits.

DEATH TO FASCISM! POWER TO THE PEOPLE! OUR TOMORROWS WILL SING! DOWN WITH RELIGION, OPIUM OF THE MASSES! We march up and down the Main Street, red flags in front, red all around. I march and scream DOWN DOWN DOWN until I grow hoarse. First grade, first year after the revolution.

CHAPTER THREE

W HEN TEACHER CALLS on you, you stand up and recite. I do it fast looking at the floor, my cheeks burn, this part is hard. Thank God, the peasant kids are worse than me, they stammer, twirl their hair, twitch and always look ashamed — either because of their clothes or the way they say things and then the class explodes, roars. At least I read fast and well from the start. It's much harder for them it seems. They, the peasant kids, always sit in the back of the class together; their clothes are made out of homespun wool, rough brown and thick even in the spring, wool stockings, rubber shoes that last a long time, never sandals like us. The girls' hair is long, thick braids tied with pieces of wool thread in many nice colors, blue, green, red. My own hair is short all around, lifted from my face with a clip. Other town girls have short hair with bows, one or two on each side. Short hair is more hygienic, teacher says, lice settle forever in long thick braids, you can't get rid of them. The girl in front of me has them; I see them crawl slowly in that white portion where the hair is divided in two parts in the back. I see nits, too, tiny, silvery. The girl scratches herself once in a while, right there on that white part, then goes on to catch them at times, right under her fingernail. You hear it when she kills them on top of the desk with her thumb, it goes "sploush," then she scratches some more. Your thumb, or rather your nail, has a tiny bit of blood afterward. I have done it myself many times.

Once a week teacher checks your hair, it's the rule. You put your head on top of the desk, she looks here and there, lifting the hair up behind the ears where they like to hide. You wait and hope she'll find none that day. Kids snicker as soon as somebody is singled out. They snicker "hi-hi" stupidly as if they had never had them behind the ear. They snicker even if they had them the week before. Actually they are happy to laugh since it is usually the peasant kids that get picked out for having lice. It must be all those thick braids, I think. Others say peasants are stupid and clumsy and ugly, don't know how to talk properly. They use different words from us, don't know how to say a polite word for "shit" or "pee." They simply say "shit," "please, teacher, I have to leave the class and shit," or something like that, then the class roars. Peasant kids walk with their eyes toward the floor or to the side. They huddle together around the stove, their feet wet. Some walk two hours to get to school. I am shy like them, blush a lot and stammer when afraid.

To be sure, I am not disgraced, they wet my hair at home with kerosene, what a horrible smell, wrap it tight with a scarf, leave it overnight, then wash it in hot water, hot enough to skin a pig. I yell and scream, it hurts, but mother insists "that's not hot at all, stop yelling or you'll get a slap." Grandma has other methods, but it takes more time. I put my head in her lap, we sit outside the house on the wooden step near the linden tree and she looks slowly portion by portion, behind the ear, in the back, on the neck, slowly again toward the front, hair by hair. When she finds one, I hear a sound her fingernails make, a very nice sound it is, then she continues some more until I fall asleep.

In the classroom, left, right, in front, pictures of Marx, Lenin and our own heroes stare at you from the walls, all in one straight line. Lenin looks sly but has an interesting face around the eyes, a bit like my doctor's perhaps, or is it somebody else? Marx is clearly strange with all that beard, just like our local priest, exactly like it, or the captured reactionaries with big, bushy beards, enemies of the people that they lead along the Main Street in chains, the crowd screaming "kill them, kill them, kill." Stalin is not special in any way, just a moustache, very much like the railroad guy from the next house over, the one who beats his kids with the leather belt. The best looking man on that wall is our hero from this town, dead at twenty-five when he threw a grenade at a German tank. In this picture on the wall he is very much alive and young and laughing; his eyes sometimes wink.

I wonder what those bearded men on the Main Street did, I wonder why the crowd gathers and spits. It has to do with the revolution in some way, that much is clear.

Mother talks about the revolution at home, with the women drinking coffee. They make sure the door is closed, then whisper, somebody might still hear. Mothers starts:

"He said to me, that young punk as I went to get my ration card for bread, may God strike me down if I am not telling you the truth, may He strike me right here in front of you if he didn't say . . ."

All eyes are on her now, waiting.

"He says to me when I ask about the family, what will happen to it, "Cut the shit, auntie. What fucking blood ties? We don't believe in those. This is the revolution, understand! Mother, brother, fathers are relatives if they deserve it. If you're not with us you are against us,' he says to me."

Women cross themselves, she continues, angry now. Women look toward the door.

"Then I say to him, 'But your mother nourished you with her own milk, you ungrateful son of a bitch, mothers are sacred, don't you know that?' And he to me: 'Times are changing, old woman, we don't believe in that crap, you can shove it up your ass.' "

The women sigh, shake their heads. One of them, the one with the gold tooth and a big wart on her chin joins in:

"If the family doesn't exist, then you could fuck anyone you please, anyone in the world, even your own sister."

"Or your own mother, heaven forbid," says another one.

"Or anyone."

"Heaven save us and deliver us from evil."

They cross themselves again and drink more coffee, which is not real coffee but half barley. As far as the revolution goes, they are clearly getting it all mixed up. At school, we are learning all about it, this revolution now and others to come later. First, we'll build the bridges, then more schools and factories, and when it's all done there will be many gardens, no poverty, ruins or hunger or disease left. Tomorrows, our tomorrows will sing, teacher promised.

"Hurrah," I agree with my whole body for those tomorrows.

Where will I be? What will I do then? Will there be as many cherries as I wish?

At home, the whispers:

"Did you hear the new song . . . 'I wear a red star red star and fight against God, but not against Christ, Communist he was.'"

I laugh aloud for some reason, the song rhymes nice. Mother snaps:

"Why are you snickering like a fool? These are Godless times. They teach you nothing but lies at school. There is no more religion left. These are Godless times."

A local priest, the one that looks like Marx, did come in the beginning for a couple of months to teach us about religion. Mother insisted that I attend the class even though it was after school and I did, with a few others. You were free to choose if you went or not; teacher said nothing, go or don't.

He came once a week with a picture book full of saints in fancy dresses, long, colorful, draped around their shoulders. They all had yellow circles around their heads, fingers raised in front and for some reason bare feet. The priest is fat, dressed in black except for the gold cross, a big scary beard makes him look like an outlaw when he doesn't look like Marx. You have to kiss his hand which he offers, the right one which always smells of bacon and garlic. Then he sits in the chair looking stern and preaches that the world was destroyed by water, the next one will go by fire. He likes saying that, and being scary, you can tell he likes the words like fire and hell. Now, grandma thinks it will be by fire also, but she thinks children will be saved because they did nothing bad yet. At least she offers some possibility of rescue for some; to perish just like that seems unjust, there has to be some reason why. I refuse to believe anything as unjust as that. Partisans died, lots of them, but they knew why—for us the kids and those tomorrows that teacher talks about.

Women were partisans too, young girls dressed in men's clothes, hair tucked under their caps with the red star in front. They had a gun on one shoulder, maybe a pistol held by a leather belt in front, a couple small bombs or anything they could take from the Germans; there was no other way, they had to steal. Italian soldiers were afraid of these girls more than anybody else, more than men because they chased them across the fields and mountains, gun in one hand, hair flying, just like Indian braves. There is a story now that everybody tells about an Italian soldier getting ready to leave for the front and he says to his wife: "Maria mia, make me big, wide pants so I can run fast when we start fighting partisans." Mother likes that story about the Italian men and anything else where our bravery is described. In her opinion we are clearly the best, there is nobody nearly as brave as us, but when told about partisan girls, she makes a face and adds:

"I bet not one of them came home intact."

Intact how? I think. It has to do with being pure somehow and Mary was pure, the priest says. In that picture book of his, Mary always sits with a boy in her lap or in her arms, looking sad. There aren't any other women saints in that book except her, and she doesn't do much. I know that women around mother pray to her to deliver them from pain when giving birth, and that's all there is to her. I don't learn much more from the priest because he only got as far as the flood and stopped coming to school after all the kids dropped out of his class. Besides, there were many things to do after school especially in the spring.

Mother tries teaching us about a few other things like Christmas and Easter and the Holy Ghost but it doesn't make much sense. Christ rose from the cross on Easter, she said, but what did eggs have to do with it, even though they were fun, or killing a pig for Christmas. As for the Ghost, I don't think she knew herself what it all meant when she said, "Take your hand like this and with three fingers, from the forehead to the stomach, right and left, see like this, you make a cross and say 'in the name of the Father and the Son and the Holy Ghost.'" Sure I do it, it's easy, but I have no idea who he, the ghost, is.

When Easter arrives the first year after the revolution we go to the woods with the teachers and stuff ourselves with meat, chocolate, cheese, wonderful things, just for this one time, all from packages that say UNRA on the top. Spring is just starting in the leaves, pale green, pale blue sky. We build a large fire out of dead wood, and burn Winter to death. Then when she is all gone, we dance around the fire and chase each other in the woods, look for violets until night falls. We are celebrating the old Slavic God, Vesna, god of spring, one of many. It is for her that we burn the winter doll and eat the food from UNRA and make crowns out of violets and leaves. She likes that sort of thing. Vesna looks like a young girl in a violet dress with long blond hair probably; Old Slavs were all very blond when they lived together in their homeland where Russia is now, teacher says. Vesna is my favorite. If you have to have them anyway, it makes sense to have quite a few gods, at least you stand a chance with one of them, I think. And then, it makes sense to celebrate the sun and spring and water. You can see it and smell it and it feels good.

I am lying in the grass; sounds of Svetlana, Senya, Mira and others are in back of me. It is spring, the winter doll is burning and the wrappings from UNRA. Far away in the woods, a bird called "Twea-twea-twee," another one answered "quonk-a-ree," then the hammering of a woodpecker. A little green worm stops on my hand lifting its whole body to sniff the air, then it moves toward another leaf and disappears in the grass. A small ant carries a piece of bread ten times its size, it's too heavy, gets dropped, then a whole army of ants come out of some tunnel to help and they carry it off together in the tall grass. I travel with it slowly; the grass is huge now over my head, a jungle, a forest, my body the size of a lady bug. I flutter my wings once in a while, move forward. There is no fear, we are among friends — large and small ants, slow insects with gold tops. A butterfly flies over me like an airplane; far away the bird calls "twea-twea-twee," another bird answers. The sun is hot on my back, are they calling me? "Anna! C'mon, wake up, hurry, we are leaving." Somebody shakes my leg. I travel through the grass, across the leaves of an oak tree. "Here I am. Wait for me, wait."

CHAPTER FOUR

W E LIVE IN two rooms on the ground floor, next to the basement, cold and damp inside. But the windows overlook the garden and if you want to escape from anyone just jump through the window and land in the bushes—something people upstairs can't do although it is nicer to live there since they have three rooms. We hear them walking, arguing on top of us all the time, have to close the windows when they shake their rugs. But then they can't jump through the window, can't see leaves from their bed.

Upstairs, on the other side, not above us where the owners are, but over toward the street, the very best spot of all because you see all the carriages, weddings, everyone passing by, there, in two rooms lives a communist woman with her husband and a child. This woman is known as "The Communist One" or "The Godless One" depending on the day or what mother is talking about but one thing is clear— she, that woman with short black hair and a pretty comb, never prayed, never asked God for anything at all, not even when she had TB of the spine, or when giving birth to her boy. Not even when she was wounded during the war. Mother looks at her then crosses herself.

"I don't believe you," she says.

And she, the communist one, to prove it is all true:

"I spit on Him, I spit on Him twice."

Mother crosses herself twice.

"If He was any good, why all the horrors, why did I have TB in the first place? Did He help you? No."

This woman is crazy to argue with mother who never has answers for things like that, yet never stops persuading her to believe in Him which is strange. Mother doesn't give up and pushes her daily to become a Christian; she, the communist one, only says "God damn" when pushed too hard, then mother crosses herself and then they go on. The woman never attacks first, I have noticed that. She has her rules; her sentences are clear, the kind mother doesn't like. As the time passes, mother nags at her less and less and even invites her over, not for the real gossip (that's reserved for special friends, the woman with the gold tooth, the one with the gray eyes, Sara perhaps), just for coffee or to see her pretty baby, unchristened yet, a hard thing to forget—so mother starts in on her all over again in spite of herself.

"What a shame for a pretty boy not to be christened yet, think of his soul, think."

To her, the cross, holy water, godparents really matter a lot. The communist woman doesn't answer at all this time, just kisses her baby and gives mother her cup. She never turns it over to look at the grounds for fortune or luck.

In the small house right in front of us, at the other end of the courtyard, Putana lives with her small son in one room. She works during the day, gets all dressed up in the evening, and gets beaten at night. That's all there is to her. In the other half of that small house, we have a railroad guy Stane with his wife Slavka who just came from a village and wears her hair in braids on top, embroidered vests, sometimes a scarf tied around the chin. Mother has to teach her everything, how and what to do, and what not, how to cook right and use polite words for pee and shit, that sort of stuff. Peasants are different from us in these small things but then they live in town for a year or two and you can't tell their children from others. They even forget how to sing or curse in their old ways.

Underneath the small house there is a pump for everyone to use; our water is the best, mother says, it comes from afar. I pump a lot, either for the washing or when a guest arrives and you serve him preserved cherries with a glass of cold water, always the very first thing, before the coffee, before the brandy. This is for special guests, not for the women who sit and drink coffee every day. The water for the guest has to be very cold, and the longer you pump the colder it gets, pump it a long time, she said, make it cold. So, pump, pump, pump before the pitcher is filled, skip while you pump, hop on one foot, don't let the voice speak, stop it in time or . . . .

Which voice?

Why, the one inside me that can make things happen, don't let it speak!

Pump before it says anything at all!

Once while watching Bratso hanging from a tree with another kid, the voice said:

Make him fall down, do!

And he did. Fortunately, nothing happened, nothing serious, no broken bones, just a scrape. But what if the voice had asked for more, what if?

Pump, make the voice stop!

Fill the pitcher, run back, serve the guest, the voice stops.

Further down from the pump, toward the creek, there are small wooden houses for pigs, everyone has one except the communist woman, then come the toilets, three of them. They seem so far away in the winter, at night. A ghost could be there waiting by the tree to get you, or a witch, especially since the creek is there, dark, whispering. You don't see the water from where you stand, it's too high up. You have to go over the wooden fence, then through the bushes, tons of nettles, and there you are, at the bottom of the ravine, the creek. There you might see a peasant woman pee standing up, her skirts lifted with one hand just a bit. She doesn't get embarrassed at all, doesn't budge, just continues the same, then moves away toward the town with a basket of cherries or apples on top of her head.

Under the window there are many flowers and a grapevine that belongs to the owner on the second floor, a fat old lady who comes to drink coffee all the time. I open the window just a bit in the summer, nobody can see my hand, then I pluck some grapes, just a few; one cluster hangs so near I reach it with my mouth. I guess you could call this stealing or something horrible like that or it could be called "redistribution of wealth" as they say in class about those who had too much and others nothing at all, before the war, before the revolution. Well, I have no grapes, she has more. You can also borrow some pears and apples from the stingy old man in a house on the left because if you don't, he lets them all rot on the ground and they are no good for anyone any more. He lives to the left of us, yellow, wrinkled, bent; his property is fenced in with tall wooden planks with nasty points at the top, not much protection really, poor guy, because all you have to do is lift two nails at the bottom, swing the planks, crawl under, nobody sees, everything looks normal, get them, run. Only the kids know how to do this, which planks they are. Past the old man with pears and apples, there is a house where the girl with one short leg lives, and a woman with big breasts, then the house of the ex-merchant, and the baker's with a daughter who looks like a giraffe. Our friend Sara "The Jewish Woman" lives there, not far, on the same street, her son Boris plays with me all the time. "Jewish" means nothing at all, you can't find out much. She says once that her real language, the one she learned at birth, is not ours but Spanish. I look up Spain on the map at school. Spain, Spanish sounds nice, far away, much further in sound than France, French. The only thing that mother ever said on the subject of Sara is that Jewish cooking is done with goose fat, ours with lard but now we have neither lard nor goose, and you could starve on what you get on our coupons and cards. We don't even get half a kilo of bread for four. Mother also believes Jewish women are beautiful when young, then fade fast. She says "fade just like Muslim women." That's about it. There are no Muslim women around, nobody to compare Sara with. She looks no different from mother, they are both dark and good friends because mother feels like a foreigner in this town having come from other parts where people are better-looking and more honest and brave and better in general. Sara feels foreign too she says to mother, but she feels foreign everywhere, in every town.

If you go past the house where Sara and Boris live, also on the ground floor like us, you can take a small narrow street full of bumpy stones, too small for a carriage to pass, almost a path, then you arrive at the tiny yellow house with peeling paint of this girl who hangs out with soldiers, the one who pretends she is a movie star and wears lots of lipstick, even in the morning. Mother says, "I'll kill you if you are like her, better dead than like that, at least I'd go to your grave." She gets going for no reason at all, talking about me as if I did something wrong while I wonder what made her angry like that.

On the other side of that narrow street, there are some more people of lesser importance, you say, "hello," "good day," know them a bit, but they don't come for coffee except maybe on the Saint's Day when everyone comes, all streets around unless you are "not on speaking terms" that year, which happens. There, almost by the creek, in a house with a large iron fence and geraniums and lilacs live a mother and daughter, both very old. The mother eats like a horse even at eighty-five, people cross themselves, it's not supposed to happen, "unnatural" they say. "Lord save me from old age like that," they say meaning either her age or that she eats like a horse. You never find out what the right old age is; they just say things like "Lord save me" but do not explain the rest.

From here, from this pretty old house, you can see the creek, the same one that flows underneath our yard; it is sometimes dry, or almost, other times large as the water spills all over the flat ground, and you jump from stone to stone with books on your back, soldiers on the left from the barracks looking, laughing, through the barbed wire. That movie star girl with lipstick stands there pressed against the wire once in a while as you skip along to school, then soldiers say some funny things to her and they laugh louder still.

The creek goes underground right here, as soon as you pass the barracks, and gets replaced by a wide short street with a movie house on one side. Can't stop to look. Not enough time. You run past it on the way to school, across the Main Street, past the photo store with beauties and babies on the fur rugs, then see the school, one side of it, big gray with a yard. You wonder if the first bell rang, you look for the clock. Still time. The river is not far from here, you can smell it. Maybe next year you will be allowed to go and swim there with the older kids, maybe she'll say yes.

When it rains a lot or gets icy, it's better to take another road to school, longer and less direct, and go past all the people mentioned but do not turn on that narrow street. You just continue walking, down past the lawyer's house and the professor of math who teaches in the *gymnasium* until you get to my doctor's house where carts stand with sick peasants inside. Mother says they go to see the doctor when they should see a priest, always too late. There our street starts and joins other streets from different sides, left and right, all going toward the hills, all ending here in front of the doctor's and the military barracks. You can't miss the soldiers no matter which way you go, either by the creek or this way. On both sides they whisper as you pass running to school, make you blush.

Senya stands there in the winter, on the corner where my street starts. Together we care less about the soldiers and whispers and she sometimes says "git" to them. Hurry fast, slipping and sliding on the ice, down past the inn with the beer and the drunks where grandpa drank all the money for songs, past the house where a young man stares in the window and has TB, they say. Smile at him for no reason because he smiles first, always in the same spot by the window, a pale boy like one of the autumn saints.

From here on, there are many smaller and bigger houses of people you don't know at all, mother does, you don't, not even to say good day to, then on the corner a pharmacy and the Main Street, where the shops are which is called *"Charshia,"* "Downtown." Turn left and depending what time it is, either take the Main Street and go straight past the photo store until you reach the school, or go by the market if you have just a bit more time and taste different fruits pretending you'll buy some, but you don't. You would buy them if you had money except you don't.

Peasants sit or stand and bargain for everything—vegetables, cherries, cheese, pigs, lambs. Town people, women, spend hours trying to outdo them in price and then they say "I got a bargain." Peasants curse a lot, wear skirts and blouses of many colored yarns. It is considered bad taste, all those yellows and greens; town women prefer navy blue, beige, gray. Gypsies wander around the market, always with a kid, always dressed in many colors especially reds but they don't care if anybody likes the colors or not. They will always stay that way which is not true for peasants who can feel what mother and others think of them and will change as fast as they can. As soon as they come to live in the town, they'll cut their hair and turn to beige or gray.

Hurry, run, it's almost one o'clock, the second bell will ring any second now. Run, you get punished if late, will have to explain why, in front of the others. You can't say "I was at the market, looking at the colors and cherries and peasants." They would just roar at a story like that but thank God it will not happen.

CHAPTER FIVE

THOMAS CAME IN the winter of my second grade carrying a large suitcase. He was tall and blond and had a fur cap just like in the Russian movies. Truck driver by profession he said and now a chauffeur for an important official here in town, from OZNA or something like that. He wondered if there was a room for him to rent; he was from the north, wheat country, his family still there, baby girl he had and showed pictures. There was no room anywhere he said, the hotel was full, most houses destroyed by the bombs didn't get fixed fast.

We still lived on the ground floor next to the basement, the owner her daughter and kids upstairs, another couple with a baby replaced "The Communist One." I don't know why he came to mother rather than those other people. They clearly had more room. I don't know why she took him either that particular day. Maybe it was the money, maybe she felt bad on account of the snow and him standing there with that big suitcase, I don't know why. It's hard to guess with her. Maybe she liked him and thought it would be nice to have a man around after all. There were five of us now before his arrival, all women except Bratso but he didn't count because of his age, a full three years and three months younger than me.

So she said, "No, I don't have a room to rent but maybe you could have a bed." Thomas grinned very wide and put his suitcase down.

It was all settled. They could have coffee to make things official. He grinned again. I thought then and now of the Russian movies where men grinned like that, big happy smiles over the whole screen. Behind them, wide open land, miles of it extended forever, instead of our own miserable hills. Here the view stopped; you had to imagine the rest.

The arrangement was as follows: mother and Bratso would sleep together, Yanna, my aunt, 17, on the floor next to them, grandma on the wooden bed in the kitchen and Thomas and I together in another bed next to mother and Bratso. The beds were twin beds, part of mother's trousseau she managed to dig up after the bombing, all in small pieces, then glued back together so they looked the same as before as far as I could tell. But, her white beautiful credenza with many fancy dishes, wedding presents in crystal was gone for good and couldn't ever be put together again. She mourned over that *kreden-ca* as if it were a person, how lovely, how beautiful, how white. That was the one she bought on credit when grandpa drank the money and she threw me across the room on the floor.

"You have to wash your hands and feet every night so the sheets stay clean," Thomas was told. We did it like that. On Saturdays a small wooden tub filled the kitchen and Bratso got scrubbed with much screaming and yelling. The water was always too hot, worse for me. I got washed first, then him in the same water. She reasoned that I wasn't too dirty, girls never are. I never saw grandma in the tub and can't imagine it at all; she would have been too big for it anyway, yet she must have washed sometimes. She soaked her feet every night in the bucket of water mixed with ashes hoping her corns would go away, but they didn't. Old people did that on account of their feet. I never saw Yanna in the tub either but she was secretive and strange and probably waited until everyone was asleep. That's how she did it, I bet. With Thomas it was different. He went to the pump underneath the house, naked to the waist in January or any other time, and washed himself there, his back very large. He rubbed himself with a piece of snow and the steam rose from his skin as we watched him through the window, Bratso and me. We talked a lot about him, who had bigger muscles, him or Stane, the railroad guy who also washed himself at the pump in January. We couldn't decide who did.

In January, that January, second grade, Thomas pumps water so mother can rinse the sheets that have been boiling in a large black kettle in the courtyard. The sheets steam on the lines for a while, then become frozen in an hour or so, then she takes them inside, very big, rigid, and dries them by the fire. It took a long time for all that, the whole kitchen was nothing but lines. Mother was always in a bad mood on wash day, complained that her back hurt a lot. Grandma cooked her yarrow teas to make the pain go away and always said, "Stay away from her today, it's wash day." All the women were mean and nasty when washing in winter. That's why we cleaned ourselves before going to bed.

Thomas chopped the wood, spitting in his palms first, to oil them I guess. He would split it in halves and quarters, perfect each time. I try to do the same, without spitting, and nothing happens at all. The piece rolls over except when Thomas holds the ax and cheats for me. He says, "There you did it. What a good one!" But I know he is cheating for me. When we have enough we carry it and stack it in rows by the basement wall, where it is protected from the snow a bit. All the tenants had one portion of that wall for their wood and everyone knew whose is what and which is which. When the snow fell, the bottom rows got wet and the fire was hard to start. You would blow and blow a lot with much smoke everywhere, then a small blue flame appeared, a good sign. Later, this wet wood smoked and squealed or sang for a long time. The ghosts were trapped in it, they might be, you can never be sure.

The wood is singing, mother irons her sheets, I do my homework about a dead partisan hero, writing carefully the thin and thick lines, large capitals like flowers in blue ink. The snow outside is high, all the way up to the window, you can touch it, and it's still snowing, big flakes. Once in a while an argument in the courtyard, from the Putana's door, or "Sister Divine," her other name, but that's not every day. Usually in the winter there is nothing but silence and the squealing of the wood as the snow falls deeper and deeper and when you wake up it is higher than the day before, almost to your waist.

Pigs were butchered in the winter—they squealed, a horrible sound, even before the knife got to them. They knew, I guess. Mother cried a lot each time, having gotten accustomed or "fallen in love" with each pig. She bought them as babies at the market in the spring, very small and thin, we fed them slop and corn carefully, then they were killed in December or January always by the same person who got a piece of leg, some lard.

When I open my eyes again, the pig is dead already, blood drips on the snow. Then they hang it up and start cutting it up bit by bit. We wait for the bladder. Blown up, it's a ball until it pops. The pig is all white and clean now, all the hair in one bunch to be sold for brushes, the lean pieces will be smoked in a special place, intestines used for sausages, lard to last for the whole year. I distribute small pieces of fresh meat with cracklings to our closest neighbors; they do the same thing for us when their pig is killed. You never fail in this, it's called the custom. Finally, there is nothing left except the balls and everyone jokes about this, drinking brandy by now to celebrate the occasion. "Who wants the balls?" somebody asks. They, my mother and others, laugh and slap their hips, thighs, their faces red, eyes shiny. More laughter about the balls. I was not certain what it all meant but the laughter was different from other times, their faces ugly.

Thomas came at night, I never knew when, and left early except on Sundays. I knew he was there in bed by the smell of the sheepskin coat that he covered us with, him and me. At times, he covered me in the middle of the night as others snored, different melodies each one, Yanna tossing and turning in a dream. On Sundays I wake up in his armpit and wonder how can he smell so good. I said, "Thomas, why does your armpit smell so good?" He laughs and says, "It must be my special sweat." Before that, I never knew sweat had a smell, very nice smell.

One day, he came early in the afternoon and said, "Let's go for a ride." He had his big truck with him right outside the house. Bratso and I run up and down the street calling all the kids, showing off with the truck. There were about ten of us, different shapes of rags and patches. Well, that was everybody's first ride and we became just a bit more important on the street from that day on. Thomas did it all with that truck. Then suddenly he was transferred somewhere else, maybe to his home in the north, maybe to another town. He didn't say where and seemed both happy and unhappy at the same time when he arrived with a can of American ham as a parting gift. The ham we ate immediately, it was very good, the peanut butter which he also brought we had to throw away because it was disgusting. We tried giving it away, but nobody liked it, not even the cats. For me, Thomas left a scarf, a large green aviator's scarf made out of wool. Mother said she'll make me a blouse out of it or a skirt, but I said, let me keep it as it is. I could wrap it around me when I went to bed and pretend that Thomas was there to cover me up. I liked him you see, in a special way.

After that, there were many arguments about our new sleeping arrangement. I refused to sleep with Yanna, she kicked like mad when dreaming, and grandma wanted to be in the kitchen near the stove. I kept thinking, but said nothing, why don't Bratso and I sleep together, and mother and Yanna, just like before Thomas arrived. Why so much commotion about finding new arrangements? Maybe Yanna was too much for mother as well on account of her dreams. But mother didn't want to hurt her feelings and pretended instead that Bratso got uncovered in the middle of the night, would catch a cold, she had to watch over him since his health was poor. It was all one big lie, that much I knew since he wasn't sick at all, big, red, chubby, much healthier than me, and she never covered me up at night the way Thomas did. Why not?

Well, since we couldn't come up with any decision, we continued to sleep as when Thomas was with us. That's how I got to have my own bed for the first time, that winter second grade, or is it already third?

Chapter Six

T HE SNOW FELL for four months or more and the school often closed
for a while because the peasant kids couldn't get to town. Our street
is one narrow canyon of snow higher than me, I can't see a thing
on either side, it is that tall. The fresh snow squeaks when you walk
on it; here and there ice patches form and you skate over them, fly.
Old people walk funny, careful, all worried not to break any bones;
some refuse to leave the house until there is no ice. Others, like grandma, tie some rags around their shoes and then you can't skid at all.
We fall and push each other, don't worry about our backs because
we are not old. Bratso plays in the snow till he turns purple and gets
sick from wet clothes. I got sick too, always in the winter for some
reason, and had to stay in bed for a long time, while others played,
shouted outside, had a good time.

The snow is still falling outside and I am lying in the bed covered
to my chin, sick. People came to visit, all women with gifts of food
for me, rice pudding, an apple or a pear, but I can't eat at all. It's
very hot. They sit there whispering with mother and looking glum,
all of them. The windows have strange ice patterns and angels appear on them running, flying around the edges of the lace curtain,
Christ is there too, having escaped from the jar but he has a sword on.

Am I pretending or do I really see them?

Everyone gets quiet and mother shakes her head.

She says, "Where did you see it, where?"

I scream, hear my voice:

"There goes my dad, there on the curtain with the angel, look! Here comes Christ!"

Women are crying now.

Mother crosses herself and says, "God help me now." She is crying too. My illness is certainly serious.

Then the doctor arrives, calls me "my pet," tells mother to stop, gives me some pills, pats my head, his hand feels cold. After that the fever drops, "the crisis has passed" and my friends appear with lessons to catch up on, sometimes a whole month's worth. They tell me the news—where they went with their sleds, who fell in the drift, where they'll go today. By now, I couldn't care less. Lying in bed is nice when fever is low and bones ache just a tiny bit. You sleep and sleep the whole day, then you open your eyes, stare slowly at the snow and the curtains, get lost in the patterns of lace, see different things in them, angels, dogs, cats.

Or better still, I beg for the picture album, a big one, it's never refused when ill. It's locked in the closet next to the blue book. And there they are—mother and father, young on a distant beach somewhere, smiling both, mother looks like a girl; he, my father is blond, thin like me. In the picture you see the water, pebbles and some other people further back. I wish I could see more, what's in the back, but you don't. Mother and father are the biggest in the picture, facing each other, smiling a bit. Then you flip a page and there is grandma in a white lace blouse, small buttons all the way up to her chin, the hair on top of her head very black. More pictures of mother in different dresses, some with hats, tons of pictures of men in uniform, their sabres dangling from the hip. How could they walk with those? Did they trip and fall? They must have. Maybe they just did it for the photos to look good with the women standing by their side, all hats and gloves even in the summer. This time, the time from the pictures, they call "The Time Before The War," or "The Peaceful Time," or most often "The Time Before The Revolution." In my memory only bits and pieces of it remain, mostly colors, pink of my organdy dress, blue slip with ruffles.

Whatever happened to all those dresses, I wonder. It would be nice to know if they were really that pink, or if I invented them too.

Now, I have mostly dark colors; clothes are very big on me especially around the shoulders; some large girl wore them before me, you could tell. I don't mind really that they are so large except for the shoes which make me feel clumsy, afraid to walk. I trip and fall in mine, lose them as well, there is so much room left behind where the heel is. Stuffing with paper doesn't work either, then it hurts in front.

Clothes are distributed once in a while, on Mondays by this special person who says they come from UNRA, nobody says what the word means. He checks to see who needs things, then they give you some stuff. Once I am sitting in class when they call my name up to get new shoes from UNRA again; mine have large holes. I get very happy just thinking about new shoes but then when I get them they are enormous. UNRA people must have big feet, I said to myself but I'll give them to Yanna, she needs shoes too. The person who distributes the shoes heard me (I swear I was only talking to myself, strange), snatches the shoes away and calls me "arrogant." I wondered what I did wrong, what the word meant.

Father is in the memory of that time before the war when I had shoes that fit. We, two of us are on the open country road, walking, going to grandpa's, stopping to eat the chicken grandma had cooked; we look at the river, taste the water, then he runs up ahead and hides behind the tree. Where is he? A bird calls far away twea-twee, another bird answers. A huge green frog as big as my hand jumps out of somewhere at me.

"D-a-d-a . . . " I run toward him in panic, but he is not behind the tree. He sneaks up and picks me up laughing. I can reach the tree branches now when he does this, reach for the cherries or apples or plums. We stop to eat again on a small bridge, big trees everywhere around us, birds sing tweee. Please help me God, or whoever, not to forget him. What would I do then, without that time, without him, without me.

He was blond like me they say. Mother is dark and strong, "He was a weakling just like you" she says "but then it's not his fault, most blond people are." Not everyone is as lucky as she.

After the illness, school seems hurried, time rushed. I can't run at all, knees hurt a lot, dismissed from the daily gym in the yard.

30

Teacher makes a big deal out of my return, how I know my lesson, what a good student and so on, very embarrassing, all of it. I look at the floor. She calls on the boy in front of me, nicknamed "Rabbit" because of his ears, asks him to recite and he stands silent, not a word. Then, on me.

"You should be ashamed," she snaps at him, "that she can answer correctly after a month of illness and you can't. What an oaf."

And to me, "Go pull his ears for punishment."

Me?

"Do it."

The class is very happy, snickers.

I don't understand, hesitate, he didn't do anything to me.

"Go on," she says, stern.

The whole class is watching.

I have to do it I guess although it seems wrong.

I touch his ear just a bit, funny feeling, warm skin in my hand.

When the class ends, during the recess, he catches up with me and hits me hard in the nose. Much blood flows and they tilt my head back, lift one hand up to make the blood stop. He goes to the principal, my nose stays big for days.

Teacher was often wrong like this but not always. She intended well but got confused along the way, just like mother did. She is tall, blond, big shoulders; she fought with the partisans and had many stories to tell. When she teaches geography and explains about the winds, she tells about great winds that blew her daughter once, just lifted her from the ground like that and thank God her dress was red so they spotted her easily some kilometers away. It would be wonderful to be lifted by the winds, carried away like that. I wouldn't be scared at all, would love it as a matter of fact. Could they blow me all the way to father, wherever he is?

History lesson next—Germans, partisans and the Soviet soldiers every day. The partisans and Soviets have big red stars on their caps and are friendly, rescue small children in trouble, give them things to eat, protect them if they've lost their parents. On the map, our country is one of many marked in red. The world will be red and the future too, just like our scarves as we march up and down the Main Street singing aloud. Our books always start with "Before the Revolution" and end with "After the Revolution" when all those things from before will be changed for good. We live in the time after the revolution (or is it during?) and are lucky because many have died so we could sit here in this class now and read instead of hiding or dying, she concludes for today.

"GLORY TO OUR FALLEN HEROES"

"GLORY FOREVER!" we yell back.

"CLASS DISMISSED!" she ends.

The monument to the dead partisans is on the hill. We visit it with flowers, stay silent a minute. Now, there is another grave where two English pilots fell, not far from our house, just behind the Devil's Stone. Mother goes there on Sundays when the weather is good and I go with her; she insists. She said they were there poor things forgotten by everyone, their poor mothers never knew where their sons fell and that's why she came there with flowers, candles and matches to help their souls a bit. She cried about their poor mothers who never knew where they were. I am not sure whether she visits them out of spite because nobody else does it, or because she found that father was in England and the two were linked somehow in her mind. I don't mention these visits to anyone; it wouldn't be good. We are not too friendly with England and the English.

Some children had fathers who were alive and heroes at the same time. That was the best you could have but there were not too many of those. I only know one. Others had dead heroes. In either case they were lucky, I thought. The books are about them and their lives seemed in order. With us it was different, nothing clear cut, whispering and secrets all around. Like that one time we went on a picnic with mother, Yanna and the woman with the gold tooth. Yanna came out of the woods carrying some large bones mother looked at and said they were human. Then, whispers and whispers about horrors of some sort. Some men were shot there and died like dogs without a grave. Mother cries remembering, reminded of something.

Graves are really important to her, and how you die, if your grave is marked or not.

"Who shot them?"

"Where? Will it happen again?"

"Shut up, kid" both of them at me.

"You don't understand the world," mother adds.

"If they did, my dear Mara, they would never grow up." The world is that bad. "It's a trail of tears." And they whisper some more.

Then we eat bread with lard and paprika on top, run around. Yanna buries the bones under a tree, makes a cross out of a branch, jumps across it three times. We gather some violets, put them on. It's spring time again, pale blue sky.

Eventually, the image of father fades and gets replaced by a partisan.

In the summer we found something in the rubble near an old house that was bombed by the war. It was an object never seen before, large like the largest goose egg, wonderful colors it had, yellow, green, red. There were five of us there on the street, me the only girl and very proud because I'm one of them. They didn't really think of me that way, but I served a function and read them stories of all sorts about Indians and gangsters, anything, inventing a bit each time, except they never guessed at all that there were my words among Karl May or Verne.

So, when I heard the low whistle, then a dog bark (that was the signal) I ran out thinking they came for a story. Everyone was there — Chedo, Marko, Niko and Boris, and Boris said, "We found something, come look."

I followed them to the house with the rubble, staying slightly behind. It was summer in July, the street smelled of dust. The church clock struck five; we waited for some reason for the last strike. The object was on the ground, yellow, green, red, shaped like an egg.

Chedo said, "Let's open it and see what's inside."

"How are you going to do it?" Boris said. "There is no key."

I said for some reason, "Don't!"

Chedo was always doing things like that, opening, fixing and would be an engineer or a mechanic he said.

"I wonder what's inside," Chedo says and picks up a large stone, starts beating this egg, smooth on all sides. There was no other way to see, there was no key.

I move from them without knowing why.

A small voice inside whispered to me, "*move*" and I did.

Chedo kept banging and banging with that stone, even had to get another one. A piece of the stone broke away, hit Boris in the leg. He moved a bit, licking his scrape.

Then there was much light and a roaring sound and screams. I ran looking for someone to tell. I am the only one unhurt. The others don't move at all or it is that I don't see them in the dust.

Toward the evening, the news spread—Chedo lost both arms and a leg, Boris an eye, the other two died right away, on the spot. Later, Boris got a glass eye but you could always tell which is which. Chedo walked around with arms and a leg that squeaked. His face was full of small green marks. Mother shook her head and wondered who'll take care of him later when his parents die, what will happen to him considering he will not marry, who'll want him like that. She always cried about Chedo, who'll never be an engineer or a mechanic.

I never told her that I was really near the grenade when it exploded and that the voice told me to move. She would have beat me had I told her the truth. That's why it is better to keep quiet when you can and lie, or invent.

This story happened right after the war but in time it never seemed different from other times; it's neither present, nor the past. Teacher lectured a lot after that, drew pictures of bombs, how to tell. The enemy left them behind on purpose, teacher said, to kill as many of us as possible.

We have to be smart and not get deceived by pretty colors, she said. There were no explosions after that. Then the summer ended and the fall came and then winter and spring. Another summer arrived as always.

In the summer, the grass is singing, you get lost in it, slowly at first. I sit on the front step, the sun is very hot. I feel nothing, nothing at all except the heat. The world is in front of me, around, hazy blue, green, then I travel to the tree tops, disappear in the leaves.

Summer nights smell of lilac and wheat from the fields. The night smells "late" something hard to describe with words. Mother, grandma, Yanna and others sit in the front facing the street, telling secrets of all kinds. Bratso and I, Boris and Ljuba run after the fireflies, catch them in our palms, then squash them on our foreheads where they glisten for awhile, then die.

Chapter Seven

Peasant women pass by the creek on the way to market, lifting up their heavy skirts to pee. Some squat, others stand just like a guy, only pulling the skirt to the side a bit. They never wear panties, everybody knows that. The creek travels toward the town, past the military barracks full of soldiers behind the barbed wire, then it disappears under the Main Street and falls into the river called "The River of Grief" where the Turks dumped kids long ago that's why it's called "Grief." Everyone could tell you that story, I am not the only one, it's called a "legend." They would kill them, then throw them in the river and people fished them dead on the shore. That was a long time ago. Turkish ruins are on the hill, one of the hills overlooking the river, not far from the monument to the dead partisans, shot there in '44.

Further north, in the opposite direction from the town, the creek is fast and deep enough to wash the rugs in the spring or summer, then you dry them on the rocks, put your feet in the water, very clear, bottom hard stone. If you follow it more, the creek tricks you, houses disappear—you are in the country where violets grow in the springtime, right by the water, and narcissus too on the hill side. Bring them to teacher, this makes her happy.

On the other side of the creek, just before it turns into the country, right by the bridge where women wash rugs, there is a butcher and his family who always have enough meat even though it was rationed, a little bit of it every week. Because they ate so much meat they, the butcher his wife and kids, all of them had faces like steaks, red big meaty. That must have been the reason. What else?

I always wait in the line for meat and milk and bread and the movies. Why me every time? Mother says: "Go wait in line, you got time, the school starts at one." You might think that's the reason but it isn't. I wait in line because people take pity on me and I come home with the goods every time, never give up like some. Mother knows this, I bet. I could bet anything she does, that's why she sends me to the line.

The milk line, like the movie line, was entirely kids, some big, others not, waiting for hours for the milk to arrive in large aluminum pots. If you are deep inside the line with many big kids around, you know when the milk arrives by the sweet and sour smell that spreads all around. Then the line, quiet until now, everyone waiting in their spot, shifts, moves like a snake, or a wave. Big kids push out the little ones even though we are the very first in line, right next to the window where the milk is sold. They kick you with their elbows, feet, in the stomach, anywhere. I am hanging on, almost on the ground, between the legs of a big pimply boy holding my former spot. I refuse to be moved. I have been there the whole morning, shit. Then I faint, or pretend to have, or maybe it really happened and they carry me off inside, put some water on my head, and milk in the container, one whole liter in my blue pot. This was not cheating since my place was always among the first ones in the line.

In the summer the milk was boiled, then it went sour, imagine after all that waiting. She would use it anyway, bake it into a bread. Other times it was boiled, didn't go sour at all, was left in the bedroom to cool, to form a cream crust. Bratso often snuck in the bedroom where it cooled on the window sill and drank it with a straw of wheat through the cream top. Nothing remained for me, not a drop. Mother scolded him through laughter and said that male children are selfish but they just need more milk and meat and everything in general. A male child cannot stare at something like a piece of meat on my plate, he cannot stare and want it and not get it. It would hurt him too much. How? Where?

She points between the legs. There.

They are fragile there. Don't hit him there! It could damage him, kill him, destroy the seeds. What seeds?

With girls it's different, they have nothing there. That's why baby girls are left to cry forever, never picked up, their bodies cannot be damaged by crying. Nothing can happen to them. There is nothing there, she says, only a hole. That's why you don't kiss girls there, only baby boys. Female children are not precious, "my precious, my boy, my little man" because "thunder never kills the bad weed," mother finished explaining with the proverb for the females and the gypsies.

If you think the milk lines are bad, you haven't seen anything. The meat line is worse but differently. Here they are, all women, many pregnant with red brown patches on the face, big bellies sticking out, really ugly as sin, waiting there, yakking all the time about husbands and stomachs and stuff. My turn comes and I deliver the same single sentence to that butcher who lives by the creek and has cheeks like steaks. I say as instructed without taking a breath, "Mother wants some tender stuff from the thigh and no bones or gristle."

He looks at me, barely to his waist, and says, "What, say it again!"

I repeat about the bones and the rest.

He winks now at all those women, then very loud, "Tell your mother I wouldn't mind a tender piece of the thigh myself. No bones for me either, only the good stuff. I don't care for those. Give them to the dogs, I say. What do you think, women, do you like the bones or a piece of that thigh."

The hell breaks loose throughout the line.

"Ha-ha, thigh, ha-ha, tender," their faces ugly just like after they butchered the pig and talk about balls. I am ashamed without knowing why, but the meat from the thigh without any bones I got. Female children are good for something.

Good for something yes but not for the most important occasions like Christmas and the Saint's Day when only a male child (and then, God forbid you didn't have one, better get a male relative to help, next best), when a male child would carry the log inside the house in a shower of rice and wheat grain for good luck and cut the cake in half with the priest at church, a very solemn occasion that happened in December, our Saint's Day.

The cake was baked out of white meal, glazed with pretend branches and fruit on the top; Bratso and mother took it to church, then Bratso wrestled with the priest to see who got the bigger half. Bratso did ("my precious, my little man"). Then the wine was poured over it, candle lit in the middle. It remained like that in the bedroom throughout the three days that we celebrate the saint; you ate it in the morning with coffee on the fourth.

Other things were baked for this occasion, depending how much food you had, but you borrowed if you had to so the visitors could pay respects to your saint. You clean the house for days first, arrange everything nice, then guests arrive, not all at once, slowly one by one, two or three, wipe their feet. They sit down, have a spoonful, must have a spoonful of the wheat dish, sweet with nuts and honey, very good. They cross themselves first, take the spoonful, drink a glass of water that you pumped cold, put the spoon in a separate dish. I carry all this on a silver tray rescued from the war, and say to each: "Please, serve yourself."

They look at me carefully, make comments on my face, hair, "how she has grown." In one corner, the icon of Saint Nicholas the protector stares at you from the wall. The room smells of cakes, incense and rosemary leaves, a holy plant.

The priest arrived before this event to bless the house with incense and rosemary for the whole year. He dips the branch of rosemary in the bowl of cold water we prepared, sprinkles the water everywhere, in the corners of the rooms, over the bed, in the kitchen, then on top of our heads, chanting in his beard, "God bless Anna, God bless Bratso, *Pomiluj*."

I do my best not to laugh, but it's hard — think about the beating you'll get if you don't stop, stop yourself.

His job is done, he can drink coffee and brandy that mother serves him on the dish; she slips money in his pocket; he leaves us that rosemary branch. It goes like that every single time. Or, he gives her his hand to kiss, extends it in front; she does it very serious, then puts something in his coat pocket. His hands are fat, hairy, smell of garlic, he expects us to kiss them as well but I jump through the window and hide in the flowers until he goes away. You can only do that if you live on the ground floor; we are lucky in a way.

In the class, this whole thing with the priest and rosemary branch is called "opium of the people," "dark ages," "our backwardness" and I think more and more they are right. The priest is fat, well fed, gets money just for throwing water over you with the branch. Nobody thanked me for waiting in line for meat and milk and bread and that was much harder. Of course, I don't discuss these things with anyone, even though my cheeks burned with shame when teacher asked how many of us still celebrated such things, and my hand had to go up. There was no way to lie about it; everyone knew my mother, "where she stood on religion." It was unfair to ask such questions since I had no choice if I celebrated or not. Children have no choice anywhere except in their heads.

A priest was necessary for these special occasions to bless and chant but he brought bad luck any other time, there was no doubt about it. Everyone said that including mother who claimed that she would postpone a trip if she met one on the road that day; she would just spit and go back, wait for a more lucky time. There was a remedy however, that only kids knew about. If you meet a priest on the street, you immediately hold onto a button, any button you have, dress or coat until he passes by and then you are fine until the next time. But imagine this:

Here I am with Bratso walking toward the river in July in our bathing suits, or rather our underpants, barefoot, here we are walking calmly thinking about the river, when here comes this blackness of a priest sliding, slinking by (toward us), grinning in his beard. Panic, nowhere to go, nowhere to hide. It's too late, he is already here, no buttons in sight, this is it!

He looks at us and says, low, "Got you this time, didn't I? Where is your button, eh?"

Isn't it funny that he seemed to know all along. He must have been a kid once too. After that I wasn't afraid of him and didn't even bother with buttons until this new priest appeared and that was different.

Old women bring bad luck also, as bad as the priest, and you couldn't use the same charm. The ones that flatter you a lot and have green eyes are the worst. Whenever somebody says, "What a pretty child" or something like it, real nice, mother always adds, "Yes, but her nose is crooked and she smells bad." That did the job, and the words couldn't get you then, had no effect. She knew everything about this, was very careful since one of those old women did something to me when I was six or maybe five. This old woman passed by the house and said, looking at me, "what beautiful eyes she has, that child." Nothing happened at first, I played as usual but then later my stomach started hurting and I cried and cried until another old woman came to the house to deliver me from evil intent. She did it with hot lead, a bullet heated in the fire, which she threw fast in a bucket of cold water where it smoked and sang for a second, then broke into small pieces of lead. These pieces contained the secret about the woman with the green eyes who cast the spell.

They are looking over the bucket, by the candle light for some reason.

"See, she lives near you and probably said, "what a pretty child.""

Mother: "Who could it be?"

Woman: "Think, green eyes, old, wears black!"

Mother: "It must be Vesta, who else, the bitch."

Woman: "I won't say yes or no, but I wouldn't have her in my house, day or night."

Mother is certain now. She remembers the woman well, how she said, "what pretty eyes she has." Half the cure is in spotting the evil person, then you chase her away from your insides.

"Devil take her away from us, from this child, to the mountains, away from the living, where nothing grows, where dogs don't bark, where birds don't sing, away and away, stay there and forever, from this child, amen." That did her in pretty well.

Now the woman makes a strange sound—"e-e-e-,ts,ts,ts," then spits three times right in that water. She orders mother to spit and mother does. It has to be three times. It's almost over, they have chased her to the high mountains, I'll be okay soon. They make me drink some of that water where the bullet fell and shattered. And that's that! I've been exorcised, they say.

I am taught how to protect myself from evil people by raising the fingers of my left hand so they look like horns, small finger and index in the air, others tucked in. You wait until they pass by, until their backs are turned, then fast, you spit three times after them, saying very low at the same time:

In your name, not mine
May the devil take you
Away from me.

Spit, spit, spit, three times after the old woman who lives near us, the one who did that thing that time. Mother knows who it is, which one.

The numbers are essential, mattered, they did the trick, but every number was different, for a different thing.

My favorite is five, always red in color. Why red? I don't know, just like that, three is green. If I count to five, something good will happen to me, five is also the best mark at school. If I count to five, and blink ten times, that's even better. Pump the water in five strokes for the guest, it has to be cold, run to the house by the time you count to five, climb the stairs by five.

How many times did I blink? No good, eight.

Other times, when counting and pumping the water, IT appears. A voice, small one, whispers: "You want her dead."

"Who?" I ask.

"You want your mother dead." I want her dead.

I didn't. It was somebody else.

Count to ten, jump up without blinking, then nothing will happen, she won't die.

"She won't die, she won't die." Jump, jump, jump.

"Please, don't let it happen, please don't. If it did happen, it would be my fault. I wished it. I did. I had to. I didn't."

The frog jumps out of somewhere behind the pump, stops the voice. I don't pump any more. I look at the frog.

It looks back at me—huge, green, big as my hand. *Suddenly* my father is with me on the road, holds me, he seems far away, a ghost. Keep him tight, don't forget! You are forgetting. Reach for the cherries. He is lifting you up. Remember the face. He is blond, blue-eyed, not strong, like me. He ran up and kissed me right away mother says with disgust, unwashed, and female at that. He was so happy that day, everyone says that, that he got drunk and fired three times with his pistol to celebrate my arrival, and kissed me then. Nobody did that for a girl child ever, but he was a weird man, she thinks, never did anything right, not like everybody else.

From him only books remain, some pictures, and postcards of strange foreign cities. I read his books over and over again until I know them by heart, many books on health care among the peasants, how to dig good wells, how to set up a room for a sick person, how to recognize TB. Books about trips to Africa with pictures of beauties from places called Zanzibar, the Sudan. Then, novels, stories about grown-ups who wander around the world searching for happiness and never find it until the very end, and then it's too late. In these books they always describe a dress or a tree or a house in a long way, it takes them two, three pages for a dress; it could get boring, you could give up but I don't, and read the description of the dress or a tree over and over again until it gets to have a real color, moves in front of me.

One large blue book is locked up in the closet with the picture album. Its title is funny, *Woman-Sex, Woman-Man,* some Englishman wrote it. In it, when you manage to unlock the closet, on the bottom shelf, there are many pictures of naked women all over the world and the information that girls in Java are the most beautiful of all because of their size and some other things. Women from Java look at me from the pictures, they eat fruit under tall lazy trees or swim in very clear streams, many flowers in the back of them, in Java. Everything is there in that book—how women had babies in Africa by hanging from a tree and men pushed on their big stomachs. Scary. Can you imagine hanging from a tree with a big stomach? You flip a page, and there is a woman with a breast on her hip, another one on her thigh, then an old man is sucking this breast to have more strength, it says. All of this happened in other countries, not us.

The book has many charts and numbers on size and age of women all over the world, when they get married, when they die. Mother hides the book in the closet but she forgets, leaves the key outside, and I read it here and there a couple of times. I have nothing to worry about, not yet, not having breasts and things that women have. I take the small mirror, mother's with a powder puff, to see if what I had compared with that God-awful sight in the large picture. Nothing to compare, thank God for that. Maybe if I am lucky I'll never grow up. Maybe it won't happen. I'll pray and count to five.

Grandma kneels and prays in front of St. Nicholas when she has time. She is in the corner in front of him, I only see her back.

God, give us good health, help us survive. I don't care about me, God, I have lived enough, you see, but it would be nice

to see Anna all grown up. Then, take me at once. She needs
me still for a year or two, she needs new shoes too, and a nice
coat . . . Make Bratso behave, I am too old, can't look after
him as much. Help us oh Lord.

She gets off the floor, huffs and puffs a bit.
"You asked nothing about father," I say.
"God, you scared me. I didn't know you were there."
"What about the doctor, you didn't say "God, help Doctor Ivo.'"
"Next time, I will, I won't forget those two."
"What about mother? Talk to him about her."
"I do those in silence every night. She is feeding us all, needs all
the extra help."
Grandma's prayers are just like her dresses, sort of simple, blue
or brown cotton. If I believed anybody, anybody's prayers that is,
I would believe hers. She knew what she was doing all the time and
women came to her for different things. Such and such tea for a cough,
such and such for nerves, a horrible bitter weed she cooks for mother
who always falls asleep after, sleeps for a long time. Grandma sleeps
well without any help from teas, only gets angry once in a while
in the mornings, trying to pile her hair on top. The braids and pins
fall down, she starts all over again.
"Devil's work, the hair, I'll cut it off," she mutters but doesn't. Her
hair is long, just a bit white on the sides, strange for an old woman
they say; she is almost seventy but you could never tell by her walk.
Grandma is tall, very straight in the back, can run fast, even catches
Bratso at times, "the Devil," she calls him. Words like pretty and
ugly don't apply to her, you better think of something else. How about
a tree of some sort, a pine perhaps. I wonder what she was like when
very small. There are no pictures of that time, none. I know that
she lived in this very beautiful city by the sea, warm climate always,
ships, and was engaged to a sailor who had blue eyes. One night,
just a week before her marriage, he drowned with others in a big
storm, they never found him, and she promised never to marry
anybody else, and that's how it was. She is not my grandma although
I call her so, but my great-aunt on my mother's side. The "real" grandma I never saw. It takes a while to sort all these things out, who
is who, what's what, what happened, what didn't. The story about

the sailor is true, grandma's only secret and she doesn't like to repeat it at all, but I insist whenever she braids her hair or when she goes to bed. That's the good moment to ask, for her to tell.

Mother has tons of secrets, some shared with Yanna about people and the land they come from, in the same country of course, but still far, in the mountains somewhere, not far from the sea. Mother and Yanna whisper and whisper before I fall asleep. I imagine these people as tall, dark, stern, maybe mean.

Before we sleep, mother washes herself, often in front of me. She does it on purpose I think to show off her body, very white, strong, big breasts. She finds a reason like "wash my back." Once a month, she is in a bad mood, ties a white rag with a cord around her waist and looks like an Indian woman in the pictures in the blue book. I try it myself in front of a window glass in the afternoon when nobody's around looking, and I see this funny blond kid with a handkerchief between her legs staring at me. I have to laugh, she looks that funny.

"You have nothing to worry about, not yet," mother says one of these days. "I didn't get it until eighteen, you won't either. The later, the better. Women are cursed. I should have been a man." On handkerchief days, she is always angry, same as when she does the sheets, she drinks more coffee, snaps at me, slaps. *Learn to avoid her on those days, stay away.*

Mother is taller and stronger than other mothers around; they are rounder and pinker and softer around the cheeks. She isn't skinny either but not soft. Her eyebrows gather in one nasty wrinkle when angry, a sign to leave the house, avoid her that day. Other women are afraid of the dark, of snakes and mice, not her, but she has her fits and faintings that nobody knows except grandma and me. Also, some strange vanity when she puts lipstick on, just partially, never in the corners of the mouth.

"You forgot the corners," I say in spite of myself. She is getting ready to go work in the hotel.

"It'll make my mouth too big if I did that." And she does it as usual, just the middle is red, not too pretty like that. You can see the size of the mouth even though she has only a bit of the lipstick in the middle.

Do I find her pretty or ugly or what?

I look at her often, while she dresses, washes, sleeps. When asleep she looks the best, mouth slightly open, black hair over one cheek.

44

She sleeps with one arm under her head, other slightly in front, then turns to the side.

Pretty, yes, she is, I think.

Once up, everything changes, the wrinkle between the eyebrows appears. She looks at me angry, "What are you staring at?" No, she is not pretty, not at all, but then most married women aren't. Small mouth, white white skin, very black hair, and dark eyes — that's my mother's idea of an attractive person, a girl. Everyone agrees with her on that subject.

"You should have seen her," they talk about some girl, "what dark eyes, like a fire, what raven hair like the darkest night, what a walk." Blond women, like the one upstairs, are considered faded, not exciting at all. A blond can be beautiful once in a while but she has to be perfect, really everything perfect, to stand out, while a brunette can be attractive with a little. Blond=weak, dark=strength, fire. I am out of luck, I know that already, but then who knows maybe I'll be that truly perfect blond, the beautiful one, or maybe I'll not grow up at all, I hope not.

A girl of my age, a peasant girl who brings us cheese once a month has dark curly hair that my mother caresses forever even though it is really coarse, can't feel good to touch, doesn't slip through your fingers like mine. (Mine is like water, or the river moss, I know it, I have touched it but she does not.)

"My pretty one, my curly one," she croons kissing this brown-haired girl with small beady eyes like a rat.

"If only one of them looked like me! Why couldn't God give me that?" she says.

"You shouldn't ask God for stupid things, or he might really give you troubles," grandma says, low for me not to hear. "They are both fine and healthy kids. Anna is even . . ." What are they whispering about?

"You are blind, look at her face." Grandma says, smiling at me.

If Yanna is around when they talk eyes, hair, colors, who looks like whom, mother looks at her sister and starts crying as if remembering something. Then they whisper about things, deaths and horrors.

After awhile, mother started saying that Bratso looked like her, even though nobody ever saw the resemblance but her, while I did have her wide mouth, the one thing about me I don't like.

CHAPTER EIGHT

T EACHER GIVES BOOKS to all excellent students at the end of the
year. My own is called *History of Glass*, how glass started, was made
centuries before mirrors, Egyptian glass, Venetian, all that work,
slow, some discoveries took hundreds of years, men who did them
forgotten now. It seems sad, all of it. I wouldn't even know about
them if I hadn't read this book. Then she gave me Russian fairy tales,
and a book by Gorky whose name means bitter in Russian. I read
his book three times, it was that good and couldn't help myself but
had to ask teacher if she had others by the same man, and she said,
yes, there are four more in the library, go there. I read all about
bums and poor and homeless people who live near a large river
somewhere in Russia, in small rooms around a large courtyard. They
argue and drink a lot, beat each other up, swear, but everyone even
the worst has a secret dream that things will change some day. I like
the way he talks about all those people; it makes sense so much I
want to cry. I read usually in a hidden spot somewhere in the yard,
or near the creek where peasant women pass on their way to town
lifting their skirts to pee, or on the door step facing a big tree. The
sun warms me, nice, the book slides from my hands, falls to the
ground without a sound; I travel slowly toward the leaves, disappear
completely, change into a bug or a leaf or a cloud. Leaves sing low,
smell of lilacs somewhere, a lady bug on my toe, green green grass.

"Wake up, wake up, wake up, what a child, you've let the milk burn all over the stove, and the bread is burned and you didn't make the beds!"

Run, hurry, get the bread out, sprinkle it with water, scrape the burnt part, wrap it in the towel, it's saved. Make the beds and fluff them as well. Turn the mattress over, once a week, take the sheets, blankets, pillows, put them on the window sill to air, to sun; the sun fights TB. Dust everything well, shake the lace doilies through the window in the flowers. When finished, look at yourself in the window glass for signs, no, not yet. Then, hurry, feed the pig its lunch. Take the slop from the bucket where the greasy dishwater is kept (neighbors contribute after every good meal if they don't have a pig; they come and say, "We just had some good *paprikash,* didn't want to waste the slops"), take the slops, put some corn meal in, cook it with potato peels or some rotten potatoes, pigs don't mind, then lift it all from the stove to cool awhile and the pig will have a lunch. The hardest part is lifting the bucket from the stove; it's a heavy one.

I make the beds, clean the house, wait in lines, cook for the pig and in addition have to watch over Bratso who does nothing at all since he is a boy and also young. I don't do all of it while grandma is alive; after, yes. He runs around, plays, trades dead frogs or pieces of junk, gets in trouble; women come to complain to mother, he beat so-and-so in the yard, did such-and-such, killed a chicken with his sling shot. He breaks his bones, jumps from trees; you have to watch him all the time. A horse carriage even ran over him once and mother worried to death that he would become a cripple but nothing happened to him, just a few blue marks.

Grandma runs after him all the time huffing and puffing, we never knew what would happen next. Then one day she got so tired of chasing him and worrying that she tied him to the tree while she went to the market. This way he was safe for a time, tied with a cord in the yard. Other kids heard about it, arrived to see as fast as they could, and there was Bratso tied like a dog. Right off they started to bark—"ruff, ruff"—and on and on, barking, until he began to cry.

Bratso had red cheeks in any season, not just winter, hands like a small baby, round with dimples. He did things without knowing why. When he cries like that, I feel bad, I chase the kids away, even though he was her favorite, it was clear to everyone.

They teased him about the tree for a while, then things were fine until the day they found out that our pig was wearing his underpants, brown ones. They went to look at the pig and sure enough it was true, all mother's work. Our pig got sick for some reason and mother decided to cure it with aspirins and these underpants; it was a serious matter, the pig had a fever, wouldn't eat at all, no lard or ham if things didn't improve. She could have kept quiet about the pants, it could have been a family secret, but she herself thought it was funny, couldn't help herself, everyone found out and laughed. For days they laughed, poor Bratso cried, then the summer arrived and they forgot.

In the summer, we travelled to grandpa's in a truck, across many hills, small rivers and a big one. The road has bumps, stones, curves, the truck shakes, smells of gas, many people vomit. The driver wears a leather vest, drinks a lot swearing at the road, blaming everyone.

"Get your asses out," he orders, "fuck this road, fuck my unlucky stars, get out, we're stuck."

The truck is stuck in the mud, all of us push very hard, then get on it again, red from the red mud. We are going high up in the mountain now, the road changes a bit, gets very narrow, the hill is to the left. Some people are asleep, others sing, then another truck appears, coming toward us. All of us wake up, the peasants start praying to their saint. It's very scary. A big, deep gorge, foamy green water are down below; our driver swears, then backs up, pulls in closer to the hill, you can touch the bank. That's clever, we think, the other one toward the gorge is the scary side, thank God we are on the left side, nothing can happen to us. The other truck moves slowly toward us, I shut my eyes, nobody says a word, we did it — hurrah — until the next time.

Grandpa waits for us in a town much smaller than mine. This town is flat and dusty and small, nothing to it, no movie houses, a couple small shops with old signs that say haberdasher, mason, dyes, two dark smoky inns full of drunk peasants — just one street, that's all. It's almost a village except it isn't. In a village, houses are not built together in one straight row, but scattered all around with land in between, with big courtyards, animals everywhere. This town is something in between.

Grandpa waits for us with his horse carriage at the market place. We hop in the carriage, he lets Bratso hold the reins, the horse knows the way, you can't get lost. Then we travel on a narrow country road where the cars can't pass, the same road where I was with father and the frog jumped at me when I was four or five. We are silent, grandpa smokes his pipe, the horse just trots evenly, Bratso is showing off with the reins. I don't think about father just then as we pass the bridge. I think, yes, this is the place where, but somehow he is nearer to me elsewhere, when I pump the water at our place.

In the village, a crowd gathers to greet us, we are known there. Girls with white kerchiefs, old women without teeth touch my cheek, say, "How she has grown." Grandpa stands in the middle, looks very proud. He is just about the oldest man around, very much liked, you can tell that, tall, quiet with blue eyes. He could look like me except that I realy look like his sister, my father's mother who died when giving birth. A beautiful girl she was, he says, with a long thick braid. You see, he was not my "real" grandfather although we called him that. It was easier than saying "great uncle," a clumsy word that can't be shortened and besides all the old men were called "grandpa" and you kissed their hand as a sign of respect.

To get to grandpa's house, you get off the carriage and walk across a tiny bridge, just big enough for one person at a time. The horse with the carrige goes in the water, not deep right there, you can see the pebbles. Now you are on the other side, then, past the sunflowers, grandpa's land starts up from the river, up the narrow red road to the main gate, a large wooden one big enough for horses and sheep and cows if you open it all the way.

A dog barks somewhere, tied. The courtyard is huge with many small buildings around and they are all his—the main house, white with a carved door in the center, barn to the right with a hayloft. There is a place for pigs and another one for chickens and ducks, and still another for sheep, a round building for wheat and corn, a small cool one for cheese and finally a john that nobody uses except me.

The vegetable garden is below the house, then the cornfields, then the river. Grandma (or great-aunt but still called grandma) sits in the garden picking tomatoes when we arrive in the yard. She wears many skirts one on top of the other, an apron, and a kerchief to shield her from the sun. She is short wide brown with a soft voice that never goes up, a bit like the other grandma except that this one is a peasant.

They had no children, saddest thing in the world even in the city. Not to have one here is a curse, mother thinks, but you can't escape your fate. It's all written up there, what will happen, the day you are born, the day you die. We know the story already from the other times, his story about the gypsy.

The gypsy with the kid told grandpa all about his future by looking at his palm; he was young then, laughed at her, disbelieving gypsy tricks, how he would marry a girl from a wealthy family, come to live on her land and will have no children at all his entire life. He tried his best to make things happen differently but one day he forgot all about it, met a girl at the fair without knowing she was well-to-do, and there it was, what they call love. Love did it to him, or fate. If he had married Yelenka, the one his parents chose for him, he would have had five sons, but you can't escape your stars.

To remedy things, they would adopt a girl from a large family (where she wouldn't be missed so much), she would stay with them and work, then they bought her things and married her off. These girls, married now, see them at times on holidays and Sundays with gifts tied in a handkerchief, cry a lot when parting, call them dad, mom. Right now when we arrive, they have Lena, with red cheeks, unmarried yet, still young, maybe sixteen. She gets up early, the first; through my sleep I hear the bells ringing as she takes the cows out to pasture. The horse remains tied in a meadow behind the garden, pigs take care of themselves in the forest behind the house. They eat all the fallen chestnuts and look generally unpleasant.

Grandma is feeding chickens, making funny sounds—pwee, pwee—when I wake up at nine or ten. We eat black bread with cream, milk with a small bit of coffee in white cups with pictures of kids on them. Grandpa drinks real coffee, black, smokes his pipe, looks for things to do under the open shed where the wood tools are. He makes us a small carriage with perfect wheels, then we harness the dog to it, but he dumps us again and again. We try it with a sheep and a goat, then give up and wheel each other around. When Lena arrives with cows we have our second breakfast which she calls "dinner"; there is still the whole afternoon left. Mother stayed for a day or so making sure we slept in proper beds with sheets (only grandpa and us had those), gave many instructions about food and rusty nails and wearing shoes. As soon as she leaves, we forget about the shoes, there is no point, too much trouble taking them off, putting them on. After a week your soles harden, hurt no more, and if you step on a nail, just pee on it, that's what Lena did.

We wander, exploring along the river, through the cornfields first, then the sunflowers, then the willow trees looking for the perfect spot. Dark shadowy deep pools right under the willow branches are too scary. Snakes might be hiding there or the ghosts of the dead girls whispering to follow them to the whirlpool hidden in the deepest part. Somebody saw one of them once. That's how the neighbor's son drowned one night as she led him to the pool. So I choose clear sunny spots where the water falls over the rocks, glistens. You can see what's what, not be afraid. Near the mill just across the little bridge, the water foams, feels cooler. Go and stay there awhile, as long as you wish, nobody's calling your name, then run to the meadow across, warm up on the grass, or sit on the white pebbles by the river, keep your feet in. Or go inside the mill, very white, dusty, and weigh yourself adding and subtracting small amounts until it's right. Then run back across the bridge, grab some cheese and corn bread and wander some more, follow the river downstream. The spring is very near, right by the monastery you see from the house. I never go in that direction, nothing of interest to see except a bunch of young men in black clothes with long hair and beards working in the fields. Nobody says much about them but you can tell you better stay away from those, they are not like us. They never marry, live together in a bunch, Lena finds it all very funny, ha-ha, she goes, pointing at them.

On some afternoons Lena and I go to the hills with sheep, picking a new spot every time, always where her friends are. They put all the sheep together, have less work. I wonder how they know which is which but they do, each time. Taking care of sheep is so easy, you could fall asleep, or play songs on Lena's wooden flute. If the rams start fighting, everything changes. Their horns clash in a horrible sound, and Lena pushes me behind her. They stop by themselves or she throws stones to make them stop or they gash themselves pretty bad.

When it turns cold, we roast potatoes and corn on the fire. You just go in the fields and find some, any field is good. Lena eats her corn very hot, squatting on her heels, whispering with the others, ignoring me. A friend of hers, a girl I know from another summer, got married in May and she told Lena that on her wedding night there was this thing like a corn cob between her legs. The girls go ha-ha in sheer delight and look in my direction. Lena shakes her head. "No," she says, "she wouldn't know about that."

In the evening Lena milks the cows, sitting on a little stool. She pats them first gently on the backs, calls them all sorts of names like "my sweet one, my bird, my plum," then she sits on that little stool and the milk goes in the bucket. I try once but nothing happens. You have to be very strong and in addition a cow has to like you a lot to let out all that milk. If they don't, Lena says, they can kick you off the stool if they wish, spill all the milk.

The wheat harvest starts in August when the weather is good. Men and women all very young arrive with their own sickles, the handles smooth and shiny from another summer, sometimes carved and decorated with flowers, red, green, blue. Girls wear their best blouses for this occasion but still no shoes. Bratso and I can help toward the end when it's almost done, but now the main thing is to stay away and watch as the big sheaves of wheat fall down, the backs of men and women go down, up. The girls start a song, one woman first, very loud, then the second voice then all the others. The songs have different words, always the same sound—oj, oj—always sad a bit. At times men sing but their songs are different, not as sad. Lena and grandma bring the lunch in the shade by the river, lay out the dishes on the grass—a large, warm bread, cheese and the cream, always a soup with meat and a barley dish. They put their spoons in the soup pot, slurp it directly, break the bread with their hands, nobody bothers with a knife. Men and women tease each other, women blush, and everybody hurries back to the field to get it all done that day in case the rain falls or hail, which would ruin the harvest.

When the wheat is cut, other people who walk behind the reapers pick it up, tie it in small bundles, then larger ones, then very large, then you cover it all up. That's how it goes, every season, if the times are good and it rained enough in the spring and you have something to harvest. Too much rain or too little is all the peasants talk about, they are always looking toward the clouds. And then if it is good for one plant, it's bad for another one. "Peasants are cursed," grandpa thinks, but the air is better here, too many people in the city.

We eat dinner around a large table with a kerosene lamp in the middle, grandpa has no electricity yet. Then off to bed. Lena leads the way with a lighted pine branch toward the small house where two of us sleep. There are two tiny rooms, one where grandma keeps her treasures hidden inside a large wooden trunk, another with two beds for Bratso and me. There is also a large loom, pictures of father as a boy in wooden frames, their saint right over our heads. Lena says, "Good night, give me a kiss." We do, she leaves. Sounds outside continue for awhile, then they let a dog off the leash, then complete silence and very dark night.

Sundays, grandpa smokes the pipe with a silver tip and talks with men who arrive with newspapers from town. I sit on his lap, sometimes hang around his neck. He likes this very much and each time he says as if for the first time, "My own, looks just like Milka, do you remember what a beauty she was."

"Yes, you can surely tell, blood is thicker than water," they say, "blood is blood."

He lights his pipe in the strangest way, not with matches as he could, but by rubbing small pieces of stone against some old wood, and then there are no flames, just smoldering wood. He likes it better this way, it's just enough to light the pipe even though it takes a long time for the whole thing.

The old men around grandpa smoke too, some cigarettes, some pipes, and talk about the Balkans and Churchill and how the English are sly, French good, friendly just like us. Grandpa met the French during the big war, the other one, when he was a prisoner on Corfu, an island, I better look it up on the map. Thousands died he said before reaching Corfu, and others died there too. Then it gets confusing—somehow, somewhere he was a prisoner and ran away from the enemy camp in the middle of the night in winter with another guy, all through the snow, waist deep, in Albania. They had nothing on except their shirts and underpants as they ran from the camp. All the men sitting here smoking know about this story and about the war. They shake their heads, look into the distance somewhere beyond the hills.

"What a human will endure," they sigh, "more than a dog." That's why grandpa suffers from the rheumatism on account of the escape in that snow in his underpants. He has many medals and documents from that war, more than anyone else around, not just in this village, but other villages around. Grandpa doesn't like to talk about it, becomes very shy. "War is hell. It always is. Medals don't help you much when your legs hurt. We are . . . a small country, not much to us. They have passed over us again and again, they will do it some more. Small countries are cursed."

"Tell about the Germans, c'mon, do," I ask.

"There is nothing to tell," he says.

The Germans took him hostage, with the other nine, then at the last moment they let them go, otherwise he would have been shot. Ten for one, that's how it was. That's in my books.

"Why did they let you go? What happened?"

"Just like that," he says, but I know he is hiding something from me, something all of them know well.

"The English are sly, you can't trust them for a minute," they agree, all three.

"They would sell their own mother for profit, Americans are the same."

"The French are just like us, drink wine, laugh a lot, shared their food on Corfu," they say, neither one of them smiling.

"The Russians are powerful. Now there's a country! All that good land and wheat."

"The sun never sets there it's so big. Think of that, brother," says one old man.

I try, but the hills stop me fast.

The world, England, France, Russia are somewhere over the hills very far away. Airplanes that pass over us once in awhile go there. Russia is like the sun, the morning sun or at noon, not later; the west or what they call western is pale blue, the color of the sun on winter days, or the sun setting. Red is the color of the east for me, the color of the revolution, but then I did see a film on that subject this year.

"Awake the East and the West Awake the North and the South
The World revolution is coming Comrades, march, advance . . ."

March, march, red flags in the wind, a red scarf around my neck, we are singing up and down the Main Street.

"Down with the bourgeois parasites!" a voice shouts in the crowd. I join in, that part is easy.

"Down with them!" a big roar, an echo, a scream.

"Down with the reactionaries, parasites, lackeys of the West!"

"Down with them, kill!"

"Death to Fascism!" from a man on crutches, next to me.

"Power to the People!" thunder, a symphony.

The future is ours, it's clear, now and forever, red.

A huge mass of people both angry and happy make huge proclamations, some older kids make speeches too with squeaky voices about their role in this revolution, then a Russian dance on the podium done by the *Gymnasium* kids, kicking their heels, falling to the ground, very fast, accordion playing, people clapping, then everything stops. A serious chorus of students in black and white appears, girls in pleated skirts. They start on a shrill tune without a melody; a short guy directs them with a stick. After that, the official celebration breaks up.

We don't do much yet, that will come, we are only Pioneers. Our duty is to be nice to people, plant trees in the park, pay attention to hygiene, don't spit on the floor (TB is everywhere, don't spit, bad) and above all—study hard.

STUDY, STUDY, AND ONLY STUDY, Lenin says from the walls.

Other signs are there too, more complicated ones.

ELECTRIFICATION + INDUSTRIALIZATION = something else. I forget what.

Or OUR YOUTH, OUR TREASURE.

"What do you want to be when you grow up?" teacher asks all around the class.

Me: "A partisan."

She: "You can't be a partisan, that's before, we don't need them anymore. You can be a worker and a hero although that would be too bad with your grades. We'll think of something."

Me to me: "I'd still rather be a partisan or maybe a doctor."

On the square, the celebration continues at night after the official speeches and slogans stop. A big circle dances, sometimes light, other times heavy, possessed. Many accordions, drums. A tall dark man in peasant shoes leads them on, twirling his handkerchief. He yells first, screams something to the others to get them going, stamps his foot, the others follow, thousands of them stamping the ground, much foot work, shoulders straight, hand in hand, head sometimes low, other times high, men rip their shirts off, bare hairy chests, sweat falls on the ground, I can see it fall, coins in their pockets keep a beat, beads on the girls' necks shake, up and down shake their breasts. It might not stop. It's too late, it's going round and round, accordions, drums.

Our whole land is behind us
Our future in front

They are singing now as they dance, changing everything a bit, and before you know it it sounds like a peasant tune.
Where am I? What is it all about? What will happen to me?
The dance to celebrate October, harvest time and the Revolution gets bigger, more powerful. I stare at the large fire in the middle of the square, flames red. Kids run all around. Women squeal.
What will happen to me? Will I get lost in all this like in the grass?

CHAPTER NINE

S HE CALLS: "Bratso, Brat-so, where are you?"

I run up.

"What is it? What happened? He's with me."

"Good," she says. "Just checking to see if he's there. I got scared all of a sudden."

I run back. We are in the yard—Bratso, Boris, Zoran and the new kid. Bratso has just cut his hand to mix blood with Zoran, become blood brothers with him, swearing to keep the secrets as long as he lives, or may his mother die, or worse, him. They had stopped being friends for two days, but today, it's sealed. I had tied their hands cut against the cut with a handkerchief; the blood must be all mixed by now, untie them. Let's go on with the game.

"Who comes here in Sherwood Forest without a pass, give me a pass word."

"The Revolution," I scream.

"Who goes there? Name your names!"

"Anna, chief commander of the fifth brigade."

"You over there, name yours."

"Boris, the terror of the seas."

"No, Boris, it's not like that! You can't be a pirate and a partisan. You simply can't. That's not how it goes. You could be a German. We have to start all over again."

"Who goes there?"

After that, we did much killing with wooden swords, all according to the rules.

"Fall, stupid, you're supposed to," I scream at him. He is always like that.

"I don't want to be the only one to die. How come it's always me? I don't want to play with you any more."

Just like that every time.

"Okay, I will die next, go touch me."

And he became Robin Hood again for awhile, me the bad guy. We count the dead and plan the next battle, who will be what, what the disagreement is. Nobody wants to be a German. We have to find a different enemy. Boris says he doesn't want to be a German, you be one. I say let's switch to Indians or Kraljevic Marko and the Turks. We have the swords ready, don't have to change much. The new kid in clean pants is a problem however; he doesn't understand the rules, even Bratso comments on that. He eats his chocolate all by himself which is not fair; we simply can't let him in the gang.

"We can't let you in if you don't share your food, that's how it was with Robin Hood's guys."

"Who is Robin Hood?" he says. No wonder he was eating it alone.

"Why he was the greatest guy that ever lived, just like Kraljevic Marko except he was English."

"What did he do? Was he nice?" says the new kid.

"Was he nice? Sure he was. He was the greatest robber that ever lived, and he stole from the rich, you know, the priests and counts and capitalists, never the poor like us."

To have to waste my play time and explain Robin Hood is silly. This kid is uneducated. He is still eating a bit of chocolate; all of us look. There is only the tiniest piece left. He takes it out of his mouth, gives everyone a lick, that's all there is. I wonder if he is one of our kind, probably not, you can tell. He can stay today but no more, Boris and I decide in secret without taking votes. A kid who shows off with chocolate like that would make others feel bad.

On all fours, we swim in the grass, then run down the slope toward the creek. Very silently we move upstream. The grass is tall, I wear a feather tied with my red pioneer scarf, Boris has one too, Bratso has one. Advance toward the butcher's house! His twins are the chief enemy—cowboys or Germans. They attacked last week by surprise, we are paying them back. Our bombs are ready and our swords.

When we come near, I wave to the troops to stop, remain silent, we are in enemy territory, don't make a sound, I'll spy and report. I crawl through the grass; only a few steps separate me from the house. This is it. I can't hear a sound. What if they surprise me, catch me from behind? I see Boris' feather, wave him to go down on his knees, I take my feather off. Then through a half-opened window I see— the butcher is killing his wife, right on the kitchen table, squashing her, she can't breathe. I see one foot, eyes fixed toward the ceiling move. I see her tongue. She moans in pain. Head rolls from side to side. I see her teeth. I want to scream from fright, it is that scary but nothing comes out of my throat, like in a bad dream.

She screams instead. Did she see me? I run.

I run back without bothering to crawl through the grass. Others run too. I must look really scared, they don't ask any questions at all as we run toward our territory. We hear a bang. We hear a dog bark. Back in the yard, only then, Boris asks, "What happened, did he have a knife?"

"A big one," I say. "And he saw me I think."

I don't say anything about the wife. When she passed the next day on the street, I knew he let her live.

"Who among you are members of *Comsomol?*" Oleg, proud, tall steps out first. Then Tanya, a blond girl with short hair, then Ivan and others. "That's us."

Tall, unafraid in front of the large grave, hands clenched into fists, they sing "The International" one more time— *"Arise you prisoners of starvation, arise you wretched of the earth"*—fire from the fascists interrupts the song, the bodies roll one after the other into the large pit, together they go, die. Soon after, the Soviet Army, powerful like a forest fire, the voice says, liberates the town, the villages, the whole land. The red flag goes up again in the sky, then "The International" again. The film ends, the story called *The Young Guard.*

The crowd disperses, goes home. Bratso says he understood nothing at all. You can't talk to him about it, or to others. Boris says it was boring.

Everybody had more luck than me, I think, walking back from the movies — to be a hero, to do something truly unbelievable, to throw a bomb or to tell a German to shoot if he wants. You don't fear him, couldn't care less. Others will avenge you sooner or later, you are part of them, a Communist, the world will be ours, you'll see. And then on the map at school, instead of many different pieces, different colors, blue, red, green — just one color — RED.

"WHOM DO YOU WANT?" a kid shouts first, always a boy.

Never me, can you imagine me?

"TITO, TITO, WE WANT TITO!"

"TITO PARTIJA, TITO PARTIJA!"

"WE ARE HIS, HE IS OURS!"

"LONG LIVE THE RED ARMY!"

"LONG LIVE STALIN!"

"DOWN WITH THE BOURGEOIS, ENEMY OF THE PEOPLE!"

"DOWN, DOWN," everybody, including me. My entire school is on the Main Street.

The most energetic kids, mostly boys, run around the town, paint the houses of well-known reactionaries with red paint. Also all the houses of people who read the *Times, Tribune,* or any other reactionary paper.

Paint them red!

That'll teach them!

They don't paint them completely, that would take a long time — just a bit in front, draw a face, put some good slogan on the wall, remind them we're here. We are the power of the people. We count for something. Nobody paints the houses except the kids.

I wear a red scarf around my neck just like the others but not a red bow in my hair which would be perfect. Mother wouldn't give me one even if I asked, and I don't.

"The red is THEM, the blue is US" — her motto, her slogan.

"Blue is royal, reactionary, the past," in class.

"Reactionaries, crazy heads, throw away your blue ribbons, replace them with red" — a song that some hum in class.

"Well," I say to mother, "I don't want the blue ribbon either," even though it would go well with my eyes, but what a horror otherwise. Nobody has one in class. So I compromise and get a yellow one that will merge with my hair of old gold as grandma calls it, make me look like a sunflower. She always finds it attractive, even washes it with camomile to make it shine.

So, back to the parade with the yellow ribbon, red scarf. We march and sing Russian songs; a boy draws a nasty picture of Truman on the wall, right on the building that belongs to one of those enemies of the people. There are still some left. How many? *Is mother one? No, not really, not an enemy. She is just a reactionary,* that's all.

Reactionaries are behind the times, in the dark ages still, teacher says, they talk of dreams, go to church, kiss the priest, tell fortunes from the bottom of coffee cups, and in general dream a lot about the times before the revolution when only a few lived well and there was nothing for the workers, their kids, no hospitals, no food. Thank God, there are only a handful of them left. The rest ran off to England or America to join the rest of the Capitalist world.

What about father? What is he, an enemy?

No, he is just misinformed.

He could come anytime if he wanted to. Some important officials wrote to him, asked him to come back, he never harmed anybody, everyone knows that.

Why doesn't he then? Why not?

The factory where many young girls work near the river belonged to one of those rich enemy guys, and a movie house, the very same one where I go, to another man; one man owned all the big stores where mother got that furniture on credit that she glued back together after the war. Can you imagine one whole factory that belongs to one single person? He, the guy who owned the factory where women make dresses and sheets, he looks like pictures of decadent Americans we saw in class— a hat on his head instead of a cap, fat belly over his belt, big fat pig face. That's how American capitalists look; they also chew gum like a cow, same ugly motion, teacher says in the class. "Don't let me ever catch you with gum." I have never seen anybody as fat as this guy; it must come from sitting around and the chocolate he ate all the time, but he has nothing left any more, just his house and he is still fat. Was he born that way, did his body just keep the chocolate?

The factory which had his name before has another name now, after a famous girl worker who was tortured and killed by Germans during the war, right on that square. This fat guy had so much land in town where the new apartments for the workers are, and other land around. He took trips to London and Paris just to get a suit, they say, or for a change of air, just hopped in his plane like that, and there he was, faster than going to grandpa's. That must have been something, London, Paris, Zanzibar.

I don't know of any other serious capitalists around. Many left, disappeared. The one who had a movie house you never see at all, he hides in shame I bet, but his daughter is in my class, tall, blond like me. There are a couple of smaller merchants here and there but they are not dangerous at all, work as employees in their own stores, just like the regular guys. Somebody had to teach others how to run things. It's hard to start from the start.

Mother says, "Everybody was smarter than your father." When they left the country, other men left their families well provided for, all sorts of things hidden in the basement or under the floor planks. Not him though, nothing but books.

"I piss on his honesty, shit on it too. You can't eat books. Look at Zekan and Marko and Stanko, and the merchant. Before they closed his store for good and chased him out, he hid a large amount of stuff, silk, wool, everything, even the thread, hid it well in the basement, in a dugout."

"His family never suffered, just one meter of English wool can buy you a chicken," the gold tooth adds.

"I bet even the commissars come to him for the stuff," mother continues. "Your father was a fool, never like others, that man."

The merchant's daughter, a little primadonna with white ruffled underpants that show when she runs, careful manners, always has clothes that fit; they are made for her, you can tell, never too big or short. Now, I know why

"Your father was a fool and honest," she says. I will never reproach him for that. *Dad, where the hell are you? I could ask you things.*

My own dresses come from UNRA, and mother's knitting. She does it for a living for a while, all day and night she knits. Her fingers bleed from the needles, once she did a sweater in a single night, she is that fast. Grandma makes her small thumbs out of lambskin to cover her own, then she goes on as usual but even those lamb's thumbs wear out from work. My mother can copy the pattern of a sweater, even very difficult ones with flowers and branches, she can do it just by looking, without ever counting the stitches, I have seen it myself; there is simply nobody like that in the whole town. That's why young girls come to us for help if they make a sweater or a dress, that's why most sweaters you see on the Main Street were made by my mother either this year or the last.

The important guys, the ones that mother calls commissars, wear nothing but leather—coats, caps with a brim in front, the kind Lenin wears in the picture when addressing the workers. Cap is proletarian, hat is not. Women wore hats before the war even when it was not cold. It makes no sense. Now these important guys in leather coats and caps were really bakers and carpenters before the war, then the revolution came to prove that ordinary people can govern themselves, and they stopped being cooks and shoemakers and got to the top. After all, mother was working class until she married, even now she is. Daughter of a peasant just like everybody else, workers and peasants. What is the matter with her? She should be happy. I don't suggest, just think.

"Underneath the leather coat and airs, nothing but the naked peasant, nothing but stupidity," she says.

Mother obviously has nothing to do with peasants. She laughs and whispers with her friends how they, the commissars, christen their kids at night when nobody sees ("so and so told me her brother-in-law got the priest to baptize his son"), and how they get married at night as well, right after the civil ceremony; they still need God, she claims. They can wear the leather coat and red star but underneath, just a regular peasant, she says.

The fat priest must be making a lot of money, I think, remembering the rosemary branch, holy water, the blessings before our Saint's Day. Maybe she is telling lies, *I have to be careful, on guard.* How does she know what people do at night? She could be just saying things to confuse me, to trick me, to drag me back to the dark ages with her.

I wear a cap with the star, with the star and I fight against God, against God. We have nothing against Christ. He's on our side, Communist he was . . .

Big kids are marching, singing. This song sounds good when you

63

sing it, it makes you feel brave strong, something you cannot describe with words. It's like color or music. This song is scarlet red.

Chapter Ten

O UR SAINT'S DAY arrives as always, just before Christmas. Other Saint's Days follow later, some more cheerful than others, some more popular. Saint George, the one who slew the dragon is a dark, tall saint with curls, a spring saint, the saint of some regular people and gypsies. The gypsies were right to pick him out, always in the month of May, good weather, dark, handsome, young. My own (you can't pick him really, you inherit him from your family through marriage, like your last name, women do, men's saints stay the same) well, mine is blond, blue-eyed, very serious looking and old. He holds his three fingers up in the air in the icon in the bedroom. A neighbor has another picture of him on a boat helping the sailors during a storm, making the storm stop. He is known as the saint of sailors yet he certainly didn't help grandma's fiancé much. If I said that, what I just did and never do out of fear, they always have an answer like:

"God wanted him, and took him away, it's God's way." At the same time, they spend their time praying so God will keep them here as long as he can. Nothing fits, nothing does.

So, here is another Saint's Day and mother takes me with her, all dressed up, both of us (if you can call what I wear dressed up: a brown skirt from UNRA and a blouse from Thomas' scarf). Mother has some white powder on, looks like a ghost, and some lipstick in the middle of her mouth. Other ladies join us as we walk down the street, mud, mud on the shoes, an autumn saint, this one. Mother still persists in her old ways, calls everyone on the street "sir, missis, miss," refers to them as "Lady so-and-so" never says "comrade" even to the commissars since they are not, will never be her pals, she says, that's what the word comrade means—your equal, your friend. We say "comrade teacher," the peasants mix it all up, start with "comrade" then switch to "sir," finally it becomes "comrade sir, if you'll please . . ."

You don't invite people to your Saint's Day; they simply have to remember when it is and if they don't, it would be a grave insult to your family, you would not visit them when their Saint's Day comes. Some saints are more popular than others, like this one in autumn and we have to go from house to house eating cakes till my stomach hurts, yet you can never say no. They would be very insulted if you refused to eat. Much preparation went into this: real butter, sugar, saving and borrowing the whole year to do it right. They talk about preparations as they eat.

I cross myself like everybody else and take a spoonful of the sweet dish with a candle in the middle. A small girl smaller than me is serving, "Have some," she says. We sit in the bedroom made pretty for the occasion, bright rug on the floor, pillows with birds on top, their picture album for everyone to see. The woman with the gold tooth points to herself twenty years ago; in the picture she wears a fancy dress, hair short, in waves. She says, throwing her head back,

"What a girl I was, isn't it true, Marko?"

Marko nods, drinks some brandy.

"Ten suitors came to our house," she says, "to ask for my hand."

"I must have had more than ten," says mother after a pause, "let me see, there was Gojko, Danilo, Rade, Rashko . . ."

In the picture album—men with sabres dangling from the hip, men with shiny hair parted to the side, babies on fur rugs, weddings in a long white dress. I remember all of a sudden: *Where is the picture of mother and father in a wedding dress? I never saw it. Should I ask? Don't.*

"Hurry fast, the wedding is coming!" Bratso shouts. Everyone runs toward the street, mother and Yanna, Putana, Slavka, everyone. If you look down and up the street, everyone is looking out, either hanging out of the windows, the very best spot, or over the fences; kids are right on the street in the middle of all the dust.

You hear a sound first, bells, carts, horses still very far. Then, a white cloud of dust up there toward the Devil's Stone. Closer now: a shout that is both happy and wild at the same time. A first guy appears, a peasant dressed like an Indian with a head piece in many colors, red, green, blue, branches, roses in his lapel, decorations all over his suit, small coffee cups attached on the sleeve. Town people, mother and others snicker:

"Look at the cups! Peasants have no taste. Hi-hi, cups."

This man with a head dress always carries a flag, a regular one with a red star, and a bottle of *slivovitza* decorated with marigolds. He pretends to be drunk or is really drunk and offers his brandy to everyone. You can't refuse. It's for good luck.

One whole cart gallops by with musicians, accordians, pipes, all playing very loud.

"More brandy, c'mon drink!"

Other carts tumble by. I count twenty, then somebody screams:

"There she is, that's her!"

Everyone cranes to see. Is she pretty? Is he handsome? – the two main reasons for looking. They, peasant couples, always look like kids, very serious; she wears a white veil over her braids. Their carriage is the best one, the most decorated, a cushioned fiacre with two white horses.

More carts, some with one horse, others with two, ribbons, flowers everywhere, scarves, embroidered towels around the men's heads, everyone red-faced, singing, swaying.

"Oh, my maiden, oh, my maiden," they sing, monotonous hum, a song about maiden in the wheat.

From our side, across the wooden fence, somebody throws in:

"And tonight, what will happen tonight?"

"Who will hold her legs up?"

"Not her mother, I bet."

"She'll call her mother for help, it's not going to be fun."

"Oj, aj, ojajaj, help!"

They laugh, slap their thighs, turn red, their faces ugly, including mother. Bratso laughs with them like a fool as if he knew what the words meant. I certainly don't, but I do know that jokes about legs and tonight are called "dirty jokes" just like the ones about the balls. Mother loves them so much she teaches Vesna, Slavka's daughter, age four, to repeat after her and say it aloud on Sunday mornings for every one to hear.

"Hey, women, did anything happen tonight," the kid yells, and here is everyone—mother leaning on a pillow from the window, Slavka, still a peasant, shy, looks down, Putana ("Sister Divine") with a large bruise under one eye, Rosa, plump, small with a husband in England just like us, then across the other fence to the right from the other yard, a thick woman with cat's eyes, wife of a railroad guy who beats her all the time. All these women are out there laughing like mad because the kid squealed, "Did anything happen tonight?"

Sister Divine, called divine for some mysterious reason, a young woman without a husband, got beaten last night, that's "what happened last night." Nothing else. I should know. Men come to see her, different ones, you hear them laughing at times, then they beat her up. She cries in the kitchen over coffee in the morning as mother looks at her bruised eye, tells her to put a cut potato on it. That will take the swelling down.

"Men are beasts," mother says, "that's what they are. If only one of them ever lifted a finger against me, just a finger, son of a bitch, I would give it to him just like this, so fast he wouldn't know what hit him."

Her fist hits the pillow.

"I would give him such a good one he would never recover. He would know, bastard, who to mess with."

She is very strong, my mother. Very very strong, you can tell. I am proud of this but Sister Divine must be feeling bad. Mother always turns everything, arguments, conversations, talks, to her advantage even though it is she, Putana, who is telling the story about the guy who beat her up.

"I could lift *her* father with one hand when we got married. See my muscles."

She demonstrates on me.

"I carried him like a baby, I was that strong, so help me God."

Then the subject inevitably goes to the same subject each time, no matter who is in the kitchen.

68

"I didn't think I would marry him until the very last day."

There were so many waiting around for her to make up her mind, the Swedish captain of the merchant marines, handsome, rich, and others. A sigh.

"And what did I do but marry this thin, sickly man" (glance in my direction), "who left me here without any food, and took his ass to some foreign land for some stupid ideals. You can't eat ideals."

"Before the Revolution the land belonged to a few . . ." I am writing my homework, trying to ignore the noise. Impossible. They talk too much. How can I think up something good when they yak like this?

"You can't escape your fate," she sighs.

"No way."

"It's all written in the stars, the day you are born, the day you die."

"It's all written," Putana sighs.

"You can't escape no matter how hard you try," their slogan, the women drinking coffee. The woman across the fence in the next house, the one with gray cat eyes, gets beaten all the time just like Sister Divine but she says it will stop.

"As soon as my oldest son grows up, big enough to fight, the son of a bitch will get it from him. My day will come then. I hope he kills him, I hope he gives it to him pretty bad. All those years he has been sucking my blood, what my back has seen."

The woman with the gray eyes gets ready to cry, it is that sad. It's three of them in the kitchen now, and me four.

What is all this? What are my stars? Where will I go? What will I do?

I will escape it all — all that horror, petty bourgeois thinking, a new world will sing, our tomorrows will, the future is ours so they didn't die in vain. They have promised in class.

I will escape it all or die. All or nothing, my motto.

"The young guard steps on the street to fight," I hum.

"Go in the other room and study, instead of listening to us."

"I'm not. I'm doing my theme."

"She is forever peering in some fucking book, what a child, bad for her eyes. And she has no interest in cooking or knitting or anything that girls do. It will all end bad," mother complains.

They examine me carefully, all three, slowlike.

"Go in the other room," mother orders.

It's cold in the bedroom, no stove is lit, my fingers will freeze, how can you write like that. They are talking about me now. Get up, listen.

"A very good student," mother brags.

"You're a lucky woman, you are."

"She takes after me, at least in that, smart. I had enough smarts for five, but see what happened. I should have been a man. Women are cursed at birth, always and forever. It's best to strangle a girl at birth."

Strangle at birth, scary. They are whispering now, it's hard to hear even though my ear is on the floor, right next to the door.

"No!" they say.

"You don't say!"

"He didn't!"

"He did."

"It can't be true."

"It is, my dear woman."

. . . ruined her and left . . . whisper, whisper.

"Bastard."

"Son of a bitch!"

"I would cut his balls off for that," mother says.

Whisper some more. Who got "ruined" where? My hands are freezing, can't hold a pencil, have to warm myself by the stove. I come out.

Won't they ever go home, all those hips, gold teeth, legs full of veins, stomachs big from pregnancies—all children's doing, they say. (Children not only worry you to death, but kill you in other ways as well, make your stomachs sag, give you those veins, bad teeth.) Vesna, Slavka's daughter, appears at the door.

"Mama wants to know if you have any of those Truman's balls left. She wants to bake something."

The women explode, stop the sad talk. Truman's balls, or Truman's eggs, are powdered eggs from UNRA, good for cooking but nothing else. You can't eat them like regular eggs. They taste bad. They send us the strangest things from UNRA like that horrible peanut butter, or plant lard. Mother gives her some of those eggs, the kid runs out.

They have passed from balls on to babies and deliveries, always at night; mother does them all the time. She even delivered that kid that came to ask about Truman's balls.

Tales of torture will start in a minute as she tells about another night when she delivered a peasant woman not far from the creek. I have no desire to listen; these stories are all the same, horrible, scary, but where can I go? It's too cold in the other room.

"She is walking all the time like a beast, afraid to soil the clean sheet I prepared for her. What do you think of that? Peasants are peasants, just like sheep. Then she says to me, 'Here it comes,' and the kid just drops in the basin."

Ouch. It must hurt when the kid hits the basin.

"I suffered with my first like a dog," the one with the gold tooth says. Now, there are four of them plus me.

"You curse your mother for giving you life. I wanted to jump out of window, it was that bad."

"But then you spread your legs for the second one, ha, ha."

"One forgets the pain."

"I never uttered a cry with either one of them, and you remember that Bratso weighed 6 kilos."

Always a super woman she has to be, the bravest, the best.

"What about . . ." whisper . . .

"Go outside like other children and play instead of peering in that god damned book. Go play."

I walk outside and sit on the stoop; it's cold. Everything seems confusing, nothing fits, but I do have a few certainties. So far it is like this: My favorite saint is St. George, because he is a fighter and has dark curls. My favorite hero is Filip, from this town, dead at twenty-five when he threw a grenade at a tank. However, before he fell he did kill quite a few Germans and he had time to scream:

"LONG LIVE THE REVOLUTION! AVENGE ME."

"*I WILL, I WILL!*"

Mother runs out.

"What happened?"

"Nothing."

"Why did you yell like that?"

"I didn't, I swear. It must be someone else."

"Don't be smart with me. You want a slap?"

She runs back in. Where was I before she interrupted me? — My favorite color is red. What will I be? Well, maybe a doctor and go to Africa or Java and Zanzibar. Or maybe an artist. I saw one in a Russian film and she looked just like me, exactly, she could be my twin. This film happened after the revolution and she, Natasha, went to Siberia where she played piano and taught peasant kids music. (I wrote a report about the film, and teacher said it was very good.)

The women are still in there. There is nobody to play with now. This year some of us go to school in the morning, some after lunch. Nobody is on the street until five or so. You can't play alone.

The women are still there. Who can I play with? Not with Bratso except when he is all alone, and today he is not. As soon as another boy joins, he changes, becomes mean. I have noticed that lately, and wonder why. It hurts me every time, even though I try not to think. Alone together, we are both separate and close; he doesn't know my thoughts, I wonder about his. He is never mean from the start like some, but I worry that in a revolution he might go to the wrong side, or betray his comrades if tortured. Something in him is missing, something I can't name, a bit like that prince in a story who had only half a heart. Will he ever change? Yes, I decide, but not today . . .

So, who can I play with?

Bosa, a merchant's daughter, the little princess with ruffles, is always sewing dumb clothes for her stupid dolls, what a bore, giving them pretend-milk. I don't have a doll. I don't want one.

Ljuba, who stares through the fence on the left side has one leg shorter from birth and a horrible stepmother who makes her work all the time. She can't play ever, except in the summer, and it's autumn now.

So who can I play with? Nobody. Not until five when we play soccer with the rag ball—Bratso, Momo, Zoran, and Boris. Boris has the glass eye. It happened after the war. I am afraid at times— what if it fell out, what then?

I get off the stoop, go inside. It's almost noon, time to eat, run to school. When I get back, the women will be gone, I hope.

When I get back they are already there, in front of the door— Zoran, Boris, and other boys. They don't know where the ball is, someone stole it, they think. We should look for the criminals soon, but meanwhile why don't I read them some books. Last year, I discovered Karl May and that was it, their favorite stuff. Gorky is my own; I don't share him with them. Karl May I read. They can read too, but not as well and they are simply a lazy bunch of boys. Here they are, all with big pieces of bread and lard, stretched out chewing the bread, waiting for me to start the tale about Old Shatterhand and Winetu. I take my time. When finished, there are many questions left.

"Is it true," Zoran asks, "that Old Shatterhand was so powerful?"

"Sure he was."

"Which one was more powerful, him or Winetu, the Indian chief?"

Boys always ask questions like that, always want to know the same thing—"Who is more powerful?"

"It doesn't matter," I say. "They both were. And besides, he learned it all from the Indians who were his friends. They were very very smart and could tell if the enemy passed just by the broken twigs here and there, or invisible footprints. Their drums carried messages of all sorts from afar, so did the smoke signals."

They are very impressed, want me to read some more but I don't. We try the drums and signals and invent a whole new way of talking, mysterious so the grown-ups will be lost, won't understand anything at all. It goes like this—you take a word like Bratso for example, divide it in the middle, then start the new word with the middle of the word. Bratso becomes TSOBRA, you see? So, here is Boris sneaking up under my window in the bushes, a goose feather tied with a scarf around his head, he really thinks he looks like an Indian, a real one, even has some war paint on his cheeks. First two whistles, very slow, it could be a bird, then a third one sharp.

That's our new signal.

Then his voice: "Tsobra, Na-an, Risbo, rehe."

It really sounds good, the new language. I get ready to answer in kind when my mother, from the kitchen yells at Boris, "Na-an, Tsobra, kingwor." Imagine that! How disgusting! She learned it too, maybe knew it all along. How can you be really different, invent a new tongue?

Then we saw a Polish film about kids who had their own tree house and I built one too. It wasn't really a tree house, though, that would have been impossible, mother wouldn't permit it, but still a house made out of wood, a hut that leans on the mean neighbor's fence. In it, a bed, place to cook things, plates, drape instead of door, no windows so far, but you can look through the planks. It's the club house for the boys and me. There we plan strategies against enemies from other streets and the butcher's kids from the creek. All of us do something, you can pick whatever you like best and are most suited for, and if too unhappy you can exchange your position for another one. I am a spy which means that I listen to people, grown-ups and enemy children and find out what they are plotting against us. That's how, in my new function, that I catch an enemy spy who was spying on us to see how we made a house. They wanted one just like it but didn't have much wood. I told him how to do it, and he said he was a spy. I didn't disclose my function, he was simply dumb, didn't know what the word "spy" meant, you don't go around giving it away if you are one.

Bratso said he wanted to be a baby, just like in life, and we let him. He liked it best when cooking was done, or when kids had to share apples, plums, a piece of white bread.

Now that everything is planned, we fight with our enemies a couple of times. You get your wooden swords ready, only two people fight for their club, it's all according to the rules, we exchange prisoners too, or those that died. Some offensives are more serious, the unplanned ones that explode all of a sudden with bombs from corn roots, over territorial rights on the creek.

We are in the yard, creeping on our stomachs the way Indians do. "Be silent," I command. Boris wears a feather, Bratso is behind a tree. Our position is better, that much is clear. They are in the creek below, we are on the embankment, next to the pigsty without a pig. We see them clear, everyone; they don't see us. Big Stojan is with them and the butcher's boys. We are outnumbered, but don't be afraid, our position is better, we can still win. Bows and arrows are ready, made out of willow trees but no poison was used the way Indians did. We are ready to strike. Stay calm!

Then a horrible sound, from the house:

"Anna, Bratso, where are you? Come home for dinner!"

"Stay put," I hiss.

"Anna, Bratso, I'll skin your ass if you don't hurry up!" Then another horrible yell:

"Bor-is! I'll break your bones!"

It's all spoiled. They know we are here, you can't strike now, nothing to do but retreat and plan another offensive another time, when they least expect us. I learned that from the Partisans.

Chapter Eleven

T HIS YEAR I SIT next to the window in class; outside carts and horses pass, a market day in town. Senya is next to me as always from the first grade on. She looks like a wet chicken in winter, sort of brown, hair unevenly cut, bangs in front. If somebody asked who is your best friend I would say Senya and she would probably say me although we never play together the way I play with Bratso and Boris. She lives four streets down, then up the hill on the cobblestone road, not far from the woman with the gold tooth, mother's friend. We walk to school together; she waits by the barracks where the soldiers are, and then back from school whenever I take that route instead of crossing the creek. When I meet her in front of the barracks and her eyes are red, you know as well as anyone that she got beaten that day, but it would be impolite to ask. We just walk in silence to school, get in our wooden seats; she always seems frightened they'll ask her to recite.

I am frightened too because it doesn't feel good to blush.

Svetlana is the best student, fast as a boy, strong arms. Her hand is always up, even when her answer is not right. She simply likes the sound of her words. You can tell it by the way she prolongs the answer, slow, firm voice, never looks down toward her feet, head straight up. I bet she never blushed, not once. Her house is near the school, her own house, not rented rooms, and it is really the best place to live. She can hear the first school bell right from her kitchen, get there in time before the second. Ljuba with the short leg sits next to Rade the Sparrow, called that because of his size. The Rabbit was transferred to another class. Then there is Anca the gypsy with very white teeth, some other kids and peasants. During recess I see Boris; he is in another grade.

Rade the Sparrow got ill all of a sudden. Everybody panicked. Could it be TB of the spine or is it something else? Something horrible in any case, he may never grow up. He lives closest to me so I get appointed to bring him lessons right after class. Inside his house it's sort of dark, cool, windows closed; he sits in a large bed propped up, all day long like that, and makes his own toys out of nothing really — bits of paper, string, small animals that walk, open their beaks. I sit on the bed next to him, try to remember what happened in class, where we are with history, who got slapped by the teacher, who had their ears pulled. His mother brings us cookies, good ones, strokes my hair, calls me "my pretty." Rade and I laugh a lot, his laughter different from anyone, small silver bells just like his voice, like a spring bird.

I bring the homework for about six months then the summer arrives and I stop. He remains inside, still ill. One day in the summer I am walking on my dusty street, is it July or August, not far from Rade's house, when this little white dog starts following me all of a sudden. It follows me to the house, sits there smiling at me.

"No, we can't keep him," mother says, "not enough food. What do you need a dog for? They are useless in town."

"Other kids have them," I beg. "Bosa has one."

"Other kids have got fathers, not you, stop bothering me. Do you want a slap?"

She never changes her mind; it's final. So I start walking again on my dusty street toward the market, the dog still behind. I never said a word to him, he just trotted along, all the way downtown, then we crossed the Main Street.

At the market on the square, peasants sit with tons of cherries, apples, plums, cheese. Town women, baskets under their arms, taste the cherries here and there, making sure they are sweet; they dip their fingers in the cream, break off a piece of cheese, eat it, then look at the peasant's nails to see if they are clean. The dog is still beside me.

The decision to sell it did not happen until this old woman

with beautiful cherries asked, by chance really.

"You going to sell it?"

I looked at her cherries and nodded.

"You've never sold anything before, I bet."

"No," I said, "never." It was true.

"Well, sit right here next to me and wait. Sit on my coat. If the customer asks, don't say he's your only dog."

"Why not?"

"They'll think you are getting rid of him on account of disease."

"What disease?"

"Like with cows or sheep. Don't you know anything?"

"He doesn't look sick."

"You just tell them you got four or five at home, all pups, just say that and you'll do fine. Here, good sweet cherries for sale!" she yells.

I sit there on the ground next to the cherries. Much time passes. The woman with the gold tooth spots me and stops to talk. She says:

"What are you doing here? I just saw your mother buying potatoes, right over by the melons, look."

She rushes by. I see mother now, yell very loud so she can hear:

"Mom, look here, look, I'm selling the dog."

She turns in my direction, sees me, looks directly at me sitting there next to the peasant, then her eyes change and she disappears in the crowd. I go on as before next to the cherries. People keep buying them, there isn't going to be much left. The woman keeps yelling, "Here, cherries for sale, sweet, hurry, buy." All of a sudden, I hear this little voice nearby:

"Mommy, why is it that they never sell dogs or cats at the market. Why isn't there ever anything for kids? It isn't fair."

The woman next to me perks up:

"Here, over here, good healthy dog for sale." A little girl appears now in a white dress, a large white ribbon on top of her head. She claps her hands together. "Mommy," she squeals, "it can't be true, here is a dog, look, just as I wished."

The mother seems happy, smiles. She says with a very fancy accent:

"We have been looking for a dog for a long time. Someone stole hers and the poor child never recovered from the shock."

They are not from our town, you can tell. I would have seen them before, nobody talks like that. They must be visitors just passing through, happy looking — mother and daughter, on vacation perhaps. The mother calls the girl "my treasure," "honey," "my sweet."

"How much is your pup?"

My confusion starts. I didn't think of how much.

"Ask more, bargain later," the peasant woman whispers in her scarf. Sure, but how much?

I calculate two movie tickets plus a kilo of cherries and ask for that. The woman gives it right away, plus a bit more for a present. I made them so happy, she says. The little girl picks up the white dog, puts him in a basket. He doesn't object.

"You should've asked for more. They looked rich to me. You should have." The peasant woman seems angry.

How am I supposed to know what to ask, it's my first sale. Maybe next time. The white dog and the girl have already disappeared in the crowd. They might travel by train to their own town, somewhere behind the hills, very far.

There are almost no cherries left. The woman gets ready to leave, packs her things. It's two hours on foot, she says, over that hill. The market is almost empty, only watermelon rinds with flies all over and the sound of a horse carriage as it pulls out.

I buy the cherries, one whole kilo, and a few more she gave me for the soul of her dead child.

Hurry home now, run fast, share them with Bratso while they're fresh. He'll never believe how I got them for nothing.

Eat them fast then run to the movies, the entire day will be good.

When the search for the lost white dog started two days later, I learned only then that it was Rade's, I swear. There is nothing for me to do to help. The dog went away with that happy girl; he was not killed; that would have been worse. I wish I could tell him that but how can I? It would mean admitting everything, explaining that it was really an accident because the dog followed me that particular day. If only he didn't . . .I keep silent, nobody knows about it except mother since she did see me that day at the market and ran away from me in horror, she now says. However, she will not tell. Bratso is no problem; he forgets everything fast. He even forgot I gave him cherries.

In September I continue to bring homework to Rade; he is still

ill. His mother brings cookies, calls me her "good child." He makes toys, small birds, we laugh as always when he makes them walk. Three months later, he is back in school with the rest of us, cured. His marks are very good and teacher says I really helped, "such a good, dedicated girl, a perfect pioneer." My cheeks burn. I look at the floor. I wish she didn't say that; it makes me feel strange. Then some time passed, and I forgot all about the girl and the white dog.

Chapter Twelve

S VETLANA TAKES US HOME one day in the spring, six of us, chosen by her, all girls from the same class — Mira, Anca, Senya, Nevenka and me. Her mother, a woman with a small moustache, gives us cheese, apple strudel to eat; they have a lot; Svetlana is an only child. Then we go to play in a large dark shed where the wood is stored next to the house. For some reason she commands us as soon as we get inside to take our underpants off. She has locked the door with a key, holds it in her hand, "I'll throw it away if you don't," she says; all of us obey. Nobody says no, not even Senya next to me. We take them off as she asked.

"Now put them far away, mix them up," she orders.

Someone gets up, mixes up the pants.

After that she says "lie down" and we do. Nobody is afraid but it feels weird.

"Close your eyes tight."

We do.

"You can pretend I'm a guy," she says, and goes from girl to girl, stops in front of each one, lies on top of her with her own underpants off. A door creaks somewhere, she gets up from the last girl, we run looking for our pants. She never got to me. Senya and I go home as usual. I think she'll say something about Svetlana but she doesn't say a word. We stop in front of the photo shop to see the pictures of the latest beauties with curls. Senya dreams of getting a new skirt she says or new sandals or maybe a new dress.

"What do you dream about?" she asks.

My dreams are neither simple nor clear. I wish I were a hero, a Partisan or a robber on the high seas. There is nothing interesting for the girls in the books. I wish I were a boy, but say nothing of this to Senya. It would be too hard to explain, and it doesn't fit so I just say:

"I guess I don't dream much," and then remembering that there is something after all, even though it doesn't really matter much but will make her happy, I say,

"If only I had shoes that fit, that would be my dream."

Soon after that day in the shed, I come home after school and tell grandma that my teacher said such-and-such—that I was the best student in the class, the very best she ever had, the most honest, the best probably in the whole school, knowing all along as I spoke that none of it was true. Nothing of the sort happened. It's not that I am bad, but not the best. Svetlana is the best, her hands always goes up in class. I always know the answer just as well as she but something stops me from putting my hand up. My hands start shaking, sweat, and by the time I am ready, convinced, Svetlana recites already and it's like that every time. I am best at silent things, those you don't recite in front of the class, composition, drawing, that sort of stuff. But here I am pumping water for grandma and telling her lies. That's what they are, you can't lie about that or that would really be lying. She just stops washing, pats me on the head, and says in a very ordinary way: "You are my golden angel. I am not surprised." I just swallow, keep on pumping, don't look her in the eye. Can she tell? It would be really awful if she could. Of all people I don't want her to think I tell lies. Then the day arrived when everything came to be true, the best of days ever. It happened like this:

People came from the capital to inspect our school and one of them chooses our class. Teacher has on a new dress with buttons all the way up to her neck, hair pulled in the back, not quite herself, she calls us sweet names, nobody gets screamed at. She knew these guys were coming and had tried to prepare for the event by telling in advance which math problem we'll have, who should recite. It's better that way, she said. These people from the capitol do not know us well, our ways are different; they'll look for problems where there are none. We are in this together; it's better not to talk about it much.

So this is the way it went. Teacher is in front of us in that polka dot dress, the guy from the capital in back, the rest of us snickering here and there not knowing what to expect. Then disaster struck. This guy listened to everything for a while. Then he did something that shouldn't have happened. He had is *own* math problems written on a piece of paper; he picked his *own* students. Everybody got confused and forgot even what is 5 + 5. Total complete defeat in math. Teacher looked pale, green; we wondered, what next?

Teacher just stands there biting her lips. We look at her not knowing what to do; her eyes give no answers, nothing but fear. She should have prepared a counter-offensive I think, but it's too late for that. The man calls on another student, then another, each time to read the same paragraph; it is getting worse. Senya can read pretty well but now even she stammers to death. Svetlana reads next, at top speed; it only took her a second. At least someone read well, thank God.

The guy has had enough, goes with the book in front of the class, coughs:

"Some of you can read, you know your letters, but don't you know the way it SHOULD BE READ?" For "meaning," he says, a new word. "Look at the text. What is it about?"

I look at it. I am not sure I know what he means to read "for meaning" but it is clear the way it should be read. I knew it all along as others read stammering or at top speed. Yes, but how shall I get my hand up? Svetlana looks down at her desk, deeply engrossed in a fly. Silence everywhere, everyone looks down, somewhere between the feet and the desk. My poor teacher, what will happen to her? She looks sick.

Grandma, help me, please, do it just once. I have never done it before, not able or too shy. *Count to ten and don't blink. Where is the voice?* It says: *Go on, speak!*

And then, guess what?

My hand stands up above my head by magic and I hear myself read in total silence.

"She stood there in front of the soldiers, a pale old woman, her face framed in a black scarf . . ."

When the paragraph ends I am still alive. Svetlana looks up from her desk, no longer concerned with the fly. He said, "Go on some more," and I did. Two whole pages, *Mother of the Partisan,* it's called, her son just killed by the Germans. The guy from the capital takes the book from me, and then he says to everyone with this happy smile:

"That's how it should be read. That was reading for meaning. Words are not pieces of wood."

The class looks at me, stunned. I am already somewhere else, where, I don't know, somewhere outside the class.

"You should be proud of her, what feeling," he says to my teacher, no longer green.

"We are, Comrade Supervisor. " She smiles at me. "I even gave her Gorky to read." And on and on.

I wish they would stop now, let me sit down. The best part is over; my blushing is coming back.

Well, from that day on, Svetlana and I were the best students in class, fought for the title, never winning or losing entirely. Some weeks she was the best, other weeks it was me, but both of us had to be ready every day since the class waited for the match to start, to see who will lose this time. And, my grades changed from A- or B+ to just plain A's all of a sudden. Was I really better, what was it? Did that guy do it by complimenting me so much, or did I want to prove to grandma that I didn't lie? You could say that I didn't lie at all, just changed events in time. Jump, jump, skip, skip as you jump, count to ten, don't blink. Make things happen.

Chapter Thirteen

Yanna was of marriageable age, they all said so. Nobody wants you too old and girls are old soon after twenty; they start to fade just like daisies. Yanna, my mother's younger sister, was dark and wore dark colors when she came to us just before Thomas. Their brother had died somehow somewhere in the mountains, right after the first days of the revolution, I think. That's why she wore black. They whisper about his death, cry and argue forever, but tell me nothing. Grandma stays silent. Mother insists that this brother was a hero, a true man; Yanna claims that he beat her with a leather strap, not a hero but a beast she says and got what he deserved.

"He's got no grave like an animal, his soul will wander in an unmarked grave," mother always cries about this.

I think all of a sudden about those bones we discovered on that trip in the country and see some sort of connection between those bones and this uncle's death. He didn't matter that much for me, just like some stranger from a book, but I am trying to make things fit, know what really happened there with that uncle, a man who was a hero and a beast. You can't trust either one to be correct—mother is too serious, Yanna too funny.

Yanna makes me laugh all the time the way she rolls her eyes or makes a face or imitates that fat priest. She jumps out of the window with me; we count one, two, three, and jump at the same time, fall in the bushes. Mother shakes her head, doesn't like it too much. You see, even though she was "of marriageable age," Yanna was as silly a kid and didn't in any way resemble a grown-up, didn't walk like them the way a girl should, sort of dignified, holding her head high. She jumped and skipped, even played hide-and-seek, ripped her good skirt on a rose bush, and was very good at hopscotch, better than anyone. Hopscotch she only played with us in the yard, mother wouldn't permit it on the street where people would see, talk how silly the girl is even though of marriageable age. They were real sisters, same parents and all but were so different from each other, everybody said that, especially mother; Yanna was the last of ten kids, "born unlucky."

I never saw the others. What happened to them? Don't ask! They don't like it. Mother didn't invent them because she tells how they fought with spoons over milk because some got more, some less. Her mother was nasty, that part I know, and she hated my mother because she looked like *him*, the very spitting image of her dad who was dark and handsome and had a moustache. He also wished mother had been a son. Even in those stories they disagree, Yanna taking grandmother's side, mother claiming on the contrary that he was good while she was a beast.

Yanna was my mother's burden, left to her by her mother as she died. It was called *Amanet* and it was similar to being cursed because if you didn't obey, horrible things would happen either to your family or families after that for many generations after yours. You simply had no choice but to carry out this *Amanet* which was really a promise to continue a wish.

"What would I wish for?" I think but can't think of anything or imagine myself dying.

People leave these *Amanets* on their death beds, everyone gathered around to hear that last wish, very clever thing to do because nobody said NO to a dying person. You couldn't even think NO at that time. Sometimes people, children too, got cursed by their parents for doing something wrong — not on their deathbed, it could happen any time — and then the kids had to worry about lifting the curse before a parent died or nothing would ever turn right with the curse on — they would get ill or be visited by a ghost at night or could have no children of their own or would have them but they wouldn't be good. You can curse anyone any time, not just kids although it is less serious with others – there is less blood involved.

The woman with the gray eyes whose husband beats her with a belt curses very often. One time I hear her in the morning from the other side:

"God, may she wear black clothes forever."

"God, may her seed die."

"God, may she walk around crippled and blind, may she rot."

Scary, mean. How could you wish all that?

Mother runs out of the kitchen, begs the woman with gray eyes to lift the curse against this woman she wants to cripple, kill her seeds. Mother says, "Sure she is a bitch but her kids aren't guilty, have heart." I have no idea how you "lift" the curse, what words to use. Do you just say: "I am lifting it," or is it something special like when curing warts or the evil eye . . . "Devil, take the curse away where nothing grows . . . one, two, three, four, five." (I wonder if it works like that, or "Devil, take the curse over the dead cat and the dead bird to the grave inside the corpse past midnight.")

Anybody can curse anybody, that's the only thing anybody can do that's powerful. But if I tried to curse somebody they would just laugh at me. Kids don't count in this at all. Grandma's opinion in this matter is simple: "You think God has nothing better to do than listen to your rubbish?" She never says rubbish except on occasions like that.

Peasants curse all the time, for anything, when unloading the wood or bringing us cheese, but they do it all the time and it isn't scary at all, just their way of speaking. You listen to them and laugh; it is that funny, no city person knows how to swear like that.

"Fuck your mother, fuck your father, your sister, your brother, fuck your mother who made you as clumsy as that (this one for a cow), fuck my bad fate, my life, fuck God and his angels, fuck each individual angel and the one who rides in the sky, brings hail and ice. Fuck them in the ass, in the mouth, in the ears, in the nose."

They just go on and on like that, and you are not supposed to listen, but we do, Yanna and me, giggling at the peasant cursing his cow.

So, Yanna, my mother's curse, or *amanet* was getting on, something had to be done fast or she'll remain an old maid because you can't marry a girl after twenty-five, they said. So, mother found a good man somewhere and arranged for dinner at our kitchen in the spring. We got washed with very hot water, they checked me and Bratso for lice, the house was cleaned the whole day long, grandma got told very politely not to fart, then they killed a chicken. Nobody said anything to Yanna which was sort of strange considering this was supposed to be her guy. Bratso said "he didn't give a shit" about the event but was certainly glad about the chicken and kept stuffing himself on the hot apple strudel even before the start. Grandma put on her best dress, black with small dots, mother a blue one. Yanna — lost in an old blouse with puff sleeves — sat in the corner humming to herself. She winked at me from time to time.

Then this guy arrives, sort of friendly, fat. I expect everyone to start talking marriage, but they don't. This fat guy doesn't even look at his bride, sits Bratso and me on his lap, says:

"Money for each kiss."

Both of us slobber over him like two dogs and sure enough here come the bucks, a lot, enough for a whole month of movies if you get the cheapest seats.

We are done with the chicken and have gotten to the strudel when Yanna looks at me and disappears in the bedroom. Now the important stuff will start. They are making coffee, that's it! They will probably kick the two of us out as soon as they start with the important words. Coffee is ready, they comment "Good, bitter, fine, you really make a good one."

Yanna hasn't come back from the other room. Mother says, "Go tell her to come back, not to be shy." In the bedroom I look everywhere. Sometimes she hides under beds when we play hide and seek or in the closet. Nope, nowhere to be found, then her head appears under the window, over the bush. She simply opened the window and jumped out, just like that.

I whisper to her to climb up, mother is going to be really mad. Yanna just shakes her head, no, no, it says, then makes a face and starts imitating the guy, how he looks, sort of painting his belly with her arms. Both of us giggle like mad. No, she said, she is not going in. She actually said "No," to mother, something I wouldn't dare, no matter what.

"I don't know where she is," I say, or rather whisper to mother's ear.

She was angry, really mad, on account of the strudel and the chicken and her good name but she covers it all up and tells the guy that Yanna is not feeling well, a very bad thing to say because nobody wants to marry a sickly girl, not even men in love. The guy leaves. But what else could she tell him, the truth? That Yanna didn't like his stomach, that he had too hairy arms and wore a greasy cap? She told me all this later as we played hopscotch in the yard, jumping, skipping around. "How could you kiss that cheek?" she says to me, goes "*Fuj!* You kissed him, you did."

After that mother almost gave up. What could you do with a girl who jumps out the window when the suitors come, and this was her first one. She did try once more, but just hinting, talking around the subject, not inviting the guy over for the strudel and chicken. The man was nice, an ex-merchant in household goods, not young, not old, whose wife had died suddenly one night and left him with a young child; he couldn't manage alone, needed a woman to cook, clean, take care of him and the child. Everyone talked about this man; I remembered all of a sudden from before, how his wife woke up one night and said to him, "Bring me a glass of water; I am dying," but he was fast asleep, didn't wake up and she went and died. What bothers me in this story is that they keep repeating he was asleep yet he remembered to tell. People either invent or lie, you have to be careful all the time if you want anything to fit.

Mother said about this man, he's a good guy, the kind that saves, doesn't drink or smoke or play cards, never beat his wife. He would marry Yanna because he respected mother so much, and even if she, Yanna, had the tiniest bit of resemblance to her sister, only one percent, that would be enough for him, he said. Mother tells all this in the kitchen, grandma stays silent, Yanna winks at me, makes a face. I knew he was not her type just by looking at him once, and nothing came of it, just as I thought it wouldn't. Yanna said he walked funny, "Did you notice that?" and went on to imitate him walking like a duck. Mother never forgave her this one, her "big chance," and years later, she still mentioned it in passing, couldn't help herself, that Yanna missed her luck because she refused to listen and be reasonable. Mother had tried her best to obey the *amanet,* the promise to her mother on her deathbed to provide a happy home for her youngest. Some people refuse happiness, there is nothing you could ever do about it. You could worry and worry yourself to death, get ill with TB just like mother did right after my birth when she threw me on the floor and had to go recover somewhere by the sea. But she is getting smarter now, and will not worry to death about Yanna. She has tried her best. Some people refuse happiness, are born unlucky.

I worry about mother a lot, worry about worrying her and making her die, but it happens in spite of everything, even though I try my best to prevent it—it's usually because Bratso fights with others or mothers come to complain about dead chickens he killed with his slingshot or because he breaks his bones. One day we are sitting in the kitchen when this woman runs in, screams:

"Bratso fell under horse carriage, maybe dead!"

Mother rushes out, then Bratso walks in perfectly normal considering that horses passed over his body. Two horses and a carriage. Mother undresses him, looks carefully for broken ribs, finds none, then she goes in the garden. We know what's coming, terror is inside me, it will happen. Where is grandma now, she would stop it. Bratso cries ahead of time, before it happens. I cry too. She comes back with a large stick and starts hitting him as soon as she walks through the door. I should go in the other room, hide, cover my ears, go under the bed, but can't move from the chair, sit there petrified, trying not to cry. If I do, even a whimper, she shifts directions, starts beating me, to keep him company in crying, she says, "That'll teach you to cry."

Other times, she sends us to get our own sticks, like the day she called for dinner and we didn't hear. You look for an older stick, the kind that breaks after a couple hits on the ass; once the stick breaks, you're free, that's the rule. But the stick can't be too old, not the kind that breaks right away, or the rule doesn't apply and you have to get another one. Finding just the right kind is important when sent to look for the stick.

She beats us with nettles when they are in season; you get it on your ass, it burns worse than a stick but nothing remains on your body after a few hours while the stick marks you carry on your arms and legs for days and other kids snicker like fools looking at you as if they never got it. Everybody gets it sooner or later on my street;

that's what it means to be a kid. Svetlana is an exception to the rule, and the merchant's daughter who only gets yelled at; her mother calls her "honey" all the time, even on wash day.

The worst happens afterwards. When the stick finally breaks and her hand gets tired from hitting so hard, she stops suddenly, looks at me wild-eyed and starts beating herself with fists this time, all over the chest, head, belly, her head hitting the wall until she turns pale and falls to the ground. Her teeth chatter, eyes roll, she is so pale I think:

This is it, you have killed her with worry, it's your fault, what now?

Hurry, run for water, make her drink, like the last time, raise her up from the floor, she won't die, she won't die, please don't let it happen, count to five.

I get her to bed, then my fear lessens; I know she is saved from death until another time, but you never know what might happen next time.

Where is grandma? Mother never beats us in front of her anymore, just on the sly.

When she gets up an hour later, she is quieter than usual, calls us her pets, then we get going as always and she forgets everything for a while. I do not forget anything at all, keep it stored somewhere inside with the voice, almost by force, in order to be sure that it is me all the time. If I don't remember who I was, what happened, then who am I?

CHAPTER FOURTEEN

Y ANNA STARTS WORKING in a dress factory even though this made her unhappy. Mother thought it was time for her to do something. Of course she could have been a happy woman had she chosen that merchant guy but it was too late; he was already married to a lucky one, from a good family as well, only twenty-one.

When Yanna started working, she got up very early in the morning and bought herself many fancy dresses with her factory money. She could think of nothing else, and would parade in front of me making all those faces, would ask, "Which one do you like best? Which goes with my eyes?" She got to be pretty all of a sudden, her hair short, curly, dark. In the evening, with two girlfriends from the factory, she promenaded up and down the Main Street. She stopped playing with me. Soon after, she met a man, tall, handsome, blond, and married him in a couple of months, still looking very pretty.

The wedding was civil without music or gypsies. Mother prepared a very good lunch and gave her a table, two chairs and some of her own sheets even though she did not approve of the guy. Too handsome, she said openly, will not turn out well. Yanna went to live in a room across the creek on the other side of town and didn't come to see us on account of the guy.

When I went to see her later—mother ordered me to spy—Yanna was all different. Her stomach looked bigger under her dress, her mouth was puckered up as if she wanted to puke; she didn't look like a girl anymore, not even around the eyes. She was a woman now and the difference was noticeable on her as well as others who were not girls anymore. Others saw these signs, not just me.

Girls were unmarried, wore pretty clothes, giggled a lot. They were usually thin. Then they got to be women, had chidren, lost their teeth during pregnancy (the woman with the gold tooth said so, mother lost some with us), their dresses and hair became sloppy as the years passed, stomachs hung low under large saggy breasts. *Fuj!* For some reason I thought it wouldn't happen to Yanna—she was too crazy, too silly and played hopscotch. But there she is now, the belly and that mouth. Can she see my thoughts or what? She says with a small laugh, "I look like one of those fat priests, don't I?" She expects me to laugh, but I run out, feeling sick.

There and then I decide, promise myself never to become a woman, *never*. It will never happen to me, no matter what, because I am smarter than that. It simply makes no sense, womanhood, marriage, none of it, I think, running by the creek past the military barracks where soldiers stare pressed against the wire. All those women in our kitchen agree on this point—the best part was *before* the marriage—they say it and look at their coffee cups. Fine, I think, you agree on this, but here is the part that does not fit: why did mother try to marry Yanna off so hard? Why do they talk about marriage so much?

What is a man good for? I wonder. For what?

Some men chopped wood like Thomas, fine, but mother can do that almost as well. She can even ride a horse just as well as any guy. What is it then? They say "poor unprotected woman" about a woman without a husband, and yet what did these men do except drink, waste their pay, beat their wives like the one with gray eyes or Putana, always bruised by someone. Nothing but tales of horror around the kitchen table, who beat whom, who spent the pay, women waiting for their sons to grow up and avenge them, beat the guy up.

What is a man good for? I wonder. A soldier behind the wire goes: "Hi, pussy cat." I go, "Git," stick my tongue out at him then skip fast to the house across the street.

I tell mother about Yanna and her stomach, she counts on her fingers, fixes coffee to celebrate. She is happy whenever she hears that someone is pregnant. She also likes yakking it up with all those women, especially now that there is real coffee around, not much, still rare, but you can at least buy the real stuff in the store and not depend on favors or the black market.

I have to do the inviting, upstairs, up and down the street. "Mother says to tell you to come for coffee real soon." I don't add "real coffee" because you don't invite people for the other one made out of grain, without any smell at all, just a lookalike. With the real one, the whole neighborhood can smell the lucky person who is roasting the beans on the top of the stove. Women stop and sniff the wind, check the direction of the smell.Coffee is so important for the grown-ups that when there wasn't any "real stuff" around in the store old women like the one upstairs had it prescribed as a medication for their heart. It made the heart go faster, she said.

I have to grind it in the coffee mill, then mother boils it with sugar and water in a small yellow *dzezva*; they drink it slowly commenting all along how good it is, how well done, just right, neither too bitter or too sweet. You can never figure out why this particular coffee today is better than others since it's always made the same way—the same amount of sugar and coffee and a cup of water for each cup. Some days it turns out good by magic, same as with yogurt or cakes.

When it's all gone, nothing left but the thick disgusting stuff at the bottom, they turn their cups over on a piece of paper and wait for the patterns to form. Everyone does it except this old woman, our landlady upstairs who likes coffee so much she doesn't want to waste the grounds, she says, and licks the bottom of her cup making me sick to my stomach. You never say anything, do not show any disgust because she is an old person and I wouldn't be considered well brought up if I made a face as she licked that cup.

There are only two important things to look out for when looking at the grounds: difficulties, when the grounds are all bunched up, stick to the edge of the cup in one chunk, except when only one small piece sticks to the edge—then it means a gift, or fortune of some kind. The second thing is travels, trips big or small—you see them in the long thin lines that go up and down, except when they refuse to form at all, it happens—then, that means tears, you'll cry about something, or your "curse" will start.

"Does she have it?"

"Good Lord, no, she is too young."

Are they talking about me again?

It will never happen to me if I try. I swear again just to be sure NO NO NO I will never be like you, just try to catch me if you can. I will escape all of you and your past and the coffee grounds, destiny stars marriage brats. Me, I am the future, still red, like in the Russian movies, fighting for the revolution, dying perhaps before the age of twenty-five.

Now that the coffee is done, there is nothing left but to sigh and talk about Yanna and how youth passes fast and who beat whom when. If somebody starts with a dream, that gets them going for a long time; I will never get any homework done, not when mother mentions the snakes. She dreams about those all the time.

"Some hidden enemy," women agree on the meaning of the snake.

"Yes, but who?"

"Who is the snake?"

There are many possibilities, all concerned with jealousies that people have, who has more of what, who has better kids or a house.

The rest is easy, always the same:

To walk up the hill in a dream is good, but not to stand on top of the mountain which is bad luck. To swim in cold clear water – good health; muddy waters – bad health. To dream of the king and queen – excellent. Children, especially female ones and blond – worry, same as in life. Gypsies – good luck in love. You'll laugh a lot. To ride a horse – good luck and victory over your enemies.

(But what if your horses are not brown or white, what if they are bright red, made out of fire, what if they fly? Is it still good luck?)

Bratso and I dream of flying a lot, over the town and the hills. Grandma says it means you are growing up, that's what flying means, and when you are all grown up your dreams of flying will stop. At times, I do dances in my dreams that I could never do in life, music in the background, on my toes, weightless, arms like wings; I move through the air like a snowflake. I wish for that dream every night before going to bed and sometimes it happens as I wished. I also learn to stop the bad dreams just in the middle and turn them into good ones. If the river is very muddy in a dream, I say to myself:

"No, that's bad health; move upstream fast!"

And there I find a clear spring. See what I mean?

But the world is full of ghosts in addition to all other problems. I have to worry about them as I go toward the john at night, even though some are friendly ones, will not harm you. Others, like the ghost of the mother-in-law of the woman with the gold tooth, are terrifying to hear about:

"There I was," the gold tooth tells, "when I hear this sound and try to wake my Marko up, but he sleeps like a log, just snores and snores."

I am getting goose pimples already, her Marko just snores, she hears this sound, then bang, bang, as the mother-in-law thrashes about, breaking all the dishes, cursing. She recognized her by this.

"And besides, who else would know right away where the dishes are? Nobody but her, the witch. We will have to open the grave, stab her with a yew stake to see if she bleeds, a sure sign."

Then another ghost visitation, always at night. The souls of young girls wander about, hide in the shadows of river banks, you see them on moonlit nights calling, singing soft, *don't look, run,* or they'll pull you toward them toward the deep deep water where they hide.

A girl is buried in my yard right under the lilac bush. They say that there was nothing there before, then when a year passed lilacs grew on the very spot. She was to be married to somebody she didn't like and instead went and swallowed poison.

Whose daughter was she?

They never answer questions like that. Some have seen her behind the bush, beautiful with long hair, still wearing her wedding dress. I walk carefullly around the bush, afraid to step on her arms. But what if they were telling me lies? They must be lies. What else? Trying to trick me and confuse me with their bourgeois lies.

Chapter Fifteen

I LIE AGAIN, only my second time. The difference between me and others, Bratso or mother, is in this—I know when I do it and feel real bad. They do it, invent as a matter of fact, the way you breathe every day, just mixing it up with true parts and you can't tell at all what is what. My lies are clear cut, just plain lies.

It happened by accident without any thinking on my part; I wasn't going to do it; it was not a must. Young student teachers came out of somewhere to observe the class, a whole slew of them, fresh from their class trip to the sea. They are gabbing with each other, about boats, the palms, the shore, the sky—none of us have been there yet, that's for later, the last year in *gymnasium* perhaps—when I say casually, without intending to, that the beautiful city they rave about is not my home town.

"Oh, that's my home town. I was born there not far from the palace."

They, the girls, look at me in total amazement and notice that indeed I look different from anybody else in the class.

"Look, what beautiful eyes she has."

"Just like the sea," says the other.

I know I am lying, but it *could* have happened after all. Grandma *did* live in that very city and had her own restaurant where they spoke Italian, German, English. Mother and father met there when he was a cadet. I have a picture of them looking at each other, smiling. It happened one day as she was passing by, carrying a basket of cherries for grandma's restaurant, and he, my father, saw her from a window all of a sudden. He knew there and then that he loved her and had to see her again and he did. That wasn't easy because people get lost in a large town and he only saw her from a window, didn't know her name, yet he did find out by asking people, by describing her to others. It must have been funny, that part, poor dad saying, "the most beautiful girl in the world," when people have their own opinions of such things. That's why it took such a long time.

Finally they met, not far from the palace; he wanted the marrige right away, mother only joked around. She never believed, not until the last day, that she would marry him, him being sort of sickly and blond, but very kind, that part she admits. She did marry him of course because you don't escape your fate; it's all written in the stars, the day you are born, the day you die; it's written.

I have never been there in that town where they met on that piazza but I know it by heart: palm trees, boats, it never rains. It's a sunny day like this one in class, as father looks all of a sudden through the window and sees this girl passing by with a basket.

Outside my window, it's the market day in town, peasants carry stuff.

The student teachers are talking about something else, men, I think.

When the class is over teacher says: "Tell your mother to come in."

And then to her, later: "Do you have a birth certificate for her? I thought she was born here, during the war."

I see it coming now. What will I do? Those silly girls.

Why did they have to blab? Will I have to explain?

Will I be beaten, humiliated in front of the others, caught in my big lie?

Please, I will never do it again, let it pass this time, never again, one, two, three, four, five, don't blink.

Well, nothing happened, nothing at all. They whispered for awhile and teacher finds out that mother did indeed live in that beautiful town, which teacher visited for a week right after her wedding. Together they remember the palms, the boats. Nobody asks me to explain at all.

What was that about the birth certificate? Where is it?

They simply forgot about me.

CHAPTER SIXTEEN

ANOTHER SUMMER at grandpa's. Bratso sleeps in the hayloft with some peasant boys without covers or sheets; he likes it better there because he can drop through the hole in the floor and land on top of the horse, so he claims but he might be just bragging. I'll never know for sure. They don't want me in there and I don't insist. My bed is still the same — in the little house where my grandparents slept after their marriage. I don't even care that he sleeps in the barn with those boys; it's better this way for me. I can look at the pictures, maybe lock the door, peek into the trunks. And besides who wants to sleep in the hay without sheets, like a horse?

Lena is bigger and taller this summer, and has larger hips. Two of us soak the hemp in the river, let it dry, then beat it with sticks until the good part remains, then grandma will make thread out of it and shirts. Lena and the girls soak the hemp and wash their own clothes in the river, wash themselves, swim in the deepest, most shadowy pools, run around chasing each other with branches. Their bodies are white with real hips, breasts, and they look like those women from Java in the book where women run around rivers without any clothes on. I take my own pants off, run with them, swim. But when we get ashore where our clothes were drying, they are not there, stolen. The girls run in panic and hide under the willows. Mile, Bratso, and other boys have stolen them, we can see them on the bank, they won't give them to us until Lena gives a kiss, and she says no.

"Kiss your pickle face," she says to Mile, "never. You just wait till I tell your father about this one, you pig face, you wait and see. Better give them right away or else."

After a few minutes of waiting, clothes fly into the river from the bank. We swim after them and float in the water trying to dress. Only Lena stands up naked to the waist, laughs, and slowly puts her shirt on. Bratso and the boys retreat. Big defeat for them.

Lena doesn't tell. She is sewing her holiday blouse at night, a pink bouse gathered all over, the kind that in town would be called "peasant," "too pink," but here it is the most beautiful blouse ever, with ribbons sewn in. Grandma has her holiday skirt out, blue with white, she'll wear it on top of the other skirts and her embroidered vest. There is still much time left; the holiday comes after the corn harvest.

Corn husking is always at night and we stay up late around the kerosene lamp, two of them for this occasion, plus some light from the stove. The electricity will happen next year, they say. Outside it's dark except for the fireflies here and there. Grandma has gone to sleep. Lena and the others giggle, their fingers work fast, off goes the corn husk in a second, men say things to make the girls squeal and blush. They push at each other, play games with apple peels then, still working fast, they start on the stories about ghosts seen here and there, mostly around the mill where everyone will have to pass on their way back. It is dark outside, how will I get to my bed?

We are husking and husking, the light from the stove flickers a bit. Somewhere a dog barks. Then we hear an eerie sound—ee-e-e-e, and there in the door stands a ghost dressed in a sheet. Women scream, Bratso runs and falls into my lap, the ghost lifts the sheet off and it's Mile, the devil, the same one who stole the clothes from the bank.

They work and work and then sing. Maybe they work the whole night. When I wake up, it's noon, Lena has already returned with the cows. I don't remember how I got to bed, did somebody take me there? Lena says, yes, a boy, tall, handsome. She winks, and I know she's making it all up.

When the holiday arrives it's easy for us, you can see the monastery from the house; others have to get up early and walk or take the carriage in. It's the only monastery for many villages around, the most important saint is celebrated there, the one who sends the thunder and lightning. I wear a white cotton dress and sandals for this occasion, Lena her pink blouse, Bratso has shoes on. On the way to the monastery we meet many girls in yellow, pink, red, blue blouses with ribbons; all have jasmine in their waists, hair slicked with water, all look shy. Some even have city shoes instead of brogans, but they walk barefoot, carrying them by the laces in their hands to keep the shine. Just before the monastery they will put them on.

When we get there, it's full of people, horses and carts. Horses sleep in the shade standing up; people sleep there too next to horses, on the ground. We are free to roam; you can't get lost anywhere. I know my way back; you can even see our house through the trees, slightly elevated, on the hill.

Grandma goes inside the church with some older women. It smells of incense inside; dark, cold saints look at me from the walls through the blue glass. Candles flicker. They light some more, some for the dead, others for the living; you have your pick. The bottom part is for the dead, where the most candles are, some thin, others thick; the top part is for good health or for good luck.

Women whisper—*gospodi pomiluj*—and bow. There are not too many men around except for those monks.

It's lighter than usual when you get out. The sun blinds you for a second, then you just follow the crowd right or left all around the monastery. One group is roasting a lamb; it smells good, will be ready by noon; a man sells candy in many colors; grandpa buys us some, then goes back to sit with the old men. They talk about the wars in the Balkans and watch the young gathered around the musicians, accordions and drums. The music is slow to start in the beginning, almost shy, then the sound gets bigger and by the time the lamb is ready, the music shouts, jumps.

Lena dances next to a man who holds her hand tight; together they stamp the earth, eyes serious, lips tight, face down. Only their hips move and her beads. I would like to try but don't. They are so big so fast so many they would trample me with their feet.

After the lunch, some sleep in the meadow by the large oak, a few women swim and bathe themselves in the river which around here is holy and can help with children if you have none. Then everybody wakes up, starts stamping the ground some more, and it goes on like that until nightfall when we go back home very very tired. There, in the kitchen we learn the latest — that so-and-so eloped with such-and-such after the dance, something you always do if the parents are opposed to your choice. "Elope" is a word used for girls ony; men have less problems with parents and choices. They never say "he elopes," it's always she. After they elope, the parents are forced to accept everything and give the dowry even if they don't like the guy because the girl who elopes is not good after that, not to anyone except the guy who she eloped with. They escape usually on a horse, Lena says, both of them on one, sometimes with help of a trusted friend if the girl is watched over carefully or if it is rumored that she might "jump." They sleep somewhere overnight, maybe outside or in a hut, he takes her home the next day to his parents, and that's that. Only peasants do this and at home in town people laugh about the whole thing, call it primitive or "underdeveloped."

"They sell a girl like a horse, or go bargain for her," the town people snicker. If the dowry isn't big her chances are small unless she is very very beautiful and the man an only son. Usually, she gets a piece of land, gold coins, or a cow. Lena says pointing to the cornfield, "That meadow will be mine."

It is almost the end of the summer, time to go back, get ready, pack; school will start soon. I am lying by the river in the meadow by the mill when the letter arrives, short, written by someone else since grandma can't write. It says only a few things:

"Mother in prison, do not know why, stay where you are until you hear more."

I can't stay here. What about school? What will happen to me?

"Why is she in prison?" I ask.

Grandpa only shakes his head; it's better not to talk about it. We have to be careful. She was working in a factory when it happened, her very last job after she stopped knitting for the second time. What did she do? Did she hit someone?

You can't talk to Bratso even if you try. He just eats, sleeps, forgets everything fast. He doesn't care if he stays here for the rest of his life; he likes it, loves it so much in the hayloft. He not only refuses to help, it's worse. He joins with the village bullies in teasing me, now that they know we have to stay. They say nasty things to me like "Hey, pussy, hey, cunt." After sleeping in the barn, he starts cursing and swearing like a peasant, even says "fuck, God damn," or "I'd rather stay here than go back, fuck it." Mother would kill him if she heard. He never tries to stop those guys.

Nobody stops him when he starts changing. Grown-ups just laugh when he curses; they think it's cute, him becoming a peasant like that. He chews on a straw, even spits after each word for emphasis, to look important the way village bullies do. His mouth soon has cracks and sores just like the peasant kids. I am afraid he might have lice.

I wash his clothes and mine in the river every week, dry them in the sun, ask him to change. Maybe if we stay clean we won't get sores, maybe he won't become a peasant. I try changing him back, winning him to my side, but have to be clever if it is to work. I say to him all alone—it has to be that way, with others he turns against me—I say:

"Bratso, let's collect all the nuts we can find, then hide them somewhere really safe. When mother comes out of prison, we will give them to her and she'll bake a big cake, the kind they don't know how to do here."

That's my tactic, it's important that he doesn't forget who we are— that we have a mother and a home and live elsewhere, and the only way to reach him is through the cake. For obvious reasons. This catches on; he starts collecting nuts and giving them to me, only I know that this cannot last for too long because he will forget, get distracted by the hay, the horse, those bully boys. It is important to repeat mother, grandma, home, cake . . . we live in town, you have a regular bed . . . with clean sheets.

When September comes, I start my grade with the peasant kids in a one-room school. They are all nice; the girls bring me gifts of apples, flowers, bird nests, and one makes a flute for me. They are older than me, yet nobody can read for shit. Teacher appoints me head of one group; he teaches the other. I have had all this before in the first, second grade.

But what's going to happen to me?

Nobody worries about me.

I have nobody but me.

Everything has gone wrong, even grandpa. He looks old and worried all of a sudden. One whole field of wheat already harvested got burned by accident when that stupid son of a bitch Mile fell asleep in it with a cigarette in his hand. There'll be no bread in the winter, nothing but corn. One cow is not giving milk.

They expect me to work now, to harvest plums, help with sheep, feed the pigs. It's not vacation any more.

I refuse out of spite.

They say: "Look at the city miss."

"You are staying here, so why pretend, put on airs?"

What will happen to me? If I start working and forgetting I'll really turn into a peasant in no time.

I write grandma a letter and to be sure it gets there, I take it myself to town on the market day.

Dear Grandma, my only one, Please come and get me. What will happen to me, what about school? Please don't abandon me! You are the only one I got.
  Anna

She arrived two weeks later, looking very old in her black scarf. We gathered my things in a bundle, took the nuts. Bratso will come later, it was decided; there is not enough food for three. Neighbors will feed two of us.

We walk on the same narrow road where I walked with father once at four. Why don't they take us in a carriage? They look angry when we leave. Nobody says goodbye; they didn't prepare chicken for lunch. It's October, mud, rain falling; all the leaves are gone. Grandma falls down several times in the mud; it's scary; how can I lift her? What is wrong? Is she ill? Both of us sit in the mud by the road, then she gets up slowly and we walk. A big, green frog jumps out of somewhere and scares me, makes me remember *him* all of a sudden. Where the hell is he? Who do I have left? We arrive in town, rain still falling, mud, then get on the open truck; rain turns to hail; my red sweater bleeds all over me.

Chapter Seventeen

M OTHER IS IN PRISON for political reasons, they say; they took her straight from her job in the factory where she made sweaters.

"What did she do?" I ask.

Nobody knows, don't talk about it; it's better to stay silent.

"Is she guilty?" I ask again.

Nobody says yes or no. I think and think and decide that she is guilty — an enemy of the people, reactionary but *only* in her thoughts. I can't imagine what reactionary acts are, what she could possibly do. (Why did I have to have such bad luck? Why couldn't she at least be ordinary?) In school, nobody knows. I would be too ashamed to tell, and when they collect for the Chinese I say to teacher:

"I have no money, mother is in the hospital."

"What does she have?"

"Oh . . ." I think briefly, ". . . TB."

"Her salary would be coming in as usual, the hospital is free."

She doesn't insist. Maybe she knows. What will she think of me? I hope she knows better than to brand me as a reactionary right away; I write the best compositions on revolution in class.

Mother can't be seen, we cannot write to her either, but we know that she is alive, still in this town. One day, we walk around the prison, a building I have never seen before, right in the center of town, a red brick with many small windows with bars. We walk right in front of it; maybe she'll notice us and feel good to see us. We wave and stand there for a long time. Then we go to see somebody, me all dressed up in my UNRA skirt, and grandma begs for mother's release in front of this man in a leather jacket with a picture of Lenin on the side. He looks at me, smiles but doesn't promise much, says words that I already know, her guilt—counter-revolution, enemy propaganda, etc.

Days pass, how many it's hard to tell, it could be four weeks or fifteen. People come and visit us with food as when somebody dies. My doctor comes with money, tells grandma not to worry. He also gives her shots. I learn that his father was born in Leningrad.

One day we are allowed to send her food twice a week and some clothes. We take the food in front of the prison, wait there with other people, nobody speaks, then somebody examines everything, then she gets it after awhile. That's how one day as the guard inspected her food I got this idea—I'll write her on a piece of white cloth, put it at the bottom of a pot with a layer of wax paper on top, then the stew over the whole thing. When she is done with the stew, there'll be the letter. What a surprise! I read it somewhere. Was it in Gorky or Monte Cristo?

And we send the food on, worrying all the time that she might not catch on, that they'll recognize my writing and then what.

A week later we get an answer, her message in the seam of the dress with the other clothes they sent us to wash. It says on a small piece of paper: "Was sick, now better, send aspirin."

We can only write a sentence or two, usually: "Don't worry, everybody healthy, saw lawyer about case."

Grandma prays to our saint every night on her knees, to deliver mother, good health for Bratso and me and my doctor who comes often to see that we have something for lunch.

No news from Bratso; he must be full of lice.

People whisper when we pass and ask, "Still there?" "How is she?"

We say we know nothing; nobody knows about the letters except grandma and me.

One night, we are writing and getting the food for prison ready when she appears at the door, looking like a ghost, pale, thin; she has never been thin before, white hair in front, over the eye. I faint, or pretend to, or I really do when she appears at the door. Was I happy or did she scare me looking like that?

Tomorrow, I don't go to school, a holiday time. People visit in twos and threes like on Saint's Day; some cry as soon as they open the door. Mother seems quiet, pats me on the head, calls me her "smart one." I hope she doesn't start talking about my letters; news could spread; I'd rather we kept it a secret and not brag how smart I was. Of course I am happy she is back, but in all fairness, I was not unhappy with grandma; we were alone for the first time and it was real quiet. And then, I'll miss those letters a bit, writing them, waiting for them to arrive; I'll miss missing mother too. Somehow over there in prison, she was not her, she became mama, mom, but all this is hard to explain with words.

Mother drinks a lot of coffee, tells stories that change each time. Some pieces fit; others don't at all. She was not *convicted,* just *held,* others went to jail, some had *electricity* on their arms, she did not. She was innocent, she says "so help me God."

There were many different people in prison and among them a well-known woman with bad morals who saved mother's life with coffee. "Whore that she is," says mother, "she managed to get coffee, even in prison. It doesn't pay to be good." All she did was make eyes at the guard and he got her coffee, which she passed along to mother. Mother was very ill at that time, lying on the cold floor without any covers and coffee saved her, that's for sure. She'll never forget her nor hers as long as she lives, even though she didn't like her morals. This woman even had cigarettes in prison, puffing them, asking the guard for a match. "What a good-looking boy you are," she would say to the guard, "how about a match, and get me a different brand the next time." "It simply doesn't pay to be an honest woman," mother concludes that part.

Another story was how this young man helped mother get out of prison or she would have stayed six months, how he spared her electricity and the shocks because he never forgot the favors mother did for him when she worked in the hotel. Even though it was strictly forbidden to bring up any female guests to the room where he lived in the hotel, mother always gave his girlfriend the key, then pretended to close her eyes. "They were both so young. I thought, why not? Life passes fast." She could have lost her job for this, the young man knew this and never forgot. He was the one that got her out of jail so soon because now he is a big shot in the Party, a real commissar.

This is all fine, but the true question remains: "Why was she held in the first place?"

"She did it all, the bitch," this horrible woman who came from the same province as mother and was always jealous of her even when young because mother was beautiful, had many suitors, this woman none; so when her good time came with the revolution, she looked for ways to destroy mother and managed to convince the authorities that mother was involved in serious counter-revolutionary stuff.

What can one do as a counter-revolutionary in town?

Never noticed anything unusual about her—I think.

Maybe at night.

Should I report her if. . . ?

No, can't do it, but what bad luck to have a mother like that.

Mother swears on heads of her children, "May I lose both of them if what I say isn't true." I hold my fingers crossed behind my back, just in case she is telling a lie, maybe she is holding them crossed too as she says, "May I lose them . . ." I spit three times without blinking just in case.

"Sons of bitches, bastards, what fucking counter-revolution?"

"When did I have time?" she foams.

"Run to work, run back home to protect my two birds and this grave," she points to grandma who does look old.

"Counter-revolution! That snake invented it all. May she rot, may her seed die, may she walk blind, may she turn in her grave and have no peace!"

Now another story emerges as the days pass. It seems that a well-known counter-revolutionary leader was related to us, and he remained in the mountains long after others were caught. He roamed the mountains like a phantom, played games with the police, left letters for them all over the place, dared them all the time, got dressed up like a peasant woman, came to town, enjoyed himself a lot. His family suffered for it since everyone believed they were helping him while they, poor people, prayed for his death so the harassment would stop.

Stories about this distant cousin are told over coffee, door always shut, always whispering, turning around to see if . . . *I remember all of a sudden:* handcuffed men after the war, right on the Main Street, led like animals by the screaming, crowd — bearded, hairy men out of bad dreams. In my school books, they did horrible things, killed people with big knives, slit their throats, got drunk.

Why would mother be mixed up with people like that?

I certainly have no luck.

Time passed. On one occasion, mother says with a wink and pride that she really *did* know what was going on, without really being part of it. *So,* there was really a reason why she was arrested, I think, but with her you can never tell; she changed her stories depending on the weather or her guest. Grandma was never like that, her truth was always the same. I should have been her daughter, but then I just didn't have good luck when it came to relatives in general.

I had to resolve the question of mother's arrest, just to make things clear, and finally, after much thinking, I decide that the verdict is NOT GUILTY — because she talked too much. They made a mistake. A truly guilty person would have been more silent like me, or a spy.

Bratso arrived from the country about two weeks later, swearing like a peasant and full of lice. We had to boil all his clothes, cut his hair short, not just a trim but everything until you saw the scalp. He looked funny, pathetic with hair like that, crusts all around ears, sores on his lips. Looking at him there in the kitchen with his small baby hands all chapped, I forgot my anger against him and that he betrayed me once. He did it at grandpa's, he will do it over and over again never thinking, never intending to, and wouldn't even understand if I tried to explain what betrayal means. He's only a kid, I reasoned. And me? I am a pretend one.

When Bratso got back, we celebrate first with our favorite dishes — plum dumplings baked in the oven with sugar and cinnamon on top, rice pudding, and grandma's spinach pie.

Mother and the women celebrate with coffee as usual.

"You'll cry for some reason, see."

"You'll get your period perhaps," says Sara reading the cup.

"How well you guessed, I just got the curse, my yogurt refused to set. It's like that when I have it."

"The female is cursed."

Then tears. All the women without exception cry a lot; any reason is good. If a kid is sick you worry to death and cry; if he is healthy, you look at him, remembering:

"If only his grandma could see him now, may his mother see him married, may she dance at his wedding."

More tears, what else? They look at each other expecting them, you can tell. They even say:

"My soul is heavy today . . . I feel like crying the whole day, for no reason, what could it mean?"

"Me too, would you believe it," Sara now. "My eyes are itching like mad . . . I'll cry."

"Ech, ach, ech, ach . . . "

"May it be for nothing. God help us, may it be for nothing."

"As long as the children are fine, I don't care about me."

"Our times are over."

"They certainly are over," says the one with the gray eyes.

"It all went so fast, fuck this life," mother says.

"Yeah, a man is nothing but ashes, nothing but dust."

"Today you're alive, tomorrow in the grave."

"My ears are ringing, guess which one, left or right?" mother asks. If they guess right, they will get a letter, if not mother will. A letter coming for her, left ear.

If your feet itch you will travel. Or if you see ants in your house, you'll move somewhere else. Or if a cat passes in front of you on the road forget it, just go home, don't continue walking on the same street, certainly don't go on a trip.

There is so much bad luck everywhere, nothing is good except the gypsies or the chimney sweep and he visits only once a year. All the rest—disasters, itchy eyes. A dog howled last night, a bad omen. The cats yowled all night on the roof; she threw water at them to make them stop. May it be for nothing, may it pass over!

I try to make up my own charms and predictions, almost always good. But my predictions are all possible, even my lies are not really lies. I mean, I could have been born in that town by the sea since mother and father met there. As a matter of fact it's an accident I was born here in this very ordinary place with mother and these women drinking coffee. And then, it's quite possible that my family is not my own at all: I don't look like her, they found me somewhere, maybe stolen and sold by the gypsies who do things like that. That would be nice. Maybe someday I'll find my real parents, maybe not. It won't matter much. I am nobody's this way. Just my own. Later, much later, when I am very famous and they ask me questions like in that book where they say that so-and-so took after his mother or father and they ask:

"Anna, who influenced you the most in your life?"

I'll say:

"Nobody, nobody had an effect on me at all since I didn't know who my parents were. I just invented myself like that you see."

That sounds good, it really does but how can you dream like that when she starts her old stories in full detail. Yackety-yak over coffee.

"I was sick for months, suffered like a dog, even though she weighed only three kilos. Now with my sweet boy, it was much easier and he was a full six."

The reason is simple—she knew all along from the first moment she was carrying a *man*, not a pisser, hole, fish, female, cursed. However, in both cases, she repeats, not a sound was heard. I bet Yanna will scream like hell, I bet she will.

It slips out of me, silent until now, listening:

"*I* will never have children. Who wants to suffer?" "That's what they all say," says the one with the tooth, "and see what happened to me. Married at 16, that's what."

"Devil got in her pants," says the other.

The gold tooth winks and starts singing the peasant song:

*"I have asked her
if she'll give me some."*

They go "hi, hi, hi, hi," laugh with nasty mouths, slapping their hips. The key word is "give" and I miss the connection; the rest becomes confusing.

"Give!"

"Give what? That's my wife."

"'Comrade, give to me,' says the Russian soldier."

And the peasant, our own, goes in the shed, gets an ax and kills the soldier who asked for his wife.

"He should know better than to fool around with a Balkan peasant. Communism of that sort is not for us," mother says, proud. "Why, once, I took the iron that I was doing clothes with and burned this son of a bitch that tried to get me from the back. He'll have a mark on his face for the rest of his life."

When was this? That's a new story.

Mother loves these stories the best, the ones that show her strong, fighting.

"And my grandmother killed two Turks with a skillet, like this on the head, then dragged them to the river and it looked as if they drowned," she says.

I know this story about the Turks and how her province was known for bravery, and how the Turks never conquered them; the mountains were too high. She added a new detail this time, the part about the river. Before, they were left to rot in the sun.

Mother attacked and burned that man because he tried to ruin her morals, I think, or something like her reputation. She doesn't like women who run around with men, calls them "hysterical," a new word. Hysterical means you like, need men too much but even in this there is a big difference between her and the others — she not only is not hysterical, it's better than that — she doesn't even care about them, period. She hopes, looking at me, I will be like her at least in this, will not care much.

"But you never know, she is partly his blood," she explains to the gold tooth. " His old man drank all his money up on music and gypsies, he never got tired of you know what."

"What?" I say.

"Nothing. Just watch your step! Or. . . .!"

Imagine blaming me for something father's father did and I didn't even know him and he is dead.

Chapter Eighteen

G RANDMA DIED one night after a very short illness. She was in
bed with the flu for a day or two, was strong enough to braid her
hair, was not really sick at all. I am awakened by voices in the middle
of the night, some commotion outside, light under the door. The doctor is there, my doctor, the same one. I can hear him, he just gave
her a shot. I open the door. He looks at me, pats my hair. Mother says:

"Go to bed now, it's late."

I go back but can't sleep. It is hard with all this happening, although
it never occurs to me she is dying. Nobody says that. They should
have, so I can be with her a bit, say good-bye.

"Look at her hands," one woman screams.

"They're turning yellow, a candle, fast."

I get up again, open the door but only see grandma's head from
the back, mother all red in the face.

A woman puts the candle right over grandma's head. It flickers a bit.

"Nana," mother says to her, "did you know that Rade came back
from England. He just came back from England to see you. There
he is by the door."

"Who are you kidding, he'll never come back," says grandma slowly.

Grandma was no fool although I know that mother is trying to make
her feel good and only lied for that reason. After that grandma

mentioned my name a couple of times and tried to say something but couldn't. Was she leaving *amanet* for me, for mother? She made some very strange sounds and I was sent to bed by force.

When I wake up again, there is the sound of water splashing outside the door. She must be dead now since they talk about her fine feet. I don't go in.

In the morning, she is lying on the kitchen table, coins on her lids, scarf tied around her jaw, dressed in her best dress with small dots, the one she always told me would be her burial dress. She also had very big white pantaloons with lace on the side, made before the revolution when she was waiting for that sailor to come back. She had one pair that was never used, and a white slip with lace, her initials P.C., all chosen by her for this occasion, stashed in the drawer, not far from the blue book.

Now she is lying on the table, all yellow, otherwise the same. Many people come, cry a lot, kiss grandma's head, then leave some coins by her side. Bratso and I eat at Slavka's, then go and play in the yard. I feel neither good nor bad. I feel nothing at all for once. People, women look at me and wonder why I don't cry, why I refused to kiss her head. "She was her favorite, and look, not a tear, what a child!" I simply can't.

Grandma said that children were angels, went to heaven right away, innocent and all.

Where is grandma? Is she up there?

Grandma, can you see me? It is a rainy day when we bury her, the red clay is on my shoes. The priest is at the head of the procession, in front of the house, then a boy with a cross with her name at the top, then the hearse with gold trim with grandma inside, then Bratso with a candle just behind the hearse, big tears rolling down his cheeks, then mother and Yanna in black and others, our whole street. I must be there too except that I am not, and seem to float over all of them, sometimes in front of the procession, other times to the side, even in the back. I see the last line of the marchers and the first. I see people cross themselves as we pass by, all the way down, past the merchant's and the baker's and the doctor's house, past the military barracks where more people join us from other streets, then still further down, the rain pouring now, past the pharmacy and the prison to the Main Street where others wait, kiss mother on the cheek. Here, we turn right.

The cemetery is far, almost in the foothill of the mountains, not far from the hospital where many TB patients are. I have never been this way before.

It's raining all the way; it rains when we get there, the clay is on my feet. They put ropes around the casket and the priest says something about her soul. The rain falls in the grave; it will be cold. Then a frog jumps in the hole, a big green frog.

"Get it out," I scream, or do I think I am screaming?

Nobody sees the frog except me, nobody tries to get it out. They lower grandma in there with the frog, then throw some mud on top. Mother starts a song about grandma, who she was, her whole life, she makes up rhymes as she goes along . . . "Why did you leave me now, why?" she sings then stops and cries some more. Yanna and she try to jump in the pit but people stop them in time.

The priest ends with "Lord have mercy on her soul, *pomiluj*."

What will happen to me, panic inside.

My life stops here for the second time. For a while it was one straight line, now it stops. This time, like the first, things have funny shapes, I am not sure I am me. Who can tell me if it's me? And if I can't remember me, then who am I?

Grandma, my only one, my sweet, I'll miss you, pray to you,
my only saint, there are no others deliver me from pain, from
ugliness, help me grow up, please. Amen.

I pray to her in silence as we go back. Maybe if I try I can keep her inside, maybe she did not completely die like that young guy who threw a grenade at the Germans when he was twenty-four.

CHAPTER NINETEEN

W HEN WE GET BACK from the cemetery, Slavka and others have
prepared things to eat, put the table in its usual place, washed
everything. Neighbors come by, drink brandy and say, "May she
rest in peace." They urge mother not to cry, but cry themselves,
remember who died in their family.

"She is out of her trouble now."

"She won't suffer anymore."

"She is in heaven now, a heavenly soul she was."

"The Lord giveth, the Lord taketh away."

Everyone agrees that grandma was good, had no enemy in the entire
town, and if there was one person to go to heaven it would be her.
Saint Peter opened the doors for her as soon as she arrived last night
and let her in. I keep thinking about the rain and the frog even though
I want it to stop.

Grandma died without any suffering, which is a good sign, the
women say. She deserved to die well while the guilty ones spend
days in pain writhing away. She also died with her eyes toward
heaven, not toward the door or another person, which is also a good
omen. You can tell by these signs if others from the same family
will die soon. With grandma everything was fine.

The room was whitewashed the next day; the woman who washed
dead grandma got all her clothes, that's the custom. She got all her

old silk dresses and big nightgowns that smelled of lavender she collected in the summer. I wish I could keep just one thing, just to touch it from time to time, but do not dare ask. She wouldn't understand. Nobody pays attention to me. It's better that way. *Remain silent, pass unnoticed,* I instruct myself. There is nothing left of grandma except that old picture of her in a white blouse with buttons. Even her shoes and pins were given away. It's the custom.

Forty days later, we go to the grave again with a smaller group this time and have a big lunch to help grandma's soul. The grass is already there, very short, pale green. I still wonder what will happen to her, what happened to the frog. They raise their glasses high and say:

"For her soul!"

"May she rest in peace!"

It's a sunny day this time, the cemetery seems larger. I can see other graves behind the trees. I wander among the graves of fallen communists marked with the red star, dead in '41, '42, '43, '44, then all the others with crosses, some with pictures from other times, inscriptions below in gold letters: "dearly beloved," "our only one." One whole family is there in black marble with oval pictures, all dead before the revolution, before my birth, before the war. One woman is pulling weeds, crying at the same time. Further down, they are digging another grave; two men with shovels, stopping to rest, drink from a jug.

The lunch is over, people will be leaving soon. Mother leaves all the extra food on top of the grave, a bit of each dish, then sprinkles wine over the cross. Gypsies will come and eat; it will be good for her soul. Gypsies are messengers in a way between the living and the dead. You see them all over, sitting on different graves, eating, arguing who got more of what. I see it clearly:

a gypsy woman is fighting over a piece of chicken with a guy; a child pulls at her skirt; mother is dressed in black; men are drinking brandy for grandma's soul. The grass is on the grave. It is not raining. I am not here but do not know where I am. The voice in me insists: It's you, listen, don't forget.

Soon after, Yanna came to report that she slept poorly because grandma came to visit her at night and shook her bed, bothered her husband. Yanna was worried about her unborn child. For once I agree with mother that Yanna is foolish—it is impossible. Mother seems offended; only bad souls wander, the guilty ones, the ones that had bad burials or no grave. Grandma was in order, everything had been done right, absolutely to the last detail, all the burial dishes, the candles, the priest, and what's more she died in peace. Yanna is a liar, we agree. I know that if grandma was going to visit anyone, she'd visit me. I hope someday she'll come.

Then I start digging again in the middle of the night, just like after the war. I don't know where I am and if they ask I say:

"Just digging, digging for the frog."

"The frog jumped in, get it out."

It all makes sense when I do it, everything fits, but the next day when they want me to explain, I'm not so sure. It's not the same. I wake up more and more tired every day; my hands seem yellow, shake. Mother says they are pink, but I see yellow like wax. I am going to die next. She looks at me from time to time, then goes to cry somewhere where I can't see. But I do see her and know it's serious. I'll die next.

We go visit my doctor who lives in that beautiful house, untouched by the war, with a large gate, with many flowers inside. In the courtyard, whole families of peasants accompany the sick, waiting their turn, eating bread and cheese from wool bags. They eat slowly, eyes fixed, the same way as their oxen outside on the street.

They don't even lift their eyes when we come in.

In the waiting room, I read some medical books on the shelves, skin diseases in color, deformed bones, enlarged TB of the lung. Here as well as in school, the signs are everywhere:

DON'T SPIT ON THE FLOOR! FIGHT TB, OUR ENEMY NUMBER 1!

Peasants are a problem; they spit everywhere, spit, spit.

Why am I here? Do I have TB? I feel no pain.

In school, we are checked for it, with a machine in total darkness; he, my doctor, looks for the first signs. There is no cure for it, not yet, except good food, fresh air. Mother worries about TB all the time, TB of the lung. She sees the doctor as soon as he examines me at school on that machine; she is the only mother around with the rest of us undressed to our waists. The doctor is on the other side, behind that machine that sees your insides. Every six months as I pass through, she expects me to have it. I can tell by her face and eyes as he declares:

"All clear, perfect, good lungs. We'll get her through, don't worry."

Mother looks at him and then from such good news starts to cry. Did she really think I would die, had it each time? The problem is that her tears in front of the kids, in front of everyone arouse suspicion. They stare and whisper:

"Anna has it maybe, why else would her mother cry?"

You try to convince them she is crying from joy. Nobody believes me, not until teacher declares, "We are lucky this year, nobody in this class."

That's why she brought me here, again. I must have TB of the lungs or the spine and will be just like that student who watches me from the window as I go by, the one who smiles at me and I smile back. He looks normal to me, a bit sad. Others say his case is a serious one, very, only a miracle would save him, or medicine from the West, but even then it might be too late. He has had it too long, and TB spreads faster in the young for some reason.

So there is a cure for TB? Somewhere in America, in the West, except that they don't care about us. We are in a different bloc, our country marked red. I hope that student doesn't know there is a possibility of cure; it would make it worse; he would get angry to know that he didn't have to die.

Now, if I have TB, I think, waiting for the doctor to see me, he would find medicine for me if it could be found. I am convinced of that. He is the only one who gives me presents every year, calls me "my pet." He has no kids himself. I have decided long ago that was it, the reason he was so nice. He probably always wanted to have a little girl like me but just couldn't, and so he gave me gifts instead. That fits.

And there is something about him I know and see—he is sad, his eyes are sad and I must look like that to him. He is the only one exactly like me.

How old is he? Is he young or old, can't tell with grown-ups, maybe the same age as mother, about thirty-four. She thinks he is thirty-four, and what a shame they couldn't have a child, such fine people would be good to a child.

When a peasant comes out of the office crying with his wife, the doctor notices us, his eyes grow bright. "Why didn't you say you were here?" and then breaks the rule and we go in even though it's not my turn yet.

He pinches my cheek, says:

"How are you, my pet?"

Me: "Fine."

"You just came to see me like that? You don't have to drag your mother along, you are getting big. Now tell me, what brings you here?" He winks.

Mother and him whisper, talk about hands turning yellow, digging at night; he smiles, winks again.

"I haven't seen her in awhile. Let's listen to her chest."

For this, I take all my clothes off, that's the rule. He listens and listens everywhere, taps my knees, bends my neck.

"Perfect," he says. "Will live."

"What should I do?" mother asks. More whispers, the two of them.

"Keep her quiet for a week or two, very quiet."

And then, to me: "What's this business about digging and the frog? Your grandma was very old, she had to die, all of us do. She would feel bad if you were not well. Let me see your hands."

He sits in front of me, looking at my hands, then he holds them in his.

"You are not going to die for a long time, I can tell. There's nothing wrong with your hands. They are very nice. They're sweet."

And now a big smile.

"All right, my pet."

We could leave now but it always takes a long time to depart. Mother asks,

"What am I to do with her? All the time with books. She'll ruin her eyes. And you know for a girl-child she hates to cook."

He tells her, just the way he should:

"I had no interest in cooking either."

Bravo for him!

"Just let her read. She doesn't have to be like others. Who says she has to marry?"

Now there is one person in addition to myself who thinks that way. Mother listens to him out of respect, no matter what he says because he has "saved" my life so many times. She mentions him in her prayers at night in front of the saint; she prays:

"God give him health and long life."

We sleep as always, me alone, Bratso with mother. For some reason nobody took over grandma's bed.

CHAPTER TWENTY

G RANDMA DIED too soon and didn't get to see many strange things take place. It started slow, with whispers at home around coffee, then all of a sudden comrade Stalin is not to be mentioned any more at school, his picture comes down in class, the song I liked so much about the "Young Guard" is out, dangerous, don't sing it, don't even hum, why I don't know; it's bad. There are no more Russian films, no more Russian music in the square where we celebrated October with *Kozachok* dances. In my reading book, only partisans are mentioned, no more Soviet tanks, brave Soviet men, no more red flags, just our own in three colors with the star. For some reason nobody asks any questions, nobody explains.

What is happening?

Why don't they explain even if it's really bad?

This is very difficult, a loss. We were big once, us and the Soviets, the whole globe. Russian fields of wheat extended beyond the horizons, Soviet scientists changed fruit in Siberia so oranges could grow in the frost. I read a book about this in the second grade, how nature can be changed to work for us. I have never had an orange.

What is left of all this? Where are we?

Here we are again with nothing but our own miserable hills, thin horses, thin, dark, mean men who beat you with a belt, the dark ages, our backwardness, how can we get out of it all alone?

The new word around the coffee is *Cominform*, a foreign word. They—the *Cominforci*—are going to jail now; mother rubs her hands, so happy, almost cries with joy.

"Oh boy, oh boy, am I happy, am I glad . . . Now it's their turn, the sons of bitches. Let them kill each other off, sons of snakes who sent me to prison for no reason at all. Let them rot there. God is almighty. He has strange ways, but sees everything. He takes his time, but sooner or later He'll avenge us."

Mother's God is often doing this, running around and avenging. He doesn't care too much for anyone, not even kids. What would grandma think if she were alive?

There are many people in the jail, some are sent far, none of our friends, mostly young people, some chief speakers from the square. "The poison took root in them like with TB," she says with glee. The young man who helped her get out of prison, the commissar, is imprisoned too, then sent to an island with others. There, horrible things happen, they whisper, not all will come back alive.

Parades stop and the slogans too. Are they writing new ones?

You can read the *Tribune* and the *Times* but not *How the Steel Was Tempered* that all the kids from *Gymnasium* carried in their packets before. You can't even talk about this book, it's that dangerous. Thank God, I read it before. Thinking about it, I try to remember what could be dangerous in this book but nothing seems to fit. It's really only about a group of young people, what they became as time passed. It happened in Russia, mostly during the war. I never knew you could go to prison because of a book. I wonder if Gorky is fine. Should I ask? Whom? There are many new stories now, how Russians attacked women wherever they came, "Thank God they didn't come here." "We liberated ourselves alone." Mother, of all people, seems proud of this. She never spoke of "Liberation" until now. "They stood up to those sons of bitches," she says, proud of our leaders.

Nothings fits, so bad that you want to laugh. She has softened up so much toward the regime, revolution and the rest that she together with others start spreading stories that so-and-so, our leader, is really an American spy, infiltrated among us to lead us to the true path. "Did you notice the way he speaks. He can't say r's, he stops to search for words. Clearly an American accent. Even his face is foreign, did you see those cold eyes?"

"Sure, I see what you mean," says the gold tooth. "I always thought there was something un-Balkan about his face."

Just nonsense. His face looks almost like mine, blonde hair, blue eyes.

Who started the rumor that the Americans are coming, was it her?

The Americans are coming, they are coming—a whisper.

It seems they will arrive in silence, probably at night, dropping this marvelous gas from the air, the gas will have no smell or color, it will not be seen. The gas is gentle and safe, and will put everyone to sleep, nothing will be touched. They, the Americans, will arrive in large flying machines and without having to bother with the usual weapons will turn the clock back, just as it was then—men with sabres on white horses, ladies with fancy dresses, gloves, everything will be as before, just as if the revolution never happened or the Germans or the war.

You truly have to be dumb to believe this story! Nothing can ever be the same, neither me or the country. I don't believe there's such a gas. They are dreaming it up.

I also refuse to believe that bit about Russians attacking the women and continue to like their music and the steppes. We don't have steppes. *Keep quiet, pass unnoticed, say nothing,* I think. It's the safest.

Our borders are dangerous now. News in the papers report how they fired at some peasant whose pigs strayed across, killed him and the pigs. Children kidnapped across the border. Shots fired on the North and East frontier. There are no more friends left; it's either the capitalists or the Cominform countries. Not a single friend, not even the Chinese. Why do I have to have such bad luck to be born here?

Then the Virgin Mary started appearing on the windows, anywhere in the glass.

"Do you see Her?" They cross themselves and whisper.

"There She is, look!"

"What does it mean?"

"Look in the coffee cup!"

"Will there be another war?"

They sit and listen to Radio America, Radio Free Europe, waiting for answers from the other side of the radio waves. There is only one radio, Stane has it, Slavka's husband, a gift for five years of good work. Mother runs there once a week to gab with the others. Altogether it's very boring, this program, just a lot of names and numbers and a boring tune at the end. I pay no attention at all what the radio says. Mother doesn't either, I bet, just pretends, makes it seem important to huddle around the radio like that, talk of "interference waves." How can you listen to the radio seriously and gab, gab, gab?

In the courtyard, they examine lamb's, pig's shoulder bones to see what they say, are they bloody or clear, will there be another war. The moon looks suspicious too with its red ring, it spells blood, bad, war. Even our games are examined, they say, "Look, see they are playing war with the corn stalks, children tell things." Some try to buy as much food as possible from peasants, store it away. You never know, it might happen, this country is cursed. We are in the middle, they walk over us, always blood and war.

Nothing much happened. Instead, the first cowboy films arrived and the new words "America," "American" became very important. It never meant much before. We knew about American capitalists in school with chewing gum and fat cigars, and I have read books about American blacks who suffered and were exploited a lot. They were often killed for no reason, hung on the trees. Women had to pick up their babies and flee on the ice. At best, they would shine shoes or play music just like the gypsies here except that gypsies look happier than the rest and mother insists they would die if crammed in one house, on the same job. They were born to roam, she insists. I don't know about American blacks.

Nobody says much about Americans, nothing at all in school. Only their films arrive, mostly cowboy ones. There are huge lines for the cowboy films, more than there ever were for the Soviet or Polish; no lines at all for ours. Kids bloody their noses to get these tickets, fight, get mean. It is as bad as the milk lines which have stopped, thank God. With cowboy films the fighting and waiting in line starts all over again, but Bratso does it now. He is bigger, knows how to fight.

Peasant boys in front of me yell, the place is very dark, only a flicker of the light toward the screen:

"Give it to him!"

"Kill him!"

"Use your left hook!"

"Don't give up!"

Peasants are always like that. Another one, who saw James Stewart die last week, kept spoiling the film for us with his shouts:

"Man, listen, he died last week. I swear on my mother's milk he died under the horse. I saw it right here."

What can you do with a man like that! Even laughing won't make him stop. It's probably only his second film, or third. We have seen hundreds, more than grown-ups who only go to very special ones without fighting or blood.

We cheer for the Indians and hope they'll win. They never do. Americans on the screen are sort of stiff, different from the Russians, even different from Italians. They smile broadly, a bit too even, showing their perfect white teeth, a bit like the doll's smile in the store on the Main Street. I couldn't smile like that even if I tried which I do when they urge me to show my teeth for the picture once a year that mother puts in the album. It seems hard to smile for no reason at all, and my pictures always show me as skinny, angry, looking to the side, or toward the ground, mouth one straight line. Nobody, absolutely no one smiles like the Americans in films; people here either look angry or mean or when they laugh they do it with mouths open, head thrown back, hitting their hips. Nobody just opens their mouths when introduced and says: "Happy to meet you," and then those lips like a harmonica and those teeth, that silly smile. Nobody says, "Happy to meet you," at all. You just stand there, look the person over, blush if you're a kid. No wonder we cheer for Indians, I think. It fits. They even stand like us, look angry, ready to fight. Americans on the screen don't smile with their eyes, something my doctor does when he sees me. Their eyes stay the same, only the mouth moves, the teeth shine.

The cheapest seats are right in front of the screen, all kids the first three rows; grown-ups are way back, so they can't hear us or the peasants who also sit in the front seats. When the film starts, right after three rings, the light hits the screen, makes it alive. I am not sure how it works, and keep thinking that the secret is in the screen, not the light. I inspect it for a second when the film ends but it looks lifeless now, like a white cotton sheet.

CHAPTER TWENTY-ONE

W INTER ARRIVED and we got a new sled, beautiful, enormous, big enough for three, curved in front, light, everything. The doctor bought it for us and just left a message in his large writing: "Hope you like it, " the note said, "have fun."

Did we ever! Every hill in town, showing off with that sled, we went far up, all the way up where the street disappears and becomes the country and you see the entire town with the river and the church. That far up, by the Devil's Stone. There, you sit down, then push just a bit, Bratso in front, then let go, down, down, high speed until an ox carriage appears in front, panic, fast, bypass it, don't lose your balance, don't fall in the ditch! The peasant curses, "Fuck the town kids! Fuck their mothers too!" He beats his wet oxen, pulls them to the side. Other kids are just flying by when we get out of the ditch, start all over again. On perfect days without oxen you go fast all the way down, past the bridge and the butcher's, past your own house, all in one single run all the way down to the Main Street where you stop.

Why is it always winter when I get sick? After one whole month of snow, the doctor arrives in the middle of the night, coat over his pajamas, declares double pneumonia, will have to save me again with a shot. He shouts at mother: "She is moving too much, she simply can't. I can't waste the shot. I don't have much penicillin left. Hold her tight."

He gets the needle out of his black bag. It's huge, as big as my arm.

"I don't want it. Let me die. I want to die."

"What can we do?" he asks mother as I thrash all around.

She whispers in my ear, menacing me with beatings as soon as I get better but I don't care if she beats me or makes me die. Then she tries something else.

"If you are very quiet, you can get something you like. I'll get you that doll from the window on the Main Street. The one that's a half meter big."

"That one?"

I don't really want a doll, never had one before, but can't think of anything else.

"Okay, buy it tomorrow."

There goes the shot in my hip; it doesn't even hurt once you give up the fight.

I get the doll the very next day, half of my mother's salary it was. That year she works in a restaurant. The doll had a real costume, all real stuff, painted lips, white teeth, and was so beautiful and perfect that I was afraid to ruin her, never played with her and kept her under a glass jar to hide her from the dust. What a waste, I think, I should have asked for something else, but what? Just plain books would be better or shoes that fit, but if you ask a person in fever what they want, they settle for stupid things like dolls.

It's my own fault, that one.

Another month away from school, lie in bed, read all the books over again, try to imagine things. *A Thousand and One Nights*, *Tom Sawyer*, *Fifth Offensive*, *My Childhood*.

Outside, you can see the snow fall. It makes a nice sound, more quiet than rain.

Bratso runs in and out, scarlet red. He grabs some bread, runs out, slams the door again, bang, bang.

I look at the album again with grandma, mother and father at the beach, watch the snow fall outside the glass, see small animals in the lace curtains, imagine things move, fall asleep.

At times I wake up because he is looking at me.

"How are you, my pet?"

He, my doctor, gives me medicine, then a piece of chocolate to kill the bitter taste of that yucky stuff, then pulls an orange from his coat pocket, gives it to me, my very first one. I have no idea how to eat it, just stare at the yellow ball. He peels it slowly, puts pieces in my mouth, it's very good, I think. He lights the fire in the kitchen, there is nobody at home but me. Mother working, Yanna gone, grandma dead, Bratso playing. It's too cold in the room, he thinks. I hear him blowing in front of the stove, getting it started with a newspaper then the wood will sing. He comes back with camomile tea, puts the thermometer under my armpit, waits a bit.

"Not much," he says.

"How much?"

"38 and will go down some more."

We don't talk much, less than when mother is around. He just looks at me, eyes dark, sad.

"Will I get another shot?"

"No more shots."

"Tell me about Leningrad," I say.

"I never saw it. My father was born there."

"Did he meet your mother in Leningrad or was it on the seacoast?"

"Sleep," he says.

He takes my hand for a second and leaves, quietly, closing the door.

I think at times when I wake up that I dreamt it all up but the orange peel tells me I wasn't alone.

In another week I get up and all is well again except that I feel funny, legs shake a bit. Excused from the gym, which is really nothing but running around in the yard. Have to catch up with all the work at school; they have finished the Greek gods, started the Romans. Other kids are absent when I get back. Senya and Mouse and Rade the Sparrow.

FIGHT TB, DON'T SPIT, signs say on the wall.

ELECTRIFICATION, INDUSTRIALISATION.

STUDY, says Lenin.

Stalin's spot is gone. All there is now is just a dirty mark on the wall where the picture was.

The winter is almost over when Bratso in his turn gets very ill. Very bad, worse than me. It happened really because mother worried so much about him being outside while she worked, that he would get ill from the snow and cold, his clothes all wet—so she hid his shoes, locked them in the closet, hid the key. You can't imagine what he did—he simply went to play in his socks and a few hours later was very sick, hot, a fever of 42, "serious," the doctor says. We put him on the sled, with pillows under his head, cover him up entirely and take him to the hospital, her pulling, me pushing as we go up that steep hill, the same one that goes toward the cemetery, all the way up, then down into another valley with a hospital for everything including TB. You can see the cemetery from here, on the hill to the right side.

We left him there for three weeks. Mother worried and worried about him, did he eat enough, did he get covered, were they nice to him there, my son. She worried much about both of us, more about him. She cries now with him in the hospital, says, "My baby, my child." I definitely don't want her to cry for me, it would be annoying really if she did. I just notice these things in passing, store them in spite of me.

The voice in me always commands: *Look, remember, there is nothing but this!*

CHAPTER TWENTY-TWO

SLAVKA'S LITTLE DAUGHTER VESNA got sick for some mysterious reason, some sort of brain fever, they whisper as doctors walk in and out, many new doctors, some from the capital, this disease is a strange one. Women go in there to visit and help, bring gifts, come back, report nothing but horrors while drinking coffee.

"May it happen elsewhere."

"Knock on wood, what a waste, what a beautiful child."

"Unrecognizable now, all her hair gone, did you see?"

"Nothing but those big eyes staring at you."

"The air inside is enough to kill you, how she suffers."

"Heaven save us, protect us from evil."

I try to study but her cries are in our room, you even hear horrible howling at night. Like a sick dog it sounds.

"It started with the headaches first, then her stomach got as big as a balloon, then it was too late," they report.

"No, the first thing was her neck, she couldn't bend it at all."

"Watch out for the stiff neck!"

"If only God would take her to Him fast."

I am tempted to go see her, everybody does, but something always stops me in front of the door.

In about two weeks, the first signs appear: my neck is stiff, can't bend it, the headache is there too, and the stomach pains. Mother looks frightened and terrifies me some more. I hear her pray for me and know it is serious but she takes me to the doctor right away, right after the signs.

We don't even wait in line this time, mother marches in, in spite of the protests from a woman with sick kids.

He does the same thing, says "undress," then bends my neck many different ways back and forth, taps my knees over and over again, very serious looking, he listens to my heart, then lifts his head up from my chest, smiles and she smiles too. I'll live, I guess, until another time.

"Just fear," he says, "nothing to worry about."

"Thank God, thank you," mother says to him.

"She is a sensitive child, you know that," he says to her, low but I can hear. Nothing wrong with my ears. Am I sensitive? What does it mean?

"Unfortunately, doctor, she is. If only God had given me a strong, tough one like me. Why, I have lived through everything, the war and prison. Do you remember when the brick fell and hit me on the head as I rescued her from the ruins? You remember that?"

"We all do," he says.

"What has she got to be sensitive about? They eat well, thanks to me."

"You are a brave woman, we all know that."

"Mother and father to them, I try."

"It's all true, you are."

"You know, doctor," (she says "doctor" the way she says "male child," likes the sound of the word), "I would go and help cook when I worked in the hotel and they would sometimes give me a piece of meat, just a tiny piece of something to fry. Do you know, Doctor, that I never touched those pieces, not once, I swear to God, may He strike me down right now in front of you if I am not telling the truth. I carried that piece of meat like a mother bird for my little ones. Just to help them grow well. They are my whole life. I have nothing else. What has SHE got to be sensitive about?"

The need to cry is in my throat, my chest. She suffered so much for us, because of us, if only we weren't around, if only I were dead. Then she could forget father, thin, weak, blond, and marry a strong tough man with a black moustache, the kind she likes. She always hints there were proposals, suitors, some are still coming, mother is liked a lot, but it seems that this one person who liked her very much didn't want us and suggested they put us in the orphanage while the two of them move to a brand new apartment. He was an engineer, good pay, could even take her to the sea town. Whenever she says "engineer," I hate it. Some words make me want to throw up just like that, because of the sound.

"*No,*" I said to him, "*never.* Part with my children, *never!* There is no man in this world to make me do that. I *never* want to see you again," she said to him, the engineer.

Doctors have to spend lots of their time just listening to people gab. Kids are helpless all the time, I just stand there waiting for the ordeal to pass.

"And so I am destined to spend the best years of my life on these two, doing honorable work, mind you, cleaning the floors, working in restaurants, but with a clean reputation not like some women we know. Mind you, I was made out of flesh and blood too, right, doctor?"

"Right, all of us are," he says looking at me.

". . . and I could have gone on and enjoyed myself like some, but didn't because I didn't want them" (us, of course) "to be ashamed of me later, of who their mother was."

I wish she had some fun, enjoyed herself.

"You are a real hero, you really are."

Mother likes that compliment the best, when people call her a hero, especially him. She needs that word I think more than any other to explain why she had no fun at all. Unfortunately, it is all true — she is not inventing this time; our life was harder than anyone we knew. Other women had husbands, wealthy relatives nearby, somebody. She only had her hands and a clean reputation for us. I wish she were inventing for once, I wish she had fun. It's all tangled up with us — what she did, didn't, and because of it I forgive her over and over again when she beats me, when she's mean. I have no other choice. It's all my fault really. If only I were not here. If only I could die.

Finally we leave, go past the gate where peasants sleep waiting for their sick, then back up the street and home, relieved.

Slavka's daughter died toward the beginning of spring. I heard Slavka wail and howl like a dog and mother cooked her herbs to make her forget. Vesna was buried in the yard, not far from the big oak, Slavka refused to bury her in the cemetery away over the hill. Later, when spring really came, a yellow flower bloomed right there on that spot. People whispered and crossed themselves when they passed the flower, which had no smell—it was called a daffodil. Slavka passed it too, watered it, whispered to her. All of this cheered me up more than anything else. Now I had a proof—a flower continued the girl, insects stopped to eat, rain gathered on the petals in small drops. I look at the clouds and branches of the trees, patches of blue here and there, the sun will come out soon, maybe it won't rain right away. I wonder if I will become a flower when I die, or maybe a branch or a cloud.

Chapter Twenty-three

S PRING ARRIVES at the end of March when all the snow starts to melt bit by bit, and the creek underneath the yard is big, muddy, a real torrent. In April the first leaves appear, it all takes forever, some wait, take their time, then the flowers arrive; violets are always the first. Toward the end of April the roads are all dry, no more mud left and you can wear knee socks, take off the big coat. By Easter, the sound of bees is everywhere, cherry trees bloom, a new one every morning when you wake up. We hardboil eggs with different plants to get different colors, onion makes them a deep yellow shade, tree bark brown.

With the eggs ready, run out on the street, take your egg, hold it in your fist and tap the egg of the person holding his, always with the pointed end. If your egg cracks, you lose it and have to give it to the person whose egg was stronger, that's how it goes, it's the rule. If they both get smashed, each one keeps hers. This Easter, a new kid arrives from I don't know where, maybe a guest, wearing new pants, and he smashed all of our eggs, every single one with that mighty egg of his. We have never seen anything like this before. You can't start changing the rules, although he can't eat all of our eggs without getting sick. The kid in the long pants got ready to leave when Boris all of a sudden said to wait. He said:

"Let me see your egg."

The kid refused, said this was not in the rules but Boris didn't listen and snatched the egg from him, then threw it on the ground. There it was — a wooden egg, well colored and all, can you imagine deceit like that?

Boris kicked him in the butt, we got our eggs back and ate them right on the street, saying that you have to be more careful the next time when some kid in fancy clothes arrives with a strong egg.

Then the summer arrived all over again, and we played all the time on the street, especially at night. You start usually with a game called "Command." You have to give something, like a shoe or a scarf, it had to be a valuable thing, not a pencil or a marble; that's too small. It had to matter to you so you would continue the game because the command can be a very difficult one, you might want to give up if it were not for your shoe. All those things get collected, put in one pile, then a person got chosen to command, with his head turned against the wall, eyes covered with a scarf. Another kid holds up a shoe or whatever and asks:

"What will this one do?"

The commander orders:

"It will run down the street, kiss the doctor's wife on the hand three times and say aloud, "I am a fool.""

That's a hard one. I am glad it's not me. Vaso hesitates, but has no choice or he won't get back his new book. We go down the street with him to make sure he won't cheat. He knocks on the door, the doctor's wife in curlers looks surprised:

"Is anyone sick?"

He reaches for her hand, she looks stunned. He kisses it, says:

"Boy, am I a fool."

We laugh like crazy. She laughs too, shaking her blond head.

Then we go back, to another command.

"Roll in the dust."

We protest. Her mother will beat her for that, "A clean dress, not fair, command another one!"

"Spit in the air three times then jump in a circle and say, "The fool is jumping, the weather will change.""

We get tired of "Command" and play "Catch" for awhile. Ljuba with the short leg runs fast, faster than me. I can never catch her. I can't catch anyone no matter how I try. This game is not much fun.

They always catch me. I suggest hide and seek, the whole street is game. Any place is fair, anybody's basement, all the yards, all the way to the creek but the creek itself is off limits.

"One, two, three, four, five . . . seven, eight, nine . . . ten. Here I come."

Boris and I hide in his basement behind the potato sack and wait to be found but nobody comes. We remain hidden, forgotten for a long time then get out to see what happened. They are playing a new game already and claim not to have been able to find us. That's the main problem with hide and seek—if you find a very good hiding spot, they move on.

When it's really late and very dark, and we're very tired there is nothing left but ghosts.

"He came from the forest, then entered the house and wondered . . . who to get first. Who do I want, he says, then he turned around very fast and said—I want YOU."

We scream unprepared when Boris points to us. The night is dark except for the fireflies. Smell of lilac, roses, acacias. Mother is near, with the women, telling stories. It's time to sleep, it's almost midnight, wash your feet.

The windows are wide open, a big moon is inside the room. I see somebody's face on it. Whose? Somebody I don't know. *Don't look at the moon, turn to the other side.* It can pull you toward him and carry you off. It pulls the tide, changes the yogurt. When it takes you away, which happens to some, you start walking in your sleep which is called being "moonstruck." A star just fell across the sky, somebody just died, grandma told us before. Everyone has one until.

Summer mornings you wake up without a single thought, just stare at the window for awhile, let the lilac come in, a sparrow lands on the window sill, look at it, turn to the other side, think about getting up, no, not yet, pretend you are asleep when she says:

"Go to the market, get some cheese and bread for lunch."

You stretch and yawn very wide, put on underpants and sandals, eat some bread with jam, get the fishnet from the hook, go to market, skippety-skip over the stones, past the military barracks where soldiers stare behind the barbed wire. They say, "That one is too old to walk around without a top." Are they talking about me? I look at myself and wonder. I am fine.

CHAPTER TWENTY-FOUR

Y ANNA HAD A DAUGHTER after two whole days of suffering and torture in that special house where only women go. After this, mother and her make up for good and she starts coming again to visit us, usually after work to pick up the kid.

The little girl, less than a year old, is all alone in that room by the creek on the other side of town. I run every morning, my classes still start after noon, skip across the stones, then a couple streets up by an old fountain, then into an old house from the time of the Turks. Nadja cries even before I come in, you can hear her on the street. Other times, she makes sweet little sounds like a bird, stretches her arms toward me, smiles with two teeth. I have to clean her up first, shit all the way up to her neck, poor thing, what can she do, it's not her fault; she is too small. I wrap her up in a blanket, then run back across the creek; she whimpers, coos, even falls asleep. All of us play with her, even Bratso, and she learns how to walk, run toward us, arms stretched.

Yanna comes from work, still in the same factory, tired, sad-looking, hair uncombed, that look of wanting to puke is permanent now; she is definitely not a girl anymore. Dumpy, loose dresses, what happened to her old ones? Mother says the whole thing was a mistake, the way she knew it would be.

I wish she didn't tell her that, she always had to be right, never admits making a mistake, not one time. Or, if things go wrong, she calls it "fate." It is never her fault. If only we had bought the house she wanted us to buy when father said, "No," if only it happened, we would have been okay, that house remained untouched by the war; she knew it would be fine. If only Yanna had married that man, the old one, the ex-merchant with a wife that died during the night—then she, Yanna, would have been happy, well-to-do, rich, etc. To make things worse, she repeats her old sentence, she always does that:

"I would marry her, he said, just because she is your sister. She must have some of your blood."

"But Yanna never listened to anybody and look what she got," she says looking at me. "You can't live on good looks—handsome and a liar and a crook, the son of a bitch."

I have looked at him carefully, but it's hard to tell. People are mysterious, hide things, turn into beasts at night. He seems fine when playing with me, swirls me around, gets me things, film tickets; he even waits in line. He talks like a kid and you can say just about anything in front of him. Large green eyes, tall, blond. It's hard to imagine that he beats that baby, broke her arm. Why? Why are people mean, what makes them do things? Will I be like that when I grow up?

I try very hard to get some order in my head, to make things fit to explain why, but she only confuses everything when she starts:

"He's not the only one to blame. If he were my husband, I would have made a man out of him fast. He would have known the son of a devil who he's dealing with. I would have said to him, "If you want to fight, fight, but with me, not the child.'" (She always forgets that she threw me on the floor, and the rest.)

She rolls up her sleeves to demonstrate to Yanna what she would do to him, how strong she is. Nobody would ever hit her. I know that, that part is true. Not a chance. She'll "forbid the bastard to touch Yanna and the child or he'll have to settle with me," she says. She is like that, tough. Proud of it too, and also proud that she never loved anyone, only weak people do, not her. Mother is like that guy in the cowboy film . . . who is it, maybe James Stewart, who leaves on a horse, leaves the town at sunset with all these women left behind madly in love with him, every one. This guy just rides the horse, all alone, no love for him, he's too good for that. He has other things to do, conquer lands, kill Indians, save women in distress. Well. . . that sounds more interesting than waiting to be saved.

Suddenly she turns to me and says, "You won't love anyone either. You are just like me."

Me? Like her? All of a sudden? Blond, weak me? She can decide things like that, whenever she decides or likes, who resembles whom, she can change her mind about anything she wants, even the color of my eyes, but if I say only:

"*But . . .* "

"Don't talk back to me, my father would have killed you if you only said that much. You are lucky I am so good natured," she adds. "Good natures get angry, but forget fast and can be good the next day; nasty natures forget nothing, just store it away."

Is she talking about me?

I am clearly *bad,* don't forget, not a thing.

From natures good and bad, the subject moves to men and here she complains to Yanna and me: "Never met a man who was my equal, not once!"

It would be interesting to meet that guy. I wonder what he would be like, maybe like James Stewart, I bet.

And she, as if hearing my thoughts, describes her favorite kind of guy:

" . . . black hair, dark eyes . . . big shoulders, like this, muscle . . . mean glint in the eye, speaks firm, when he speaks, not much . . . big black moustache . . ."

I scream without knowing that I have actually opened my mouth: "Just like a Turk. That's what the Turks were like."

She, angry now (how am I to know that the person she describes is her dad), reaches for the broom to hit me with it, but the broom hits the stove instead, spills the milk.

Mother is in a rage. "See what you made me do, you devil child!"

Grandma did it, I bet, to punish her. She is up there watching over me. I know she is.

If I were to tell mother what my book said, that the old Slavs were all blond like me and dad, but when the Turks came everything got mixed up, she would burn the book, beat the hell out of me. It would be a terrible insult to her family, to her father whom she loved so much, and to her grandmother who killed those Turks with her skillet.

You can't fool around with words like "Turk," worse even than "German" because they didn't stay long, not like the Turks, five centuries. Our backwardness, you can't forget that.

Parents can kick you, send the broom after you, kick your ass, pull your hair, but still it's like this, these are the rules:

> *"If a kid has a mother he has both parents." "If you lose your mother, you lose everything." "Fathers don't give a damn, let you run around in rags and lice." "You better watch out and don't lose me." "Your poor dad had a nasty step-mother who didn't feed him and he remained weak." (I am weak too.) "She, the step-mother, didn't care, it wasn't her flesh and blood."*

Flesh and blood, blood is thicker than water, my blood—words like that do something to my stomach, make me choke. Can one get sick on words?

CHAPTER TWENTY-FIVE

B RATSO STAYED OUT OF TROUBLE after an illness or a big beating then everything got started all over again as before. He swallowed a penny and thought he would die but didn't, it came out; he killed chickens with a sling shot. Women came to complain, mother beat him as always.

Once, we go, two of us, to get some good pears from the old miser on the left—you just lift a couple boards at the bottom, then go under, there you have the pears. Well, he crawled under as usual, I keep guard. It's all done; Bratso hands over the pears, I put them inside my dress having tied the waist with a string; it's just like a bag. Just as he is ready to come back, the old devil yells somewhere:

"I'll get you, you little thief."

Bratso gets confused, hurries under and we hear a distinct "rip"—we both know what that means. His brand new pants, the only pair, made out of "Devil's skin" to last a long time, very tough material, toughest there is, went like nothing on one of those nails on the bottom plank.

Bratso's ass is showing through as we run. What to do? Think fast! We have two more hours left until mother comes home from work, run fast to Zorka, the one with the gold tooth; she has a sewing machine, can sew well. She laughs pretty hard at Bratso's ass but gives us cookies, fixes his pants with a nice patch, same color, you could almost not tell, but you really can. And we go back.

After dinner, Bratso walks around the room in a funny way, like a dancer of some sort; each time mother comes near him, he darts away, sort of swings to the other side, protecting his ass. I want to laugh, but how can I? She would ask: "What are you laughing at?"

We wait for the worst, just before going to bed. She can see the pants as she goes through his pockets and then!

She never noticed it, not until much later when the pants got too worn and then she said, "That's a pretty good patch. When did I do that, pretty good job." The two of us explode and tell, but nobody gets beaten. It was simply too late.

Poor Bratso, always hungry, always in trouble. He needs so much food, way more than me. When finished with his plate, he just stares and stares at mine until I throw it at him in disgust. He lies a lot too, all the time and can't separate the lies from the rest. I suppose that's the main difference between us when it comes to lies — I know when I do it, they are only a few, almost always the same — his change a lot and could never have happened, which is really a lie. The perfect example of the difference is "The Story of the Apples," that's how it was called. It happened like this:

Mother bought some special apples, called "winter ones," stored them well to last for months, and then in the middle of winter when there was nothing fresh to be eaten, she went in there to get some. To her horror they were all gone, to the last one. She checked and double-checked and even thought she was going mad, maybe she never bought them, just dreamt them up.

"Good Lord, I am going crazy, I must be," she said.

I came to her rescue, and then she remembered as well, that she did buy them from that handsome peasant with a black moustache who swore on his wife's head they will not rot, not until May, if well stored.

"Do you remember, he gave me one free?"

"And then he carried the apples in a huge bag and you gave him coffee to drink and you said he reminded you of your dad?"

It's settled; she bought them all right, but now what? They didn't rot, but disappeared altogether, not a trace, not even an apple core. She wondered and wondered and asked around, no clues at all. Nobody else had a thing missing and we shared the basement with others.

A month passed, then a pile of money disappeared as well from a special little place in the linen closet right under the sheets. This was serious; she questioned everyone: Slavka, the people upstairs, us. I swore I didn't touch it, she knew I wouldn't but she had a stick ready just in case. Bratso volunteers the information all of a sudden:

"I remember that two days ago I was dreaming about Nena," (the woman upstairs who replaced The Communist One). Bratso knew mother suspected her of stealing our wood.

"Yes," mother says, putting the stick down, "what was she doing in your dream?"

"She was . . . sort of sneaking around our wood . . . right by the wall . . . you know the spot."

"And then what happened?" Mother was curious.

"I saw her in the dream and she saw me and then she starts chasing me and as she ran . . . the apples drop from her blouse, one by one, red ones."

Bratso looks at us, describes, "Her blouse was very big, enormous, red too."

"And then what? What does red mean in a dream?" mother wonders.

". . . as she runs, she trips on a piece of wood and another piece fell out, and there in the dream I saw the money."

Mother believes the dream, I see it on her face. I can't stop giggling to myself, silently.

All three of us go outside now to inspect the wood. Nothing there but the same old wood on the spot where Bratso saw the money in the dream, but mother thinks that one piece is missing perhaps. Is that a red thread over there? Maybe her blouse got ripped as she ran.

She tells the story about the dream to Slavka who is too polite and respects mother too much to disagree with her but her eyes are laughing, I can tell. There, at Slavka's, they invite the guilty person to visit, all of us waiting. Mother seems convinced.

The woman came for coffee that Slavka prepared and mother doesn't say: "Why did you steal my apples, my money, my wood?"

Nothing like that. She drinks coffee and tells the dream that Bratso just told, adding a bit here and there, the story wouldn't be good if not, and then she asks, looking at her, if she knew perhaps what the dream meant. "Children are innocent. God reveals Himself to them more readily than the rest of us."

Bratso seems ready to leave the room, wants to go and play. The woman stops him, holds him by the collar.

"You devil, what lies."

Now Slavka starts laughing, then the woman, then me. Bratso just stands there with the same look of hunger and fear of the stick. Mother had to admit that he ate all the apples, slowly over three months, took the money as well. Some money was found in the woodpile, as he told it in the dream, but in a different row of wood, what a silly place to hide things.

No, he didn't get beaten on this occasion because his story was good, and after a few days when she was no longer angry, she laughed and laughed about his lies and his dreams. There is no justice at all to her beatings, none at all; I think, you get it if she feels like doing it, that's all.

Bratso deserved it this time, and nothing happened. I get it for no reason at all, just for crying aloud when she beats him. It's enough that she calls me, and I don't run in the very same moment, or if I answer, "What is it?" . . . instead of "Please." She pulls on my hair, pain spreads over my old scar.

"That will teach you to answer me like that. My father would've killed you if you said, "What is it?' You are lucky to have me . . . but you won't for too long if you worry me to death and I die, then you'll know what's what, when they put you in the orphanage, you'll see . . ."

The beatings are worse with grandma gone but in time, they'll stop. I will learn not to care, not to get upset by words or sticks. That's what growing up means to me. I am going to be tough and strong.

Chapter Twenty-six

For AWHILE nothing much happened. People stopped talking about Russians or Americans, rations got bigger especially for bread, there were new things in stores, I even got shoes that fit but after waiting so long didn't care that much.

The Main Street got asphalted, ours was left the same, many new houses were built, Senya got a new blouse, Boris is getting taller, Ljuba curls her hair once in awhile, we continued to live in the same place, mother changed several jobs. From the factory to a restaurant to cleaning offices, back to knitting again as before. Bratso is clearly getting out of hand, she had to be at home.

Slavka has another child, delivered by mother in the middle of the night, then in the morning over coffee and knitting it was told in full color, blood and guts, how she ran around and the baby fell on the floor, how mother tied the cord, how the baby was born in the caul and will have good luck. Slavka came to see us all the time, to get recipes for cakes, to ask mother what to do for a cough; her house got neater as the time passed and she stopped being a peasant altogether one day and did as others—scrubbed, cleaned, dusted all the time, was upset about cups and saucers and such. Now, in the kitchen she whispers and cries to mother about her husband, a railroad guy who travels a lot and met this woman on

146

one of his trips out of town. This new woman has magic power over the poor man. Slavka begs:

"Please help!"

"How do you know she has all that power?" mother asks.

"It's not hard to tell . . . you know . . ." Slavka looks shy. "He doesn't come to me . . . in . . ."

"That's serious," mother says, then to me, "You go to bed."

Bratso is in bed already, reading a comic strip, a new thing since we broke up with the Russians. Everyone is obsessed, even Senya; they bore me. I hear Slavka leave, mother calls Stane over and they talk but I can't tell what she says to him. He doesn't say much. . . and with Bratso awake I can't listen at the door.

Next day, in the morning, she gives Slavka something in a little silver box, tells her to repeat things when the moon is full. Is she turning into a witch? In front of my eyes, like in my old book:

"Then the old witch said to undress completely, naked as the day of birth, no pins in the hair, no rings . . . then in the middle of night go to the grave of a dead virgin, gather some dust from the grave, ride back on a white horse and if you meet someone, say "I am stealing his soul back.""

(My questions are—what if you don't meet anyone while riding that horse, what then, does it matter? There aren't that many people out after midnight. Is it the dust or the horse or the person you meet that does the job? What if you met a priest while riding stark naked on that horse? What if?)

Mother didn't tell her to ride on the horse—that would have been too hard around here—but she did tell her to spit three times in his soup, make him drink this powder with blood when he can't see.

Poison, I think. *They'll kill him, should I tell?*

Nothing much happened. Slavka got pregnant again, Stane seemed sad when I met him at the pump. Mother and Slavka did something to him, I bet, let him live but poisoned his soul, made him look sad. He never did before.

If you want to do someone in, someone that stopped caring for you—you just have to have the right combinations of tricks, horse's hair, blood, dust from different types of graves, even a shirt can serve the purpose, the witch says things over it, you put the shirt back where it was and the unlucky person will love you or die. Magic is everywhere all around us. When it hails, to make it stop you throw out the poker or anything made out of iron. That does the job.

We have thrown our poker out long ago; it's still hailing, all the fruit will suffer, there won't be any left, mother fears; from upstairs they threw out a pot, Slavka her pan, anything iron to appease the God of Thunder who also likes nails.

"The price of vegetables will go up," mother shakes her head. It is hailing really bad, pieces of ice.

"Come on, Bratso and Anna, pray that it stops."

"I don't know how," Bratso says.

"It's just the cold air in the upper portions of stratosphere that forms the hail . . . and snow is . . ."

My lesson for tomorrow. I have been memorizing it for hours.

"What do you know," she snaps.

"It's here in the book, you want to see?"

"Book . . . shit . . . stratosphere . . . Trying to sound important as if you didn't come out of my ass. Both of you pray!"

I really don't know how to except to grandma, my only saint. But grandma cannot stop the hail, it would be silly to ask and besides I feel I can ask only for a few things from her—help to survive, get out in time.

"Why did you leave me, help me get out," I pray in silence to grandma.

CHAPTER TWENTY-SEVEN

A GYPSY CARAVAN ARRIVED in the spring spread their tents on the other shore of the river near the small yellow houses. The circus starts at night, during the day they roam around in town, the women always with kids in their arms.

"Madame, may you live to be a hundred."

"May you dance, may you have good health."

"May you dance at your daughter's wedding, may you sing."

"May you have a good life."

"Give me some food for my little one."

Mother always gives something, it will bring us good luck, but she watches over the gypsy's shoulder to see she doesn't steal something. They can do it really fast while talking to you, just with one hand. They can also fix things, pots and pans, sharpen knives. The women beg, wear bright colors, sing at times, then the whole caravan disappears and goes somewhere else. I wish they'd take me with them. I wish I were as dark.

The story how I tried to become a gypsy with dark hair is a very old one. It happened when I was four or five; some of it is in back of my head, just a tiny bit, like a color of some sort. The story means one thing to mother and the women listening, another to me.

It started with the smokehouse where they cured ham, where I sat for hours hoping my hair would turn black, but my eyes only became red. The next thing I tried was to pour black ink in my eyes and turn them from blue to pitch black. They hid the ink, afraid I would do it and become blind.

"Heaven save me from this child, where did she ever get an idea like that," mother tells.

"She'll be the death of me. Imagine, my dear woman, ink in her eyes and to have a blind person to worry about as if I didn't have enough bad luck."

"Children can kill you if nothing else will," they agree.

"Lucky is the one without them."

BUT, get this: if a woman doesn't have a baby soon everybody gets crazy, cries over the woman, what will she do? Her seed will die, and all think of ways to help her, either with words you say or jumping over graves.

Nothing absolutely makes sense. If children can kill you, why have them? Why all the fuss about having a baby? I should really give up altogether this whole thing about making things fit, trying to make sense. Maybe I'll just go and run away with the gypsies after a while—they travel a lot, that would suit me fine. A gypsy woman touched me once on my head just like grandma did, said, "My pretty one," to me. Was she doing the evil eye on me? Nothing happened, I guess not.

The circus is fun, more fun than anything else, better than the best of cowboy films. Both Bratso and I are united on this as we roam around waiting for the show to start, peek inside the tents. Inside one tent—mirrors that make you different sizes, fat, skinny or a dwarf. In another—a fat gypsy woman with chains that she breaks like nothing, in one try. She asks everybody to inspect the chains, some men do and try; they are real enough. Then she goes "Zavoum, zavoum, crack," and on the ground fall the chains, broken. She stands there in a two-piece bathing suit with stars and just looks tough. "Who would want a woman like that?" men say, jealous, I bet, of her arms.

Another gypsy, a skinny man, swallows a sword and eats much fire without getting burned at all, then the bear dances to the sound of the drum. Tam-tam-tratam goes the drum, the bear has his feet up, a chain in between his teeth makes him move, lift his feet, bare his teeth, tam. People laugh, scream, slap their hips.

150

Tam-tam goes the drum. We move on toward the rides, the very best in circus, called *ringspiel*, a foreign word.

The problem is money. Where to find it. Mother did give us some but that was ages ago. The *ringspeil* spins around and around, all lit up. How to find money, that is the question. Think up something fast or you won't fly, think well. I am thinking hard when this gypsy woman passes by with her child. I look at Bratso. Our problems are solved.

It's not that hard, he never looks clean, crusts on his knee, bare feet. I close one eye, pretend not to see, half blind.

"Can you spare some change?"

It's best to ask for less. Nobody says no to us, we are that pathetic, "Poor children," they say, sorrow in their eyes, "some parents just don't care."

In about an hour, after much hard work, avoiding all the familiar people who could tell, we have enough for a ride up there, on the *ringspiel*. Foreign word, sounds good.

The wheel is huge and high, you wonder "What if I fall, what then?" before it starts. When it starts, slow at first, then faster and faster, you don't think at all, you have no time. It is that fast. Somebody catches you from the back, on the turn, or you catch somebody in front, then when it's going really fast, the fastest — they let go of you — you fly away from the others — you scream and close your eyes. It's scary and good at the same time. That's what the *ringspiel* is like.

At home, mother says, "I never cared that much for the circus. Your father did, just like a kid. What a strange man. How come you are so late?"

"We had to wait in line for a long time," Bratso says without blinking. "You should have seen that line."

He lies so well, he is tops, the best, and if you asked him tomorrow why we came late, he would believe it himself that we waited in that line. I have never met anyone like that in my entire life.

Chapter Twenty-eight

I start *gymnasium* in September; this means you are no longer a small kid. Everything from now on is going to be serious stuff. Mother stands there on the street with a pitcher of water and throws it at me, saying aloud:

"May school go like the water flows."

She did this when I went to the first grade.

She did it for Bratso too, the magic to make it all go well, easy, good grades. Now, I go to one side, he to the other, and she throws water over both of us. Other women, the whole street is there with pitchers and water; Boris is getting it too and so is the merchant's daughter, hair all curled up. *I remember all of a sudden*—we were supposed to eradicate this, that was in my first grade, our backwardness, dark ages, but nothing happened, nothing at all. Here we are with pitchers. What will happen to me? What about tomorrows that sing, and the revolution? Nobody talks about the revolution anymore. Instead, it's blouses and skirts and clothes and food; May First is not as big in sound, not as red anymore.

I wear a black uniform for the new school. To get here, you no longer go across the creek but straight down by the crossroads, where Senya waits in front of the military barracks, past the inn where drunks and gypsies sing, by the window of that young man with TB, dead now almost a year; mother went to the funeral and cried. Then still further, past the shoemaker's and the watchmaker's, past the prison and the hotel where mother worked and got us that meat, then you arrive at the small park tended by the young man who loves flowers and knits, strange, they say, "Like a woman." The school is there on the left by the park, much larger than the other one, three stories high. In front of it, directly in front, stands the church and a large fountain built in memory of a girl, dead young, her parents' name on top.

The main street is right here, only half a block. You look at the stores during recess—later, maybe next year, you'll promenade with others up and down. It's still too early for that, you are still too young.

The river is two blocks away from the main street; it curves around, passes through town like a snake, some parts are deep, others not. If you take a wooden bridge, where the water mill stands, you are in the neighborhood of small, yellow, crumbly houses that get flooded in the spring, something you have to consider when you get jealous of people who live there near the river, just jump in from their front step. From here, you see the factory, a gray noisy building where Yanna works.

There aren't that many houses on the left bank, except for those few by the river, because the mountain is very steep at this point and people don't like to walk up and down. This whole section of town without any houses, dark, thick woods, is called the Park, a cool place even in summer.

The Park has many paths, large fir trees; further up it becomes part of the large mountain range that frames my town entirely on that side, stops your view to the north. You can get lost there easily if you don't watch out, and if alone. Part of the hill, bare white stone with a narrow path right underneath is called "Devil's Peak" because it tempts people to climb it and fall in the river, big and foamy at that spot, forming a gorge. Right there, at the very end of the Park where all the paths come to stop and you can't go any further, right on the very edge of the river, over the foam, they have just opened a little restaurant that mother says was there before the war. We often go there with her after a Sunday walk in the Park and drink lemonade while she talks to her friends. From here you see everything—Devil's Peak, the mountainside, the water under the bridge and even a train as it comes through the tunnel and enters the town. I wonder who is on the train, where they are going; the people on the train wave with handkerchiefs, everybody waves back. The train stops for a minute or two then hurries away, disappears behind the trees, just the hole of the tunnel left.

I hear the train at night, very faint; my town is a link between eastern and western provinces, the geography teacher says. You see the same train in summer from the river further up; it passes over the bridge and disappears in the tunnel, a different one, as the rivers curves like a snake. Young people, big ones, not kids, girls with breasts, go swimming far upstream where the river is very big because of the dam. To get there, the only way possible is across that bridge which is only made for trains, doesn't have a walking path. What if the train arrives, what would they do? They must be terrified every minute as they cross over, except they look very happy, sing songs as they pass, watching the rest of us with contempt. You have to be much older to do that, maybe last year in high school. Some go even further than that, past three, four tunnels, almost to the spring of the river, ten kilometers or more. Some day I'll go there as well, but not yet.

The Main Street divides the town in two uneven halves and in both directions it becomes a road that goes east and west. To the west you take the street to get to the hospital and the cemetery, past one neighborhood where many gypsies lived and people were shot right on the hill in '44. I know only one person from there, a gypsy girl named Anca whose father plays bass in the band.

Hills dominate everything really, most streets are on a hill of some sort, all except Main Street and those houses by the river shore. Anywhere you turn, left or right, there is a hill, some smaller, others bigger, different colors as the seasons change. You can't escape the hills; your view stops anywhere you turn; you have to imagine the rest.

Our town goes back to ancient times, teacher says, as far as the Romans who had a name for it ending in "us." Turkish ruins are on the hill as well as the snakes. "Don't go near it, danger," we are warned. The monument to the dead is on another small hill, not far from the snakes and the Turks. On May First we go there and stay silent for a minute. We were the first liberated territory in WW II the history teacher says, way before anyone else, way before Paris, Brussels, our main reason on the map. Everyone is happy about this because we did it alone without anybody's help. In addition, town people like to brag that we have better water, air, smarter, healthier people than anyone else. It is hard to tell, not having seen much else.

If you ask the kids where they would like to live the best, if they had their choice that is, all of them would say the Main Street, without any doubt. Everything is there — shops, the movie house, the river not far, and you can see all your friends as they pass by, yell to them to come and play. All the houses on the Main Street are new with showers and toilets inside, you don't have to walk in the snow to get to the john, fear the ghost. Yet, if forced to choose, I would still choose the same street, mine, because of the creek, and the way the street ends, becomes the country with violets and trees. We have linden, apple, oak trees in the yard; on the Main Street you can't have that, and forget about pigs and chickens and chasing the butterflies. And if your mother chases you, you can't jump anywhere from the fifth floor, you can't land in the flowers the way I do, the way Yanna did.

My composition called *Our Town* gets me an A+, extra-special praise from the teacher, they even take it to the upper grades. She asks, "Did anyone help you with this?"

"Nobody, I swear."

Who could help me, mother only went up to the fourth grade, but I don't say that. She wouldn't like to have it known.

I just tell her about the A+ and how they asked if anyone helped. She gets almost angry at me.

"It's not my fault I didn't go to school. I wanted to, was very smart, smarter than you I bet, but she wanted me to work, take care of the other kids."

"She didn't like you , and she was not your step-mother at all?" I know nothing about her.

"No, she didn't like me too much because I looked like him and he was quite stern."

"Your dad?"

"Yes, him."

"Stern with you?"

"No. With her."

Today she is quiet, almost soft, remembering; she tells me her story for the first time:

155

This happened in a village in another province, far away from here, where men are very proud, have dark moustaches, wear guns at their waist. Her mother had many children, one every year, poor woman. It was hard, she did have a horrible life with that many to take care of every day. And then there were sheep and cows and the fields. One day, on her way to the mountain, she, my real grandma, took mother with her, led her to the forest that was very far. She left her there under a tree and went away. Mother is very small, four or five; when the night falls she is afraid and cries and cries. Luckily a deer came and sat beside her, licked her face, she fell asleep on his stomach and was no longer afraid of the dark.

Meanwhile, her father came home and asked what happened to his favorite child, and her mother started feeling bad and said, "I will go and look for her, maybe she got lost in the woods." When she found her, after walking many hours, mother was still asleep at the foot of the tree but the deer was gone. She was carried back, put to bed, called soft names, but never forgot that her mother tried to get rid of her this way. Mother forgave her in time because she said her life was so hard, but could never love her, no matter what.

I am crying when she tells me this story, when she comes to the end. She is crying too. Why is there so much nastiness everywhere? Will it ever end? We were going to change things, the future was bright red. What about the new socialist man? When is that?

CHAPTER TWENTY-NINE

THE FIRST LETTER arrived from father, from England, beautiful handwriting just like mine. Even mother says, "It's just like yours, look." Blue ink on blue paper, a photo of him in a large raincoat against a shop in London with English people on the edges of the picture—is that him? It's hard to tell. I look at the handwriting and the photo again. The memory of that road with the green frog is far away now in back of my head; is that the same man? The picture shows a short man with lines around his mouth and eyes; she has similar ones in the same spots. I guess much time has passed since the road and the frog.

We photograph ourselves for him, mother in the middle, arms around us. We sit there like this then the guy says, "Smile and hold," and goes in back of the shop, puts his head under a black cloth, sticks it out again, puts our three heads closer together, wants us to smile again, a difficult thing to do, we have been smiling for a half an hour, my mouth feels frozen, paralyzed. We send this horrible picture to father, me looking as if I had swallowed a fly, but he answers right away, pleased, tells how much he liked the photo, how I am the only one that looks the same, would recognize me anywhere, same face and all. Bratso he couldn't, he admits, he was only a baby then, and mother must have been different except that I don't remember that far.

Letters arrive regularly now, every couple of weeks, then small packages of coffee, then Gillettes, fountain pens, fabrics. Mother stops working, knitting, and opens her own shop, right in the kitchen. Tons of people arrive to buy this coffee that mother weighs on her small scales, then cooks some for the customers before they leave. The smell of coffee fills the yard and the street. We have it more often than anyone else. She loves this inviting, and I do it for her, knocking on the doors, up and down the street. "Come over, mother says to come," all the time now.

Big girls appear next. The news has spread. In the kitchen they examine whatever she has received, none to be found in the store. Raincoats, thin, transparent, in many different colors and cuts, with hoods or without; nylon is precious, touch it carefully, it's foreign, better than anything of ours, they say; ours isn't worth a shit. They say "shit." English wool, English nylon, silk, anything from "there," from the West is better, lasts. Then stockings arrive one day, "real" ones, different shades of beige and brown, some with butterflies on the back, some with seams, some without; all go fast in two days as girls pass in and out.

Mother keeps nothing for herself, not much, a pair of nylon stockings that she is very careful with, then mends when they rip. The rest is stashed in the wooden closet next to the blue book. Mother inspects it, checks it, she handles pens and stockings with affection— you can tell she likes having the closet full of so many valuable things. When Bratso is outside she shows me the money; it seems a lot to me, big bills. She'll have a tombstone built for grandma with some of this soon, she says, proud.

"If only Nana lived to see it happen. Good times are coming."

But, stockings, raincoats, coffee changed things. People seem to look at us differently now, with envy I would say, that's the right word; we have someone in England, abroad, and items that nobody has except us. It is as good as being a hero's daughter in the second grade, or almost. Nylon coats are embarrassing really, make you feel funny as three of us descend slowly toward the Main Street, mother in the middle, two of us on each side, not a drop of rain anywhere, just some small clouds.

Mother walks erect, head high, like an Indian in films, she really likes this part the best, that walk toward the Main Street hoping the rain will fall, for her enemies to see her now with her healthy kids, dressed in almighty nylon, all three of us, different shades of blue, mine too large.

As we pass open windows, women look up.

"Holy shit," says one woman later, "I was on the street to get some air the other day, and what do I see but Mara with her children, all in blue nylon."

"Let her be," says the woman with the gold tooth. "Her time has come. She has suffered long enough. It's only fair."

My time is coming soon, I guess. You can't prevent it, it will come.

"If only Nana could see you now. All grown up, all dressed well."

Grandma sees me, I am convinced; nobody knows it except me. She watches over me in difficult times like that old woman in the Italian film we loved so much. It was about homeless people in Milan and one particular boy who lived with others in the shacks right outside Milan. When everything else failed and they had nothing left, the old woman who liked the boy so much and was already dead arrived on a cloud and lifted them all into the sky and took them somewhere else. It was called *Miracle in Milan* but things like that never happen in life.

Grandma speaks to me through the branches in the spring, when the wind blows or the grass sings in the summer by the creek. I can't say she said this or that — it isn't that clear, mostly like color or smell or music which seem to tell me something new every day.

Your time is coming, it is, it is, they say. *Don't be afraid, Anna, it is okay, we are here, we are.*

The time has started speeding, flying, running fast. I hear it in my ears. A buzz. I hear the clock. They ask all the time: "What then? What will you do? What will you be then?"

There is less time than before.

When is then?

I will not marry then — I know that.

I will not have kids — that much is clear.

I seem to know what I don't want but not what I do, that is the problem.

The gym teacher says, "She should dance," but there is no dance school in this town. Will it be too late then?

Dancing would be fine even though she made a mistake. I am not strong enough for it even though my arches are perfect and my legs long. Could I improve on my strength? Dancers don't marry, live in different towns, always move a lot, have many admirers who send them flowers; when the curtain falls they thank them for the flowers with another dance, but never love anybody in particular, only the dance.

One thing is enough, after all. That would suit me fine. I imagine them happy. Of course things did get complicated in *The Red Shoes* and she went on to die but that was because she made a mistake in the beginning having fallen in love with that guy. Not me, never.

In these decisions about the future, nobody helps. They only get me confused. If I say I might dance, they, the women, make a face:

"Oh, God, no. It would ruin her legs. They all have legs like men." The nerve, I think, with their own stubby miserable ones ruined with veins and kids.

Or:

"No, no, that wouldn't be good. She is a fine student. Why waste all that brain? Dancers are dumb."

Dancing ruins your legs, theater is no good either because the make-up ruins your skin. And then, actresses are not really considered "good women," the way mother sees good — too much make-up, too many towns, too much of what she calls "stormy life." She doesn't volunteer anything that would be good for me to study although I know she likes words like engineer, adjutant. These words she pronounces in a special way, making them sound big and fat. Some words make me sick to my stomach, their sound does. Other are pleasant to the ear like firefly, moss, daffodil.

CHAPTER THIRTY

O NE PACKAGE CAME with a pink and white silk dress, just for me, with a note written on a card in blue ink. It says, "Happy birthday! You must be growing up, my bud." Him. My dad.

Of course you can't wear a dress like that to school, it would be unfair, make others jealous. Maybe on Sundays when I go to the Park with Bratso and mother. At school we are all dressed in black, white collar if you wish. It has to be black, but you can choose any style or wear it over another dress or slacks in the winter. In addition there is a beret now with the number of the class in gold letters on top, a hateful, ugly hat you stuff in your pocket until a professor appears, then, fast, put it on any old way because if not, a whole point off for bad behavior goes in the big black book where all the grades are.

We fear all the teachers here or rather most; this is a serious place, you can fail now; nobody failed or was left behind before in the other school. We have so many of them, one for each subject; the schedule changes every day, you have to look up, be prepared when called to recite. There are many new girls in class, plus Svetlana, Mira, and Senya who sits next to me.

The class is larger than the old class; the stove is bigger too; my seat is by the window again, you can see the church without lifting your head. My reputation is clearly established after only a couple of months—excellent student, the "best in the class," which means that when they have gone all around and no answer was given, they ask Svetlana, then me. I am the last one and know all the answers just about all the time. I don't even lift my hand up, why bother, they'll come to me if nobody knows, and it's usually a very simple thing to figure out. My answer, always told in clear sentences, correct grammar, perfect conjugations, only the essentials—makes me feel good while I say the words but afterwards there is embarrassment as they gape at me as if I did something truly fantastic which I didn't at all. It's all there, in the book, you take it out, put it in your words. I am not like the rest, their faces gape at me. How, in which way I don't know. Something in me is different. They know it. I know it too, but it simply has no name, not yet.

It is probably connected to the excellent grades and my answers in front of the class but that is not all. They believe, think that I know things by magic while it's really a question of figuring things out. They could do it as well. For example, if we have a written composition in class, one hour to write the essay, they shouldn't waste their time sitting there and biting their nails, get crazy what to write about. They are biting their pencils, rolling their eyes, saying, "I can't think of a single thing." I figure out things way ahead, the day before when I say to myself:

"Okay, the last composition was called 'The Winter Charms of My Hometown,' the time before it was 'My School,' before that 'The Spring,' so it can't be those three."

Then I think a bit and pick several different subjects, several possibilities, each different. In my head I make an outline for each. Beginnings are short, simple, introduce the subject, drop it, move on to the main part, more and more of the main part, then finish with a short paragraph that's different from the beginning yet has some of its thought, make it uplifting, they always like that even if I don't. Leave always five minute to check the verb agreements, plurals, the capitals and that is all.

I watch Mira spill her ink all over the paper, run to the john. The one in front of me is still on the first sentence when the bell rings. I am surprised others haven't figured how things work, they would all get excellent grades. It's important to have a plan. I wish to tell them about it but do not dare, too ashamed they will see how much everything is planned. They think it comes to me from the sky as I write. It is true that the math problems do get solved in a dream once in awhile, but it's because I worked before falling asleep. With French it's the same.

"Are your parents French?" the new French teacher asks. She is young, pretty, her hips move and sway when she walks, dress tight. The class snickers already. They have heard this one before. (French, ha, aha, hee hee hee, her parents are French.)

"No, Madame, they are not."

"So surprising . . . please come in front of the class and recite again so the others can hear."

In front of the class, looking nowhere, over them, I recite:

Les sanglots longs de l'automne blessent mon coeur monotone . . .

"Stop now . . . see what I mean, class. It is *eu* like in *coeur,*" she pouts, her lips like a flower.

"Say it again, all of you . . . *Eu eu.*"

The class tries. *Eu eu eu coeur.* They sound like dogs.

"Anna, you may go back to your seat, my dear. Your accent is perfect . . . you might want to study languages later in the capital. To speak like that shows a musical gift."

"She is like that in everything, even math," somebody from the rear seat. Then snickers.

"Oh really? How wonderful," her eyes wide.

I turn red at that point, cheeks burn, then the neck, it almost hurts, feels as if I had too much sun. My condition is so bad that the biology teacher demonstrated the conditioned reflex on me. He says after having explained about the nerves:

"She'll turn red when I say to blush." I do.

I will have to learn to stop it somehow before it spreads all over, say *"no"* to it just as it starts, either in class or on the street when men watch me and say things as I pass by. I will have to learn to look at them straight in the eye and not blush. I blush, not because I am ashamed of something, that much I have figured, but because their eyes examine me in a way I don't like from outside as if I were a cow, a dog or a cat.

Recess time—small recess in the courtyard, just enough time to pee while another girl watches on guard. Some boy is always hiding behind us or, worse, three at once.

Big recess—half an hour—either run and drink some water from the fountain or sit on the bench in the small park. Run back when you hear the bell.

Chemistry is taught by a small dark woman who limps. "Who'll marry her like that?" mother asks to nobody in particular when I say she is very nice. Men limp here and there, especially older ones who were in the war and proudly show the leg where the bullet went. Most of them are married as well, but with women it's different. Men don't have to be good-looking at all, she says. They are currently whispering about a girl, a neighbor who has one smaller breast, has to stuff her bra with wool but that won't help her later on when he rips it off. Then what? Some women have no hips, others have no stomach or their breasts are uneven. I have nothing at all, thank God, not yet, just very long legs and arms, Desa says, when she makes me the dress. "Is that good?" I ask mother about the length of my legs. She doesn't say no or yes.

I do know she approves of my grades though, my offerings every year, celebrated with coffee, the rows of straight A's without exception; nobody has that. Her enemies know this and are suffering to death. I serve some function after all. I am pointed out to other kids as an example of someone good, with a great future, the child who'll be somebody some day instead of "You poor nobody . . . with your grades . . . nothing but the factory for you." A parent says all this to his kid with his arm around me. Both the kid and I look toward our shoes. To work in a factory seems just about the worst thing one could do now that we don't have many heroes of labor left or pictures of workers-heroes on their jobs. The worker is never said to be "a good catch"—but doctors and engineers are; a professor in the gymnasium is fine but not in the grammar school.

Our home room teacher reads our grades every couple weeks in front of the class. Until this moment nobody knows for sure what her latest grade was. Each professor grades us every time we recite, but then they hide with a hand what they write down, not even those in the first rows can see if it is an F or C. It's hard to tell why they do it that way, why you couldn't simply say, "Today you got an F," or "An A." So our home room teacher is the only one who can tell us what is what, and he does it in front of the class, big black book in hand, leaving me always for the end. Once in awhile when reading my grades, chemistry A, French A, Math A, he pauses for a second:

"What's that? An A- perhaps?" A worried look toward me.

"Oh no, I made a mistake, just a smudge."

Then he reads on and on all those boring grades of mine after having read tons of Ds and Fs. His mouth makes a funny pout when he says an A, sort of licking his lips as if he were eating an ice cream cone or something very nice. He likes saying an A so much, you can tell he likes the sound. No wonder the class looks at me with strange eyes. Svetlana is good too, but less perfect, I can say that. She can be surprised and not know her answer which never happens to me. I function like a perfect machine every day, ready, catch me if you can, it's almost a game. Nobody knows I play it but me.

Svetlana has gotten big all of a sudden, combs her eyebrows in front of the window glass, not embarrassed at all by this, and together with others gossips about boys, small miserable creatures of our own age, in short pants, cow licks, nothing to gossip about. I never do, with anyone, about anything much. *To talk against others is bad.* My slogan remains the same as when that guy in the Russian movie said to the Germans: "Shoot me if you wish, I won't betray anyone, we are not cowards." Actually, I have nothing, nobody to betray, but I wish I did, so I could say things like that in front of the firing squad. We were born too late, nothing was left for us. It all happened before. What bad luck. You can't be a hero in the middle of the forest, alone, or sitting here in class. Some generations are less lucky than others, some are heroic, others ordinary but it's not their fault. It's one thing I know I can't invent, or make it happen by working hard—history you make with others, united in the same thought.

Everyone is collecting pictures of movie stars, the present rage. They waste hours getting addresses from each other, always somewhere in Hollywood, writing the formula letters in English, asking for a picture of God knows who . . . Charles, Gary, Dean, James. They say, eyes rolling so you can see the whites: "Oh, I just *adore* Charles Boyer. Whom do you adore?" Very embarrassing question because if I say I adore nobody that immediately sets me apart, but how can you pursue a subject like that and not laugh. Adore! All my heroes are dead.

Or: "Don't you think Elizabeth Taylor is the most beautiful woman in the whole world?"

"Did you see her lashes?"

"Did you see her eyes?"

"If only I could be like that!"

"No," the other one, firm, "*I* adore Ava instead. Did you see her waist, and her legs?"

"You are both wrong," the third one now, "Maria Montez is the best."

They have forgotten me now, thank God, and who I adore. Then Sveltana rushes in with a picture of ten different stars, just their legs, nothing else, photographed like that, cut at the waist. She wants to know, it's urgent:

"Which ones are the most beautiful of all, which ones are like mine? Look at the calves, look at the ankles, and the thighs."

She lifts her dress up. It's all perfectly ridiculous since all the women in the foreign pictures have all these funny poses, one leg over the other, or one leg stretched holding the other one at the knee cap. Or kicking up both legs up in the air, often in dark silk stockings and high heels. None of the stars stand simply, legs apart, knee socks on the way we do, so what kind of comparison is that? I notice suddenly that the women in the picture have no hair on their legs but nobody questions that. Americans are like that, they have no hair.

Legs are the most important item; men look at legs first, says Sveltana, then eyes, then mouth. "If only I could have Silvana's mouth." She pouts in front of the window pretending she is a star from *Bitter Rice*. If a girl is just a bit pretty, she carries on like that with the exception of the peasant girls who continue to look the same.

Recess time is over, history next.

166

CHAPTER THIRTY-ONE

THE HISTORY PROFESSOR marched in carrying that large black book. He didn't say "good day," nothing at all, just sat in his chair, opened the book. In a bad mood today; it all spells bad mood; things don't look good. It means he will not lecture but will give an oral exam instead. The book is open; he glances toward us. The class whispers. He leafs through the big pages, each marked in different ink. The first row communicates the information to the rest. He says, "Shush." Where is he in the book, is he in the beginning or the middle? Nada, whose father died in '44, is in total panic, shivers, not prepared today, hopes he will pass over her until the next time so she can correct her F. He is on the R's now, they whisper. Her name starts with S, bad. She buries her head in her lap.

Others, those with names from A to R relax, he is already on S. Heads go up, the danger has passed. He'll call from S to Z.

He looks up, smiles with one corner just a bit, then zip, zap, changes his mind entirely and announces quietly:

"Alexic, in front of the class."

Nada relaxes now, lifts her head up.

"Miss Alexic, let's see what you can tell us today." He reflects.

He is on A's now but you never know where he might go next. They can call on you anytime they wish, your grade can change from A to C. You have to be prepared all the time, every day, know the entire year's course, not just what we did last week. Of course the written exam counts for half but that's only twice a year, not enough to change your grade if it is really bad.

"Why don't you tell us, Alexic, about the first uprising against the Turks and the life under Ottomans. You must know that."

(God, that's an easy one. Turks . . . our backwardness, small crumbly houses, small windows with bars, women hidden behind them, watching out . . veils . . . They kill us for no reason, take the kids away, the very small ones, mothers cut their sons' arms to make them less perfect, those that go and come back after many years in Turkey, the Janissaries, are the worst, the cruelest of all. They torture us by splitting a man in half, tied to horse's tails and torn apart, or impaled on a stick. One whole tower is built from our skulls, not far from here, only ten kilometers away. Then—we rose and fought and got killed *en masse,* five centuries of it, our backwardness, our under-development, they call it. Why didn't anyone help us then? Teacher said that before they came and enslaved us, our kings had silver spoons while the French ate with their fingers, and we even had the most democratic constitution for that time . . . we were all equal and peasant . . . The first uprising was led by a man with a black moustache who looks like St. George; they met under a large tree and planned how to strike the enemy . . . strike . . . strike . . . equal and united in their hate . . That's what I would say if called.)

"Yes, my dear, you are taking your time."

Mira Alexic throws frantic looks toward us, eyes asking for help.

"What are you waiting for? Why all this shyness, I saw you a minute earlier, you were chatting away or is it you talk better to boys?"

"Well . . . " Mira starts, " . . . it was against the Turks and, well . . ."

"Show us everything here on the map," he demands.

Teacher gets up and walks toward the window as if to give her more time. She unfolds the map. It's raining outside, November rain on the windows, tap, tap. The church from the First Uprising is right in front. I see it well and the fountain, and the priest now goes in, then an older woman in black.

The class whispers to Mira as soon as his back is turned to us. She starts all over again.

"The First Uprising was against the Turks . . ."

He, from profile, not bothering to look:

"And when was that?"

Mira rolls her eyes, makes a silent plea for dates.

The class sends messages with their fingers . . . 1 . . . 8 . . . 0 . . . 4

"1904."

"And then? . . ."

We are sending bits and pieces, she only deciphers a few things.

Class: "Dynasties."

Mira: "And dynasties. . ."

Class: "A pashalik . . . "

Mira, completely gone by now:

"They were against dynasties and pashaliks, that's what they were against . . . and . . . well . . . it happened in 1904 or so." He, the history teacher, looks as if he had eaten too many cherries.

"You make me ill, truly sick to death. How can you amount to anything, you cretins, if you don't care about your own history. Pashalik . . . dynasty . . . 1904 . . . pathetic. Alexic, back to your seat . . . You won't have to ask your homeroom teacher for this grade . . . zero for today . . . If I had a lower grade, I would give you that, and I see you didn't forget to curl your hair."

Mira does have pretty brown curls. Many girls are curling their hair, the only special thing permitted in class. No make-up, no jewelry unless your ears were pierced at birth. Mine were not. My dad wouldn't allow it.

He sits down again, looks toward us for another victim; Mira cries without a sound. I whisper to Senya what she ought to know just in case. She looks pale today, eyes red, might muddle it. Her arm has a bruise from a stick, right around the wrist. "Boinovic!"

A peasant girl in rubber shoes, probably wet, a thin girl who looks like a plucked chicken, stands up.

"Boinovic, tell us about the last offensive against the Germans. You had that last year."

Boinovic stands straight and recites without looking at anyone, hands clasped together, her voice a singsong, a bit like a priest.

" . . . And then the Comrade T with the Partisans liberated the whole country . . . we did it alone, nobody helped . . . "

She looks a bit like the photo of a peasant girl from my first grade book, the one who was hanged right on the square when the Germans arrived. Nobody mentions the Russians anymore, neither mother, nor others, not even me, much. Of course we did liberate ourselves but why tell us in the first grade that the Russians helped? Did they or didn't they, that is my question. Why can't things be certain?

Political hour is once a week, led by the same home room teacher who reads our grades in class and teaches drawing as well. He brings pots and pans, says, "Draw this." He is a tall, handsome man who always licks his lips in a special way, beautiful long fingers that can draw anything in a second. I never thought hands can be beautiful before seeing his—hands were always neuter, mouth, eyes, legs were considered pretty or not, but never fingers. He never gets angry at us, it would somehow take too much effort, distract from the general happiness he feels, shows in his eyes. Once a week, he teaches us about the system with questions like:

"How do you decide who'll sweep the floors in our Socialist system?"

"How do you decide who'll get paid more, who less?"

"Not everyone can be an engineer. Do you think that is fair?" This is not for a grade. You could say anything you wish, absolutely anything and still survive, he will never get angry, not him, yet there is always this deadly silence in class. Girls look toward the desks, twirl their hair, scribble, pretend to be reading their books. My turn, again.

"To each according to her needs . . ." That was from the second grade.

My answer pleases him, he repeats it twice, sort of caressing each word, licking his lips like a cat.

"According to the needs and capacity of the person, said Marx. Correct."

I come from what is referred to as a "reactionary background," rather than a "progressive" one like the heroes in my books. The teachers know this, know my mother and her mouth, yet there is never any mention of this in school, at least not in front of me. Mother was sort of surprised, expected me to have all sort of difficulties when her enemies took revenge. I was warned it would happen in gymnasium, should be prepared. When it didn't happen at all, she didn't know what to think.

Mother never understood how I could do well on "political line" or give the correct answers to questions about the revolution and such. She still didn't guess we were on different sides.

CHAPTER THIRTY-TWO

S UMMER RUSHED IN as always and the postman brought a package
with material for a blue dress; father's writing said, "A happy birthday, my pet." When we unwrap it all carefully, there is also a white
slip inside, the most beautiful one in the world, just like the movie
stars wear, and almost hidden, wrapped separately, one very small
bra that mother looks angrily at.

"He'll spoil you, that man, you don't need that yet. What have you
got to hold with a bra?" she says and snatches it from me, puts it
in the drawer, but promises not to sell it. The blue material will
become a dress when we take it to Desa, the seamstress, near the
river in one of those small houses on the left shore.

There they sit and sip coffee; I look for catalogues to find my dress.
I get to choose although they make suggestions about what is suitable,
what will last several seasons, always a large hem. She measures
me several times, comments as always on the length of my limbs,
"As long as mine," she adds, then cuts the material in front of us
on the floor, very fast, with firm sweeps. After that it will take a
long time. God, I hope by the end of the summer, I get to wear it
at least once.

There is a first fitting with pins, then the second one with most
parts sewn in, then we arrive again, drink coffee, and she hands over
a dress on thin tissue paper, glowing with pride. There it is! She

has even made a handkerchief out of blue scraps and blue ribbons for my braids.

"Turn around," she orders when I put it on.

"It's like sugar, isn't it?"

"It's like honey," mother agrees.

The dress reaches to, almost covers the knee, but not quite, a suitable length for my age. Little girls wear it shorter, way above; women's dresses cover their knees altogher; my age is in between, a tiny bit of knee showing through.

Desa has some good *paprikash* on the stove, we stay and eat, then go to the river, then I take a nap on her couch.

"Does she have it yet?" she asks mother, my eyes closed.

"No, not yet, soon. I didn't get it until eighteen, maybe she won't."

Her machine goes clippety-clap, bare feet on the pedal, clippety-clap. I will sleep some more, yes, I will.

When I wake up they are still talking, the blue dress is on the table, they both examine me very carefully. For what?

Wear the dress, go with Senya, see *Fernandel*, or maybe *Stagecoach*, yes, if we can get the tickets. There is no line for ours, all in black and white, all about the war and peasants.

"Fuck the war," mother says, "who wants to see more of it?" Instead, they like things like *Intermezzo*, or the one about the young composer with TB, whose blood fell all over the keys, or anything very sad so they can cry and say it was good.

We, Senya and I, go mostly for Indians, or Robin Hood or Fernandel or Chaplin. When they kiss on screen we laugh or whistle; there is an uproar in the front seats. It lasts as long as the kiss which seems to go on for a long time. I never saw anything like that in life, maybe they only do it like that on the screen, or in Hollywood that's how they kiss. In Russian films kisses were short. In this film, they look at each other first, slow, dumb, then their mouths open as if they wanted to bite. It doesn't look like a kiss to me. Everybody kisses around us, but you hear it, a loud smack on the cheek and it looks and sounds like a kiss. This other thing in American films is completely different. Senya and I discuss this when the film ends. She says her older sister who is sixteen has kissed already—a boy. She says not only do they open their mouths to kiss, but worse. He stuck out his tongue at her and shoved it in her mouth.

"Yuk," we both think at once.

"I would vomit," I admit.

"She didn't."

"Why didn't she slap his face?" a thing I am instructed to do if anybody comes near me. Mother said "If anybody touches you, or comes near you in any way, just slap him, the son of a bitch. That's what honest girls do. They'll have respect."

"Why didn't she slap him?" I insist.

"She didn't say why not," Senya says.

In my blue book, the one father left, there is nothing about kisses or kissing or how to kiss. They just describe different parts with medical words nobody knows. Nobody around me kisses in that special way. Stane and Slavka never, maybe Yanna would know but would she tell?

As we walk from the movie, dark already, no lights anywhere, when we turn toward my street, there, in the shadows by the acacia trees, we see them not now, but at other times, often, couples pressed against each other, only one person visible from here, a man, his back. A woman is against the wall, or a tree, you know she is there; you see one leg with a shoe, sometimes a bit of hair or one eye. You wouldn't recognize them in the daylight, it's so dark. Maybe it is someone we know, we think, separately, Senya and I.

These must be people that "walk together" as the term goes, maybe girls in the senior class, that's quite old, or the students from the university on vacation in their home town. Who knows who they are.

Time seems faster now, seasons hurry, speed, just rush past me. Something is pulling at me like a torrent. I wish grandma were here, she would know what to do. I wish she were. Everything is faster even the bugs and leaves. Bratso's games don't interest me as much, same goes for Vaso and Boris. I can't even stare as much at the trees. What is going on? The sun is too bright; my skin hurts, sounds are too sharp. What is happening to me? Can grandma see it? I don't even think much about her anymore. Where is her face? Where is my old voice? I don't count to five anymore. I am scared. If I can't remember who I was, then who am I?

Mother whispers with others as always. Her voice is far, I barely pay attention yet I am not thinking anything else, nothing at all. Am I sick? I must be.

"She didn't have a stitch of her own."

"You know what I mean."

"He chased her away, the other day."

"Really, he did?"

"He didn't!"

"What a disaster!"

"You can't be a virgin twice, that's for sure."

"She should have told him ahead of time."

"How could you, my dear, say a thing like that?"

"Just packed her up and returned her to her folks."

"Said to them she wasn't intact."

Slavka does her washing today, from the window I see her at the pump. Bratso runs in, face sweaty and red.

"Hurry, we are playing Tarzan, want to come?"

I don't really care, could just as well stay here, read or sleep instead. Maybe. Why not?

In the ravine, not far from the butcher's, they have hung ropes from two large trees, and they fly over the creek screaming, "Oh-aoha," pounding their chests, pretending they were the lords of the jungle, I bet. This game doesn't interest me much. I watch, lying in the grass. Far away a bird called "Tewa-tewa-twee." Another one answered, "Quonk-a-ree," then the hammering of a woodpecker. The butcher's wife opens the blinds; they go klank-plank against the wall. She shakes the sheets. Boris goes "Oh-aoha," over the creek and then plunges together with the rope, the branch into the creek. He is not hurt when he crawls up, but I know and he doesn't, he has lost his glass eye. It just fell out, maybe it wasn't properly attached. It, its place, looks awful, you want to scream, just skin where there should be an eye. I don't scream but look at him and he knows I guess because he runs down to look for it, we all do, nobody says a word. We look for it in the creek, among the pebbles and sand, it's hard to find, but we do; it was resting on a leaf. He couldn't put it on again or continue the game and he wore a black patch for awhile then again the same glass eye.

CHAPTER THIRTY-THREE

I WENT OFF to a camp in July, to a mountain village, two hours by truck. We sleep in a large gray building, one room for the girls, another one for boys at the end of the hall. Everything gets sprayed the first day for lice.

We did a show for the peasants with their costumes on, my part was a dance number from a film. When it rains, there is nothing to do the entire day. When sunny, we hike up the mountain, something that's supposed to improve your lungs. The last week I get ill and am sent home, just as well. The doctor examined me again—liver problems, he said, and prescribed mineral springs.

The train leaves at five in the morning, we are there at four, warned to pay attention, or else. At four, there is nobody on the second class benches except a peasant woman asleep with a basket of chickens by her side. As minutes pass, I doze off, then wake up. Hundreds are already here, locked behind the gate waiting for the train like us. Now it will happen, somebody screams, "Don't push." I hear it, it's arriving on the third track. "Pay attention," mother commands. "Watch out."

The crowd moves forward in a wave.

Mother holds Bratso's hand, looks upset; I have a suitcase in mine. The locomotive appears now, enveloped in bluish smoke. Beautiful, like on the screen. Two peasants jump over the fence, over the fence, run toward it. It hasn't stopped yet. A uniformed guard opens the gate, and everyone rushes out toward the train, some tripping and falling as they run. Mother holds my hand, I the suitcase, we run along.

At the entrance to the compartment, it's all blocked. Men and women elbow each other, kick, push, shove. The important thing is to get in somehow and we do. Now the train can move even if we have to stand.

The train starts, then stops again. A woman runs toward it with chickens in her hand, somebody pulls her up. Then a whistle, then we go. If there is nowhere to sit, you sit in the corridor. Even the WC is taken, a big woman sits there asleep, her piglet tied to the bowl. Nowhere to pee. Bratso doesn't care, he pees from the train standing up. Mother holds him from the back. I hope I don't have to, what then?

Someone passes the cheese, then a fried chicken leg to eat.

Women talk of operations, children's diseases, boring things.

Many tunnels all along, smoke enters the train, close the windows, kid, keep them shut; women worry about drafts.

Kids wave as we pass the river shore. We wave back. We stop, get out of the train, run with others to catch another train. Here we even have a seat, and there is nobody in the john. At the end of the day, a horse carriage takes us to the springs from the train station.

We are in a large hotel with red carpets, marked as a hotel of the B class. All of us have our own beds. Tomorrow we start the whole thing, the cure. First a doctor is assigned to my case, he prescribes the baths, and water, hot and cold, three times a day, plus a special diet.

We eat in the hotel with many different people. We know none. I have diet A which is less good than mother's; Bratso has N for normal meals. I get lots of cooked carrots, cooked fruit, nothing really good, no cakes or fresh fruit. When you look around you see waiters carrying different plates. Some people have no fruit, some no meat. That would kill Bratso, that's all he likes. Soon, in a day or so, you find out who has what, all stomach diseases of some sort. Some illnesses are vague like a "nervous stomach." Mine is a real one at least. He felt it, the liver was too large, swollen, he said.

Women also have problems connected with births. Births and pregnancies follow me even here. You can't escape it. Whenever women get together it's like that, even in the hotel of the B class. Of course, they change fast to newspaper topics, politics, as soon as a man appears.

Mother likes it here, never shouts at us, calls us "dear" or "sweet" in from of others; "My only treasures," she says. Her new friends at the hotel are all from the other times, "before the revolution" — God,, nobody says that except them. They say, "I was a major before the war," or "I was a deputy sub-director, financial *chinovnik*," or names like that. They say things to each other like: "Madame, you dropped your hankerchief," or "Thank you, sir, you are so kind."

One even kissed mother's hand once.

The entire town is like that, not a real town at all, just a make-believe one with villas and gardens, a very orderly river with linden trees around, more gardens and flowers, peonies, roses, geraniums, on my way to the fountain where I drink that water every day.

You have a breakfast first, nothing much, things like bread and jam, then you walk along the lindens and acacias to the spring, drink exactly a cup of bubbly water from the fountain full of coins that people throw in to make a wish, to get cured or who knows what.

After this, you sit in the sun for hours and watch the most unbelievable costumes pass by, wide skirts from the North, veils. By this time it's noon, you have lunch, very nicely separated portions of spinach, carrots, a very thin slice of chicken for me; Bratso has pork and rice.

Then comes the nap until two, get up and drink that horrible water — the hot one this time. It tastes, smells of eggs and sulfur all mixed up but is the only one that's doing you any good because the cold one doesn't taste bad.

We promenade a lot, it's good for your stomach. Everything is light-colored here. Even when it rains, the clouds lift up fast, the earth smells of linden trees and pollen. Bratso and I chase butterflies, mother watches or chats, then it's time for us to go to a pink building with a dome where we have baths.

A girl brought a glass jar full of sand, turned it upside down and said to get out when there is no sand left at the top. This is my very first bath of this kind if you discount the wooden tub, and I suppose I should be amazed or something, but I am not. I have seen baths like this in books, and new buildings have them on the Main Street. Mother always enters it with me even though she is not ill. They were not prescribed for her, just me.

She seems to delight in undressing in front of me, the very last thing I wish. "This is you," her breasts say to me, quite large, both of them. "This is you in time." She shows me her scars, on the breast where milk stopped at birth, and the large one on the stomach where the skin bunches up, her appendix cut. To make things worse, there are some hairs on me where it used to be all white. It wouldn't bother me if they were left there alone just for me to see. The fact that she sees those hairs in the bath is what makes it no good. She'll go and whisper to others about it, betray me to the one with the gold tooth. Everyone will know I have them, and before you know it the news will spread, boys will not play with me anymore.

Or worse—those women around coffee might think I am one of them and might include me in their talks. I want to stay outside of that talk. Women's talk, women's bodies, everything about them makes me ill. It would have been so much nicer had I been a boy, let's say a gypsy boy, tall, lean, fast.

There are some hairs under my armpit too. Good Lord, no way to stop it, there is no way even if I try.

Small silver bubbles gather around my stomach. Mother says those are the sick parts where the bubbles are. It makes no sense. How is the water to know where the sick parts are, which part is sick, which not? Better say nothing, she always has to be right and might snap back with, "What do you know, you came out of my ass, trying to sound more important than me, well, you are not." I say nothing, dry myself, we leave.

We photograph ourselves by the picture of the window overlooking the sea. The man says something to mother about me, they both look in my direction for awhile.

Two braids in front, blond, not too thin anymore, that's me!

Other people look at me from time to time as we pass, say things about me, to me, all weird. Mother thinks they are talking about Bratso, even gets frightened one day and confides in me.

"Look, over there, that strange couple, they've been eyeing him for over a week. Did you notice the way they stare?"

"Where? Which one? The one with the dog?"

"No, no, over there, by the rose bush, don't stare, it's impolite."

I look at the couple she whispers about; they don't seem strange. As a matter of fact, the woman has smiled at me several times already, even said to her husband:

"What a pretty child, look at her eyes."

Now, they are clearly talking about me, but I say nothing to mother about that. She thinks we better be careful, stay on our guard, they could steal Bratso from her. Some childless women are desperate, not everyone could have a boy.

"Stay close to me, " she orders Bratso, " and don't accept candy from anyone!"

Who would want to steal Bratso, you couldn't give him away for free, the kid that fights like mad, knees full of scrapes, nose bleeding, horses run over him. He spells trouble in general, not mean at all but clearly not as nice as me. She must see some of this or is she blind? They were looking at me every day and she never saw it! Who cares anyway, I think. I know they did it; it would be silly to insist.

After one whole month of bathing and drinking and eating the carrots, I am pronounced cured, but my liver will have to be checked every few months and the diet kept up.

When we got back, a letter from father said he is in America now, where she asked him to go, and he will do what he can to get us to New York. I realize that she has been plotting things without telling me anything at all. Now I know at least, but I also know that it will not happen. Our government will say, "No," the way they did for another woman who wanted to leave. I will have to write him, tell him to come back.

Toward the end of summer, Boris, Bratso and I found a dead baby in the creek. It was blue, not pink. It was just born when it died, mother said, and forbade us to play by the creek. Someone killed it, some unfortunate girl. She saw the marks around the neck. We buried the baby; it was left to us. We didn't really bury it. Boris put it in an old basket, then hung it on a tree to dry. He started crying for some reason when he came down.

"Indians did it like that, you remember when you read to us?"

Boris is growing up too. He must be. I have never seen him cry before for reasons that were not clear.

CHAPTER THIRTY-FOUR

"CAN YOU IMAGINE, he slapped them and took their clothes off."

"Right in the Park!"

"As naked as the day of their birth, hit them too."

Could it be true? I perk up. The man who lives not far away, someone that I have seen, he probably saw me as well, this man did horrible things during or after the war. He volunteered. Now, all those ghosts come to him at night, he can't sleep, howls, and worse. He gets up and roams in the woods, especially in the Park where the young couples are at night, amongst the trees, pressed against each other. He sneaks up behind them (he is very strong, was a butcher before), surprises them like that, and before they have time to know what's what, he tells them to undress, forcing them with a knife in his hand. Then he takes their clothes and leaves them naked in the woods.

"Sometimes they are undressed when he gets there, my dear," the gold tooth says.

"That's what he hates the most. Then he sees blood, blood-thirsty man."

"It serves them right," mother now.

"Come on, Mara, you were young too."

"Didn't go in any woods," mother answers. To me: "I don't want to catch you in the Park after dark, not even with Senya."

And the police, why don't they do something, I think.

The women, as if hearing my question:

"Nobody would touch him. He can do as he pleases. He's got all those medals for you know what."

"Who would testify against him, my dear. Would you say you were naked in the Park at night?"

"Nobody dares," Sara says.

"He won't bother an honest girl, I know that," mother concludes as if for me. They stop. I do the French verbs, memorize another Verlaine.

At school, same seat, same black dress. Biology hour, a large frog in a jar, snakes in jars, scary even though you know they can't bite. Then one day the professor came with a large black object, put it on the table with respect, and said, "Look at it carefully, don't touch! It's called a microscope." We all look at it from three feet away, then it gets whisked away to another class. We go back to jars, insects on cotton, prepare our own exhibits for the end of the year.

While waiting for the large gym to be built by the river (it will even have a swimming pool), we can only do two things in physical education, same as before—run around the Park when the weather is fine, or stay inside when it rains. We do headstands on the greasy floor that smells of tar. You do whatever you know best—bending back until you reach the floor, this is called the "bridge," or the "wheel" for which teacher moves the table to the side. I do splits, my specialty, perfect ones each time. To do all this, you wear ugly blue shorts with elastic all around the thighs. They are big, all puffed up, and make you look fat even if you aren't. Peasant girls cannot afford the shorts, so they do their number, their headstands, with dresses tucked in around long wool stockings so that nothing shows that way. But, this doesn't always work, the dress falls down and you see underpants full of holes. Svetlana wears a real pair of shorts gotten somewhere, short, white, a size too small. Her breasts point at us already, small pears. I still have none. Maybe it won't happen.

Math hour everyone fears; the nightmare of numbers every day. Senya stands now in front of the room, her little dog eyes asking for help.

"Square root of . . ."

182

For one small fraction of a second the teacher turns toward the window, looks at the rain. I whisper the answer, she relaxes, writes it down on the board. Good. He, the snake, turns around and to me:

"For you, Anna, zero for today." The class groans:

"Unfair."

"Silence, this will teach you to whisper. And that's not all. You'll have to give me a perfect answer every single time for the next five times if you want your grade back."

The contest starts for the next two months to see if he can catch me once. He likes this, smiles, turns to me all of a sudden when he thinks I am somewhere else, or when lecturing he stops abruptly:

"Anna, give me . . ."

I know it each time.

This kept us going for awhile, then nothing much happened all the way through the spring. Anca the gypsy came to class with a necklace and was sent home at once. Bratso's handwriting is getting worse since they tied his left arm to the chair. Now he can't write with either one, I do all his drawings at home because he can't draw a cow's waist, he says. For those he gets a good grade, but what if he has to do them one day at school, what then? I worry about it. Why won't they let him use his best hand?

Father never answered my letter that asked him to come back. Maybe it was never sent. Our government said NO, we can't go, mother can if she wants, but not us. I knew they would refuse. She has a lawyer now, will insist.

Slavka got another child. Her whole house smells of baby shit all over again even though she tries. Putana got married to a captain in the navy and went to live in one of those new apartments on the Main Street.

"Whores always fare the best, who'll pay me for my honesty?" mother said when she left.

CHAPTER THIRTY-FIVE

H E EXAMINED ME AGAIN, alone this time, I am big enough for that. Naked to the waist, he taps my back, says:

"Cough now."

"Again, again . . . say 33."

"Nothing wrong with the chest, all clear."

I lie down, he checks my stomach to see if the liver is swollen. I don't like this part, he'll see my hairs and say something the way he did the last time. He'll say:

"You are getting big, my pet," or something embarrassing like that.

He doesn't say anything, just smiles, gives me a kiss on the cheek.

He always does it the same way as when I was a small kid simply because he likes me or wished I were his. That would have been nice, I think; I wouldn't have minded that, that would have been fine. If he wanted to adopt me that would be good. What silly thoughts.

"You are doing fine, nothing wrong with you, dress."

He kisses me again, on the neck this time. His wife walks in with a big piece of cake for me and him to eat, then I run out and another patient comes in.

"You have to stop running around like that," mother says, referring to my underpants or the bathing suit. We were passing by the military barracks when they said something about "Her small tits,

184

too small yet." Mother called them names, "Sons of bitches," they made me feel ashamed for no reason at all. "It's too bad you have to cover up, the sun is good for the chest, fights TB but you have to have something on top." And she gave me a cotton scarf for the top.

I am sitting alone thinking what to do – go to the river before or after lunch. The sun comes through the windows, doors, Slavka sings and washes diapers at the pump. I reach for mother's mirror, the one she uses to powder her nose. My forehead is hurting; there must be a bruise there when I fell into a whole with Boris last night during hide and seek. Sure enough, there is a large blue mark just over the right eye. I see the bruise in the mirror, but I also see very blue eyes with small white flowers inside, long black lashes, pale pink skin. I see this girl smiling at me, quite pretty, white, even teeth.

Is that *me* really?

Is that what others see when I pass?

Why doesn't *she* think I am pretty? Because I really am. At least in the mirror I am.

I can't see all of me in the mirror, nor what others call my tits, barely visible things, no bigger than a nut. I wouldn't call those breasts. They are simply enlarged nipples, like everyone has, even Boris.

I put the powder puff back, look at my legs in the window glass, my image together with the trees that the mirror reflects. Yellow scarf, brown pants, long arms, barefoot. You don't need shoes until later when everybody promenades.

To get to the river, you cross the Main Street and the market, dust on your feet, then over the bridge to the left bank where the willows are. There you put your book in the shade; later, others will come for lunch. If you get there early, about ten, there is no one anywhere yet – the river is yours. First sit on the pebbles, warm yourself in the sun until you can't stand it anymore, then enter it slowly, water cold, transparent, a pale green shade, deeper green where the willows are. Swim around, or whatever else you call the splashing you do, still nobody here at eleven. Completely frozen, warm yourself in the sun on the pebbles, watch small lizards, ants, fall asleep.

Others appear, kids first, and Bratso, which means I'll no longer have any peace, will have to watch over him; mother worries a lot. "Make sure nobody hurts him, pushes him in the deep water." Her enemies could do things. He doesn't know how to swim. "It doesn't take much." When she finally shows up with stuffed peppers for lunch, I am relieved. She can watch over him now, I can be just like any other kid.

There are quite a few people now by noon, all in their usual spots. The river meanders, leaving pockets of pebbles and sand here and there, different spots to sun and swim. One whole section under the willows is called "the pensioner's beach." There, the very oldest sit, men with rheumatism, legs lost in the war, older women in black slips, whale-like. They sit mostly in the shade, drink coffee they fix right here, play cards, read a paper or two, discuss Truman and the Korean War. They must be the only ones paying attention to that distant war; it has nothing to do with us. We are on neither side even if at school they collect for the North. Nobody really cares; it's too far. The Russians are no longer fashionable, Americans aren't either; even though there is nothing but their films in town we are still not on the same side.

Further up, away from the willows in the clearing, some men are playing soccer in their bathing trunks, two small pieces of cloth held by the button on each side. Their muscles bulge as they kick the ball.

Older girls, swinging and swaying, walk near us on their way to the dam. A train has just passed. Younger girls swim in their underpants and a scarf or tie a string to the scarf and pretend it's a real bathing suit. Boys, like Bratso or older, have either underpants or the modern chic ones the older guys have, the ones that show their entire ass, even the crack.

Mother wears a suit of the thin material that was once her dress, three buttons on each side, and a bra. She is very white, whiter than me. With the peppers gone, she sleeps now in the shade, hair covered with a scarf. She always looks nice this way. I chase a fly from her face. I would like to kiss her but then she would wake up. I think about it, then change my mind.

A man is soaping his entire body, rinsing himself, doing it all over again. He puts his hand inside his trunks.

Boris dives from the wall, Bratso after him, legs apart, Svetlana next. She is the only girl that does this, the others are too afraid to lose their top. She is clearly an exception; she swears as well, says fuck, god damn. I find her unbearable now, her wiggly walk, her

186

bathing suit, the way she rolls her eyes at boys, the whole thing is too obvious, she has no shame, she even told the entire class the day she got IT, as if it concerned us. There she is, pretending to be Esther Williams, jumping from that wall, as if she had been swimming in an American pool all along.

"Goal!" the men shout from the clearing.

Mother wakes up, yawns. The conversation will start soon. Women, or all those called women, not the old ones by the willows, but women who are neither young nor old, actually anyone who is married and still puts lipstick on, they sit together in the same spot with mother and watch over the kids. They sit by the water, feet in, head in the shade and pour water on their breasts, find the water "delicious." God, how I hate that word. Some of them seem okay, their bodies firm, others have the most unusual formations on their legs, skin like orange peel, huge cheesy breasts. They say slowly: "Honey, soap my back," "There, good," "Stop."

Women talk forever, you can fall asleep, wake up, and it is as if they never stopped.

"Is he?" they say. "What a son of a bitch, with such a fine wife."

"Men are beasts." Mother knows.

"Look at those brutes there with the soccer balls, nothing but beasts."

I look at the men playing ball. Muscles. Fast. Hair. Beasts.

They say that so-and-so, nobody I know, is no longer innocent, got ruined this summer.

"Ruined her and now what?"

"Who'll want her this way?"

"What about the bastard?"

"Oh, no, he won't marry her either, they say."

"He doesn't want to marry a loose woman, I bet."

"Did you hear, Kosa's daughter got a real fine match. A doctor."

"From a good family, too, with connections, they had that even before the war."

"*There* is somebody with a good head," mother approves, "not like my poor Yanna who married for love."

"Young people are stupid, don't listen until it's too late."

"Love is like a stone."

"Try and eat it, you can't live on love."

"Yanna could have married anyone, a wealthy man, but what

can you do, you can't escape your fate."

Who got ruined?

How?

"Goal! Another goal!" the men shout.

It obviously happened during the time when the couples stand pressed against each other like the ones in the Park or when I walk home from a film. *What* got ruined? *How* are you different from then on? My book that has pictures of women in Java doesn't say anything about that. There is no mention of that word in the book. I did look it up. Can *men* be ruined?

Nobody says, "She ruined him and left him." *Why not?*

Mother chases Boris away; he has been sleeping by my side.

"He was looking under her scarf. Did you see that? Men . . ." she says to the gold tooth.

He was only sleeping, the way he always does. Boris and I slept together at five. He's like a small pup, my wordless friend. Why pick on him, accuse him of things, make him ashamed? Adults are funny, they lie and lie. I try my best to make things fit, but nothing does.

Trees, flowers seem to have a pattern, after winter the spring, flowers bloom and die then get born again. With us it's all different. Nothing fits. My future, or what they call "future" is somewhere far, over the hills, it has no shape. It's like color or smell. It has no end.

What shall I do later, what will I be? These questions occur all the time, everyone asks. Obviously, I'll finish high school and not stop at grade eight. That is for students with C's. I will go on, but what next? Why is time running faster now, faster than when I was nine? Who can tell me that?

Svetlana knows already that she'll be a doctor.

"I could be a doctor, how about that?" I say.

"Your health is not good enough, on call all the time, all those hours. Svetlana is tough, you are not."

She mixes up things even further by adding: "When you marry . . ." or "You should know how to cook, who'll cook when you are married?"

None of this applies to me, but who can argue with her. I give up. *Keep silent, glide through.* Still, the question of that future profession remains. So far things didn't turn out well – failed as a partisan, it was too late, failed as a dancer, too late for that even though they say I have this gift, still . . . maybe a doctor . . . if I get tough enough . . . or maybe an actress, not in the theater but film. Theater is out, too much banging and hammering between the acts. How can you imagine anything good if you see them working there with hammer and nails . . . And always the same actors, no matter what they do. The big-nosed guy who played *Hajduk Veljko* against the Turks two months ago is doing *All My Sons* now, sounds just the same as before. He comes to buy ties from us. How can you imagine anything if you know too much?

Actresses from the theater wear more make-up than anyone else, that's why the expression "to be painted up like an actress." The pudgy one from *All My Sons* comes to buy some butterfly stockings or "Anything interesting," she says and giggles. This woman with blond hair in sausage-like curls is full of small gestures that make you think of small dogs, poodles perhaps. "That's what the ladies from big fashionable cities are like," mother says with respect. (Her own gestures are large, direct, nice.) If actresses are like this one, I am obviously not fit for the part. It's the wrong profession for me. And to be perfectly honest, I can't imagine myself standing there in front of all those people blushing like mad. It wouldn't work. Actually, when I say I think of being an actress I don't really mean performing in front of others at all. What I really like is the story part on film when picture and music go together so well as the actors walk in the park, or beach, in any season, in color. I wish I could get inside that screen. There, everything has a purpose, fits; the music in the background helps with the important parts. How can you know what to do if nothing fits well? There is no music in life.

Today on the street, something in me whispers:

This walk, right now from the river, dust on your feet is not like any other, never will be. This day is the only one like this. Look, listen!

Is that my old voice coming back to me? It has stopped for awhile. Is it grandma speaking to me? I am alone on the street; it's July. The street curves at the corner, houses are on the right, linden trees on the left, a peasant cart is far away, the smell of bread and linden in the air, Boris in front of his steps. The church clock struck five.

Something sharp catches me, holds me by the throat, something brand new; it has no name really, but resembles sad music. Am I getting ill? "Boris, oh, Boris, I'm getting ill," I scream past him and run home.

Chapter Thirty-six

I N AMERICA, the happy land without any wars, the land of gold, mother's father worked in the silver mines for a long time. This is all new. She never said anything about that before. If only he had stayed on, she would have been born there as well, wouldn't have suffered at all; he had a plan to bring everyone there, five kids, her unborn. Then, an accident happened in the mines and they were going to cut his leg off in the hospital, but the night before he had a dream that told him what to do:

"Escape from the hospital," the dream said. "Leave America, go home, bathe your leg with the water from the holy spring three mountains away and your leg will be saved."

And that's what he did. He left America, did everything according to the voice and his leg was well again.

Women cross themselves, drink coffee, get ready to cry.

He never went back. It wouldn't have been right. With money earned in the mines he built a beautiful house, made it himself; he was good with his hands. Italians destroyed it in '44 together with all the documents and pictures that she could remember him by. Of course she remembers him enough in her head.

"He had large shoulders, big moustache, what a chest." And of course he liked her the best, because he always said:

"I have three daughters and this child, my best." If only fate didn't turn the wrong way, she would have been in America from the start, would have never married father in that town. Who forced her? Did anyone? Why do they argue? Why does she cry and argue with Yanna about things I know nothing about? There is so much blood and horror where they come from. Nobody tells me. Yanna knows but wouldn't tell. Those are their secrets, nobody knows but they. The two of them argue all the time, their stories clash, that's why they argue so much, trying to convince each other that such-and-such didn't happen. Each swears on their children's head that she is right; it did happen.

"How you lie, disturb his poor soul for nothing."

"He was a snake," Yanna insists. The same story which never becomes clear.

"You'll leave me all alone when you go there," Yanna cries, pregnant again.

"If only you had married a decent man, instead of that crook." Mother floats on her special cloud since America might happen after all. Something else to make her enemies jealous with, when she departs and leaves this shitty town for good. Onward to America! You'd think she is already there. Women discuss how in America one lives so well, that even if you get killed there in the army as a regular soldier, your whole family gets new clothes, a flag, a silver watch, and a pile of gold.

"I'm telling you, that's the place to be, not here in this hole."

"What about me? I'll have nobody left," Yanna cries, my poor aunt.

What about *me?* Nobody asks me anything at all, just another year gets going along with September rain.

A Mexican film came with Dolores del Rio, called *Malkerida*, or *Poorly Loved*, about a mother and a stepfather who fell in love with her daughter; he got killed, the daughter went to the convent. The song in the film is very beautiful, sad; it catches on for some reason and everywhere you turn someone is humming this forbidden love. The girl who is forever pressed against the military barracks and not married yet, starts looking like the star of the film, hair, eyes, everything; she is clearly the most important woman in town.

Anytime she passes by, people turn to look:

"God, she *does* look like her."

Then *Gilda* arrived a month later and this girl stopped being as important since her hair was very dark; she went back to the barracks. With *Gilda*, all the women went wild over the haircut from the film: one side is cut so it falls over the eye, hides part of the face, makes them look like a star. This style is called "free and loose" because you don't need any combs or pins to keep it in place. Mother disapproves for health reasons.

"They'll go blind pulling it off the eye."

"Devil got in their pants."

All the bigger girls get one however, and when you see them on the Main Street at night, they are always moving that hair with one fast head jerk.

"Just like the bunch of mares," mother's opinion of the new hair style. She doesn't approve of the new fashions in sleeves which show the armpit and hair.

"What next?"

I want to tell her that these are American fashions, not ours; she ought to be happy, she should like it; America is her favorite place. Of course in the American films women have no hair in the armpit, and those sleeves are more suited to them.

There is more lipstick on the street, worn by university students on vacation or women with kids. For us it would be an F for bad behavior if caught, either in school or on the street. However, in class, girls bite their lips to produce an effect, Svetlana does it all the time, licks them too in front of the window glass. They tighten their belts over our black uniform to make their waist look small, so tiny you wonder if they can breathe at all. Our new biology teacher lectures one whole hour on the belts:

"Girls, it will ruin your bodies, make pregnancies hard, it's silly and stupid, women's garments should be comfortable and loose."

Everybody listens politely but they ignore it the next day.

What does she know, a big dumpy woman with gray hair. This is the latest fashion, straight from the films and a tight belt is the only thing allowed in school. A tiny waist is important, small red mouth, white teeth. Hair and eyes are still supposed to be jet black, but because of the American films blonds are okay too even though it is not our national look. I am noticed.

Svetlana has larger hips, most girls seem to be changing for the worst—getting to look the way their mothers look. This is called "well developed," hips and stuff. I am almost the same as before and hope to remain.

At school, more French nouns, more chemistry without chemicals, just books and formulas, professor says this is not the way it's supposed to be but we do what we can; the next generation will have better luck. In history, uprisings continue one after another, kings killing kings over crowns, marriages to form alliances with foreign countries—too many kings, queens, killings, and dates as if it made any difference that it occurred in 1887 instead of '86.

The October revolution was the best, total change, a new world, red, but that was long ago in grade school. We never studied October again. We seem to be going backwards and were meant to advance. People, girls, nobody cares about the color red as much anymore, if you want to wear blue you can. Speeches have disappeared from the square, or they seem official, sort of like holy days. There is no dancing or singing as before or bonfires. Even the word revolution before or after or during you don't hear anymore. The word is pale pink, or beige.

"Who goes there," the voice screams in the darkness, in the book.

"Nous, les proletaires," Gavroche answered.

Wrong, I am getting it all confused. This is from *Les Miserables* for the French class, not from *October Is Red*. He doesn't say *"proletaires,"* but *"la commune"* in there. It's not the same.

We are going back and back. History is really not interesting at all now, maybe it never was. Maybe I got confused. I understood it to mean something else, events that can happen in your time. You make them happen. You see the change with your eyes. History for me was in the present.

In biology, we study all about flowers, collect them, press them in books to make an exhibit for the end of the year. Pistil and pollen, how insects carry it, deposit it, then it travels inside. Some plants are male and female, something I didn't know, it seems better that way, or you have to depend on the wind or bees to make it happen. *I remember all of a sudden* from the grammar school: in Siberia, they were going to change some things so that oranges could grow in the snow. I wonder if they made it by now? Nobody talks or thinks about Russia anymore, just me trying to make things fit and because I am stubborn—a new way to describe myself to me.

The class giggles about anything, pollen or pistils; even when two butterflies meet on the window sill it is enough to disrupt the class.

"What is the matter with you, girls, where are your heads?" teacher asks with a smile.

We finish the course with the fertilization of eggs. An egg in color looks like a large sun. Titters in class everywhere. What's the big deal, I think, just an egg.

Nobody pays attention, girls look out the window, stare, get together with their best friends, whisper a lot.

I don't think hard either when solving the math problems, my old books don't help much, words just float over the page. When Bratso and Boris want me to read about Indians I have no desire left; it seems too far. Nothing is near, not even the bugs or branches.

Some have IT clearly, but nobody admits it except Svetlana; she was the first. Senya must have it as well, but she doesn't say yes. I discovered IT one morning when I woke up, and knew what it was, but then thought, "If only I keep silent about it nobody will know." I took the sheet to wash it at the pump, but there was no way to hide it, it grew worse each day; she found out, then took me aside and demonstrated how to do it with the string and rags she had already prepared.

She looks at me with anger and pride as she shows how. I know how, I have seen her do it so many times, in front of me. I wish she would go away, stop talking about it, leave me alone.

This must be the end, the worst. Maybe you can't escape your fate. I thought I could.

Everybody will know about it, all the kids and Boris; how can I play with them and not die of shame? They'll make fun of me, I'll never again be a friend.

The women celebrate IT with coffee in the kitchen and look at me in a new way. You're one of us, the gold tooth seems to say. Well, I AM NOT, not in my head, that part is still me even if the body betrayed. She shouldn't have told them; it makes it worse. Everybody must know about it for sure, they are probably discussing me left and right as they see me rinse those god-awful rags, hang them to dry.

Is this why the female is cursed, something they repeat every day?

She even wrote to father about it, worst of all. Why am I not just my own? Will the boys laugh?

I test Boris and the others one day. They play the same, couldn't care less, say "Pass the ball, hit it with your head." I don't seem different in any way. Maybe it'll pass, it only happened twice. I hit the ball, score the goal with my head.

"You better stop playing with the gang like a boy. Women are making fun of me, you are the only girl on the street," she says.

And: "It wouldn't hurt you to learn how to cook, you know."

"The doctor said I don't have to, remember?"

"You better stop playing with the boys. I don't want to be laughed at."

I play hide and seek still, once in awhile, but soccer doesn't seem right anymore, not if you have to be thinking about IT and mother and the women watching me play.

Chapter Thirty-seven

"DIDNT I TELL YOU this morning you'll get something," Sara said, proud. "I saw it in the cup, didn't I?"

We didn't know what to make out of it in the beginning. "Bathing suits for Bratso and you," father said in the letter. There were two items, a pair of yellow pants with mesh inside, very delicate. Mine was this scratchy thing in many colors, no bigger than a glove, pretty, yes, but clearly the wrong size. "I thought he knew I was getting big!" I think, disappointed, but don't give up and go in the bedroom to see if anything could be done. It stretches like an accordion. I put one leg in, then the other; it fits. How strange since it's no bigger than a glove.

I walk out for everybody to see this new bathing suit that makes my waist very very small, stretches softly across the hips.

"Mother, look please. Don't I look like Esther Williams, look, don't you think I do look like her?"

I simply look wonderful, can see myself in the window glass, then run upstairs to see myself in the landlady's big mirror. Marvelous!

"Watch your step," mother only says. "If you stop looking like a child now, at your age, later, when the time for marriage arrives, they'll say, "Why, she has been grown up for a long time, she must be old.'"

"I'm not . . ."

"Just watch your step." But she lets me wear it instead of selling it since it was sent for me.

The yellow bathing suit is a problem; we can't figure it out. Women examine it carefully, and all of them decide that father made a mistake: pale yellow is not a male color, the fine mesh inside is too delicate for a boy to wear. And besides, it doesn't look like a bathing suit at all — it's too big, all the way down his thigh; boy's suits are tiny, show the entire buttock. He made a mistake and sent shorts for me, "These are girl's shorts."

At the river bank, general commotion about my new suit. Girls cross over from different sides to touch it, to see. Svetlana makes a nasty comment:

"It's easy to look good and have a small waist in a bathing suit like that," as if the suit hid me entirely.

I wonder if Senya is jealous too. I look at her. She says nothing, swims fast in her underpants and scarf.

Afterwards, the suit travels around. Women take it home, copy it fast, think of ways to imitate the elastic.

Mother said, "I don't understand why he sent you that, to you, you have nothing, no breasts or hips. He should've sent me one instead."

CHAPTER THIRTY-EIGHT

"GET US SOME COLD BEER on the way back. It's only a step away. Wait, here is the pitcher. God, is it hot. Wait, put on some clean clothes."

I have to have another check-up before school starts. In my yellow shorts and a yellow blouse from America I wait in the lobby with a sad-faced peasant. The pitcher is embarrassing; it's too big to hide. This will go fast, one more person. The peasant blows his nose, goes in.

I stare at the pictures on the wall when the doctor's wife walks through, dressed to go out. "I have some good cake in the kitchen, go get it, it's on the blue plate." She closes the door.

I come back with the plate, eat while waiting for the peasant to leave, then my turn comes. I go in with the plate and the glass pitcher for beer.

"I am so tired of everything," he says washing his hands. "I am tired of disease."

"And you, my pet, how are you?" He always says "my pet," or once in a while, "my dove." He kisses me on the cheek, a new timidity is in me, worse.

"You have a cake mustache," he laughs, wipes it from my mouth.

"Go undress, you know what to do."

"Do I have to?" I don't want to.

"How else can I examine you?" he says, his eyes very black.

I put the pitcher on the floor, unbutton my blouse, he listens to my chest as always.

"You are growing fast," he says. "All tanned, rosebud, you are." I feel cold for some reason, put my hands around myself. He kisses the back of my neck. Well, so what? He always does that!

I don't like the way he lowers my pants to inspect the hair, more of it every day. He always does this when we are alone. With mother there he only winks at me and I wink back. He says with a wink, "You are my friend, I am on your side, no matter what she says."

Now, he does the same thing as he dances around me, tapping here and there, stopping to kiss my shoulder, my back, my chest. He always does that. It is neither pleasant nor unpleasant, sort of strange. It tickles.

"We are almost done," he says. "Now move over here," pointing to the usual place, his medical bed. I lie on the bed, he examines my stomach.

"Your liver is fine," he tells me. "We got you over the hill."

His hands on my stomach feel sweaty, warm.

"You were a very sickly little girl, but no more," he whispers. "You turned into a rosebud."

Well, I might as well get up, I think, the cold leather is under me. He is at the foot of the bed now, touches my foot all of a sudden. I look up: he is standing by the bed, his pants unzipped, the bluish thing, like a horse's, is pointed at me. He has a shirt on. I can't see his face hidden by the shadow of the blinds.

Am I frightened, what do I feel, do I know?

"Danger," the voice in me screams.

"Run!"

Is it grandma warning me, or is it me? I grab the blouse and the shorts, put them on fast, already at the door. He is zipped up now, but I can't see his face.

"I better go now," I say, polite, normal. The doorknob is behind my back. (Why do I feel sorry for him all of a sudden, why do I pretend that nothing happened?)

"Mother will worry about me," I say. "I better go now . . . and Bratso should see you about his knee."

"My rosebud," he says, his face trembling a bit. I pick up the pitcher from the floor.

"So long, see you later," I say, all composed. He says nothing, slides in the chair. I close the door, pitcher in my hand.

The street is luminous like in a dream. It's summer, late afternoon, August. Something is different on the street, and in me. It has no name. It's like music in back of me or the blood rushing in my head.

When I get back they are talking about vampires and how to kill them forever; you have to pierce the heart with yew wood, but the blood from the heart can't touch you at all, or you'll become one too when you die.

"You can't let the butterfly escape from the heart either," mother says. "You have to catch this butterfly, that's the vampire, they are always gray."

"Mother, please, come to the bedroom." My legs are shaking, now, can't make them stop.

"He tried."

"Tried what? What are you talking about?"

"He . . . tried . . . to . . . ruin me, I think."

"Shh, who tried . . . don't shout so loud."

"He . . . the doctor . . ."

"Doctor, your doctor?"

I nod.

"You're mad. That man has seen every woman, every girl in town. Nobody ever said such a thing, never. Why would he pick on you with all the women around, his own one is good."

"Mother . . . he did . . . please."

"You are inventing things. Better stop that."

"I am not. He di . . ."

"He saved your life so many times and Bratso's, gave you medicine when I worked . . . You should be ashamed of yourself telling stories against a man like that. Ungrateful!"

"Mother . . ."

"I don't want to hear another word, you hear, an honest man like that."

"He did try . . . I'm not . . ."

"What happened to the beer, did you get some?"

I point to the empty pitcher. She makes a face, says, "You better go back," then slams the door. The vampire stories go on. They are laughing hard now. Pain is in my head. I am alone in the room, light from the window falls on the bed. It is late afternoon, August, a bug lands on my hand.

YOU HATE HER, the voice says.

YES, I HATE HER, YES, I DO. It's not the voice. It's me. Me and the voice are the same.

I hate her more than him. For him, only regret that he betrayed me; he was a friend. You shouldn't do that.

What do I want her, wish her to do? Do I know?

Yes, I do know what, it's not that hard. I want her to hold me tight, very tight, to cry over me, with me, tell me it is okay, that I am all in one piece, to stroke my hair, to love me, but she does not.

"Je te deteste," I say to her, pick up the pitcher, walk toward the inn to get the beer. It is something I have never said to anybody yet. I must be getting brave or grown-up, but my legs still shake a bit.

A month went by. In biology the teacher took the frog out of the jar and we started to cut it up when Senya passed out from the smell. She put the frog back and drew diagrams on the board. Mother went to the capital alone for two days. Bratso got a red ball from father and became very popular with all the boys. I wrote another magnificent composition, this one on the river and the train, called "Summer Light."

Whenever I met him — it only happened twice — both of us looked down and walked on. Then he was gone suddenly, and another doctor replaced him, a very different man who only talked to grown-ups.

CHAPTER THIRTY-NINE

I N OCTOBER I am just sitting in the Park thinking about nothing in particular when this tall blond man runs up to me, sort of throws a piece of paper in my lap, a tiny piece folded many times. He just breathes "From a friend of mine," and then disappears as fast as he arrived. Two girls are there on the bench, can't read the note here, go read it in the john.

"I want to know you better. Saw you at the beach this summer many times. Love, D."

That's all. I go inside the class casually as if nothing had happened but those two from the Park have done it already, spread the news. Anca snatches the note from my pocket as two others hold me, then reads it in front of the class . . . making fun of each word. This is the first love letter in class. Everybody is surprised that it should be me, shy and all. Svetlana asks, "Are you sure it was sent to you? Maybe it's a mistake." Everyone wonders who this D. is. We examine all the Danilos and Dragans around us but find nobody suitable. We think about it, I think too, then we forget it. Maybe it was a prank, the most likely thing.

Senya and I go out to the Main Street just about every night, then run back at ten. She meets me by the barracks and we proceed down, dressed in our best. She has stopped looking funny, has grown velvet-like, still silent which suits me fine. The whole town is there when we appear at eight – older girls in nylons, hair still cut free and easy, walking arm in arm on one side, men walking on the other, swinging their shoulders, hair all slicked back. Some men stand in front of the pharmacy, hands in their pockets, and comment loudly on eyes, legs, hips. Older people, or married couples just sit in front of the hotel where the music plays, and drink.

So here we are, two of us arm in arm walking up and down, from the old school to the small park, toward the new photo store and where the new buildings are. Then back again, the same way.

"Who is that man?" Senya asks, interested all of a sudden. He is good-looking, well-dressed. "He looks like a college student to me," I answer, thinking about the capital and what it would be like to be there. "Oh, ah, student life," everybody sighs.

Nothing but mystery in the capital. Dances, lights, adventure, love. "She had so many adventures there, many," they say of certain college girls. Even Mr. Rudin, who gave me an F for whispering awhile back, even he softens up suddenly if you say to him:

"Mr. Rudin, come on, we have had enough math, why don't you tell us about your student days?"

Or: "Mr. Rudin, tell us about the capital, do tell, *please.*"

He doesn't do it right away, we have to beg. Svetlana does, knowing his weakness for her and that he won't refuse if she rolls her big eyes. His own grow misty, he lights up a cigarette, smooths his hair back, looks through the window, in profile like Boyer himself, then he goes, is gone – out of the classroom, somewhere on that bridge on the Danube where he met her one foggy night, mist in the air . . . She was unbelievably beautiful and was dressed in black, he stresses that.

"Was she in mourning?"

"No, no you don't have to be in mourning to wear black. Things are different in the capital . . . but you wouldn't know that . . ."

"And then?"

He saw her on that bridge night after night even when it rained and when the snow started to fall, she still came. They talked about everything that mattered – Chopin, Dostoevsky, Mayakovsky, Blok, then one night when he came as usual, she was not there. Gone off somewhere . . . where he didn't know . . . he had no address

address . . . the capital is big . . . you can get lost.

"She found somebody else, you talked too much," Anca screams trying to be funny.

He thought of killing himself in the Danube after that. He hints at that, says, "I felt like . . ."

"It was too deep," we scream to tease him, it's permitted.

"Cheer up!"

". . . but came to your miserable town instead . . . which amounts to the same thing, as if I had jumped . . . What do you know about life?" he concludes. "What a fool I am, telling you all this."

Then suddenly: "Alexic to the board. Find me the square root of . . ."

The mystery is out there, you can find it, if careful. Right now, it is mostly around the Main Street, up and down, in the faces of others that we search for a clue. Senya and I walk, look; blue pleated skirts on both of us, a pink sweater on me; she has a white one. Knee socks, knees showing a bit.

Her sister passes us with someone. They are going together, it's official; we would be too young for that, maybe later at fifteen or sixteen. We are fourteen and a half.

Rade says, "Hello," dressed in his long pants. He never found out about the dog; at times I am tempted to tell.

Bratso is out there with all the boys his age, little wasps yelling at couples, asking for spare change. Mother always sends him along, but we split up as soon as we get to the Main Street, thank heaven. What would Senya and I do with him around?

Svetlana, with two other girls, belt tightened to burst, barely breathing, just gallops by, excited to the hilt about something tonight. She slugs me on the arm as she passes, says, "Kiddo," as if we were friends. Ljuba, a real beauty, I think, limps along with another girl, always together, those two, her best friend. We could have become friends but didn't. She only trusts that other girl, older than her, three grades up.

Up and down.

The gypsy band in front of the hotel has just started playing "*Dark Eyes*," their usual number, when this man materializes in front of me like a ghost and says:

"I am David."

("David who?" I to myself.)

"I sent you that note with a friend. He gave it to you, right?"

Where is Senya all of a sudden? She has gone, disappeared in a split second; it's the rule we know by heart: if a man comes over to talk to you when you are promenading with another girl, she has to leave. Still, it seems silly. She shouldn't have abandoned me now even if it is the rule.

I search for her with my eyes, then, not knowing what else to do, we, me and this man, start walking in the middle of the crowd.

I still don't know what he looks like, only see his shirt.

Senya floats by through the haze, Svetlana and Boris stare. I think it's them. The math teacher smiles in a sad, mysterious way. His eyes tell me, "You are not a child anymore, this is it, it is starting."

"You know you look like Grace Kelly," he says as we turn toward the photo shop.

"I don't know her."

"An American actress. She played in *High Noon*. Did you see it?"

"No, I don't see those."

"What do you like then?"

"Oh, cowboy films." I say the first thing that comes to my mind. "Or detective ones with murders." I say it even though it's not true anymore. I can watch other films too where they kiss and all, but for some reason I want to sound tough, boy-like. And to say "cowboy, detective," is good for that. That's what Bratso likes. I don't want him to think that I am one of those silly girls that pine and swoon over movie stars, write to them. I am tough.

More courageous now, I look at him for the first time. He is tall, dark, a man-boy with very green, gold eyes, a bit like a gypsy. He smiles now:

"We could go and see a detective film together then."

"If mother says yes."

I have no idea how long we walk up and down. His eyes produce the strangest effect on my stomach, like sledding from the hill. Bratso runs up to me, says it's almost ten, we better run.

At school, the next day, it's as expected. Anca demonstrates how we walked together. She takes my jacket, parades with it across the floor, kissing the sleeve as she dances.

"What beautiful eyes, my dear," she tells the jacket, drops it on the floor, kissing it like a fool. "What a mouth, what eyes, what hair."

The math teacher arrives in the middle of this dance and says to no one:

"This class promenades a lot, it certainly does. I wonder if there's any time left for math?"

The class roars, excited to a peak.

I have barely put my books down, taken off the black dress, when she looks at me with hatred, slaps me very hard. It's so sudden, so unexpected, I fall. She has stopped beating me, what is this?

"Devil's blood, you have been out with a man!"

Is that all? Did Bratso tell her? He signals, "No," with his head.

"I just walked a couple of times on the Main Street with a boy. That's all."

"For everyone to see, I bet, for my enemies to rejoice!"

"Why is it bad? Should I walk in the Park?"

"Shut up, devil's blood," she slaps me again, hard. I don't fall this time, prepared.

"Mother, what did I do wrong? I did nothing wrong."

Soon the council arrives, the gold tooth and her Marko, mother's friends. She gives them brandy, they joke for awhile about this and that, then they start on me, all three of them at once, sort of finishing each other's thoughts. They saw me as I walked, they say, nothing wrong in that, but there are many horrors ahead if I start seeing boys so young.

"Your grades will suffer."

"And her future," Marko says.

"What next?"

They are here for my own good; David is older than me, three whole years; he can take advantage of a child. Before you know it, he'll ruin me, then leave. Their words pass through me, nothing stays. They are all wrong. *I will see him, she can slap me if she wants.*

And I do. Nothing happened to my grades, happy to report. I am not sure however that I see him because I like him or because he likes me. In any case, he is shy, quiet, a bit like me. We don't "go together," that's for older girls, but I see him on the street by accident usually, we stop to talk, or after class. Actually, I do all the talking, he stares at me, smiles, his eyes really beautiful deep deep green.

This winter I am no longer on the sled with Bratso, that was left behind for the younger kids. We go far up in the mountains by the Turkish ruins, all the way up with a bobsled, one person on the brakes, one on the wheel, six of us pressed against each other we descend, danger on the curves, watch out not to hit the horse carriage, swirl fast to the side. We lose Senya on the curve once, then all of us fall in the big drift by the roadside, snow to my waist. Everyone laughs, wet. David cleans my face with his handkerchief, laughs, looks at me. It feels good. I feel really good, entirely fine, all in one piece somehow, there is no bad feeling anywhere in me. My time has come. Maybe this is it. Is this their fate or something else, I wonder, not knowing for sure.

We celebrate the New Year at school for the first time, everyone together—Senya, Anca, students from the upper grades, even some professors are here; Rudin smiles a lot and whistles a tune. A band, half gypsy, half students plays the latest American tunes. Big girls with a touch of lipstick here and there swing their hips to a rhumba.

"When I kissed you for the last time, the cherry trees were in full bloom."

"Cherry Blossom White," a rhumba, everybody's favorite. I have never done this before, never been to a real dance. We are permitted now being old enough. But how do you do this? I have never danced *with* anyone. What if someone asks me and I don't know how? I'll just die. Senya says: "Just do two steps to the right, two the left, the rest is easy, see like this, listen to the drum." She shows me on the side.

It's not hard at all. I dance with a tall boy with pimples, two to the right, then to the left, concentrating on my feet. Most girls are dancing with older guys. Our own bunch, the ones we knew from the first grade on, seem pathetically small and not mysterious at all. Boris watches me dance, looking hurt somehow.

I spot David in the corner as I dance with this pimply guy. I wonder why he is not talking to me, what is wrong? When the rhumba stops he tells me that my mother wrote to him, and to his parents as well.

Told him, warned him to stop "messing around" with me, that I am too young, and if not, she'll use her own methods to make him stop. He doesn't know what to do, what would be right.

After that, we just stand there without saying much and I don't dance anymore.

The church clock struck twelve. The lights go off, everyone shouts then another number starts. Bratso and I go home together, the streets are all ice. I shiver, get under the sheets, see that he is covered. Mother is not here, will be late. She is celebrating with grown-ups in a restaurant that just opened up. The window has bluish light, patterns of ice on the glass. Bratso is asleep already; his breathing even, soft, one round chapped hand on the pillow. Why am I crying now, I wonder. Why do I feel so sad? Something terrible will happen to me, something I cannot stop.

"Why are you crying?" Bratso says, opening one eye.

"I'll protect you next year, I will," he says and turns to the other side.

Chapter Forty

B Y TRAIN to the capital it takes the whole night. Then, after much walking we are in a tall building with large cars in front. Mother knows what to do, they know her, us, our last name. They tell us to go to another office where a man sits in a tall chair with a large hawk in bronze behind his back. He is very pink, no hair at all, face like a baby sort of. He points in my direction and says something horrible while smiling a lot. The woman next to him translates:

"He says you have a pretty daughter, Mrs. Stefan."

"Yes, I do," says mother, "and a son too, right here. Nothing but these two. They are my only treasures. You know, dear madame, you tell him that I suffered like a dog to raise them well . . . Thank God, we will go to your happy land now, get reunited with their father. My time has come finally. You tell him also that my father was there too and . . ."

The woman goes on and on in English. The guy smiles. Mother thinks they are interested in her. He is only polite. Behind him, almost over his head, there is a photo of another bald guy, next to that hawk. American women behind the typewriters have pink faces with lipstick and glasses. Nobody has glasses in my entire school. Even old men have hair. This must be a strange country, I think, watching that guy open his mouth, show his teeth. He smiles and smiles as if something were funny.

No, I don't want to go there. I don't care about father anymore. I used to long ago in grammar school. Now, he is less clear. He can come back if he wants us together. I don't want to go there. Mother speaks loudly as if to herself.

"I am going there for these two, not myself. Bratso needs a man to get him in shape."

The woman examines Bratso as if he were a dog. It's not fair. Nobody asks me anything. I am like a book or a package.

An American doctor examines us around four. We have not had anything to eat yet, but mother is happy.

"See, they don't want any sick people in their country, they are right, they know what to do, smart."

We have to be perfect to get in, she insists. If you have a single bad tooth, they make you fix it, or pull it out, she was told. Mine are perfect and Bratso's too, thank God. This man comments on our perfect teeth, says, "No chocolate, no candy."

Lungs are checked next, very carefully, then stomach, eyes, many blood tests. Even our heads are measured for size. I wonder why. Are we getting hats?

Back to the embassy, main building, tired, hungry. This is a political question, the woman standing next to that bald guy tells mother. *This* one she ought to pass, I think.

"Has anyone in your family been a member of or a sympathizer with . . ." (What a stupid question to ask in a country that just had a revolution. Of course we have.) They ask me nothing. Mother answers proudly, "No, never," for three of us.

At home, she is triumphant. America here she comes! She tells over and over what happened at the embassy, and what they said and what she said and how they examine you carefully, even measure your head, how they said what fine children she had. "I can hardly wait to leave this dump, my time is here."

Everyone seems jealous of our departure. It's uncertain when, maybe in May or in June. Bratso is ready to go, anywhere is good for him, he says. Yanna cries and cries. Her stomach is big already, still married to the crook. Grandpa arrives for a day and cries as well. I have never seen him cry. Mother forgives him for something, I don't know what.

Panic hits at school as Senya and others prepare for the big exam, the first *bac* is coming up in June. If you don't pass it, that's it: you go to the trade school. The rest continue, not many, toward the twelfth grade and another *bac*. Everyone panics. Voices are shrill. They have stopped promenading. Not many months left. The exam is hard—everything you have learned until now in all the subjects, any question can come up. Any date in history, not only ours but Roman and Greek too.

I give them my own very perfect notes, underlined in red ink, and relax completely, stop studying for good. Why bother, we shall leave in May anyway even though May seems still far. Can it be stopped, all of it, or is this what mother calls fate? She says you can't escape it no matter how hard you try. I could if I were not a kid. Fate applies only to children and people who are very poor or sick, I decide.

Nobody pays attention to me anymore. In the kitchen, she screams with joy over coffee. At school, they are memorizing the dates. I sit for hours and think nothing at all. Time sits still. Then, I see David again on the street and we start seeing each other again. Nobody cares now. There are no more slaps. We go to the circus, funny mirrors make us laugh, we go to movies together, even up and down on the Main Street at night.

One night, he walks me home from the promenade. I have always gone with Bratso before but now he is already in bed. It must be eleven o'clock. The street is dark except for a few houselights and the stars.

"Are you really going away?" he asks.

"In May, she thinks."

"Then I'll see you when I get back. Do you want anything from the coast?"

His whole class is going to the sea. I can't wish for anything now.

"Bring me some shells, okay?"

I see his eyes in the darkness. Can he see mine? We are very close but do not touch. That would be another, more serious step, I think, if he touched my hand. Something runs through me, some sort of current never felt before. It's everywhere, my head, my chest, my limbs. It has no name really, I have to find so many new words for all these things. Can he see me tremble? I hope not. What would he think? He only says goodnight, then leaves, disappears by the barracks. I want him to kiss me, to hold me, but do not know that's what I want.

CHAPTER FORTY-ONE

W HEN THE DEPARTURE COMES it's like in those films we saw and never believed it happened that way and you say, "It's only a film, it doesn't happen in life." A telegram from the capital said — "All clear, get ready to leave in a week. The boat sails from France."

I try reaching David for three days. He is somewhere on the coast, but they move every day. I give up.

I run to say good-bye to grandma — pluck a few weeds, stand there hoping to cry but can't. A whole army of ants travels across her name carrying a spider. Her picture in a white blouse looks at me. A woman dressed in black is hitting her chest, falling to the ground. That's on another grave. I see no gypsies this time.

I forget to take with me anything that matters, no notebooks, no books with the teacher's dedication for excellent grades, nothing of mine. I don't know what I did with David's note . . . I leave the doll under glass, still pretty, untouched for Yanna's daughter, the bathing suit for Senya, she must have wanted it a lot. We take some clothes and pictures, two suitcases in all. Everything else remains, all the lace curtains with funny patterns, pillows with roses that mother made as a girl, the icon with the patron saint, Jesus in the glass jar given to grandma by the sailor she loved.

The suitcases are ready, we walk out into the courtyard. On the street, others join us, everyone. It's sunny, warm, the end of April.

The mud has dried. Yanna walks with us at the head of the procession, her stomach big, her face patchy from pregnancy and crying. Sara and Boris join us at the point where the street curves. Then we move on. Senya waits in front of the military barracks with soldiers peering out. She takes my arm; we walk down. The whole class is waiting on the Main Street together with the math professor and the teacher of drawing who gave us political education once a week. They stand in front of the new store. David's friend is here as well, the one that gave me that note.

I am here and not here. I see the beginning of the procession and the end. I see me. *Look, listen, don't forget,* the voice in me shouts.

We walk down the Main Street, past the photo store, past the gymnasium, a sharp turn across the bridge, toward the railroad station.

"There is still time," I think. RUN. Nowhere to run. We are there. Trapped by the station.

Yanna cries some more. Boris starts a tune on his harmonica and everybody weeps some more. Even the railroad men are crying. I can't. I think—it's not fair that I have to leave, nobody asked me. It's not fair. Where is David? I was so happy, finally. My time had just about come. Nobody kissed me yet. I kissed no one. It should've happened here, in this town. I never went across that bridge to the dam. That was supposed to be next year.

Nobody leaves like this unless they die.

The train arrives fast, people rush to get seats. David's friend is with me inside the train, but he can't talk. He is crying too. Why are my eyes so dry.

One minute left. I look at him next to me and at Boris still playing a tune so there would be music in the background the way I always wished, Senya only a blur among the others on the platform. I turn to the boy next to me, him still sobbing, and kiss him hard so it hurts my mouth. Better him for the first time than some stranger in a strange country. He holds me briefly and jumps out. He didn't have time to kiss me back.

Then the whistle went, very sharp, killing every other sound including the tune Boris still played, then a tunnel appeared and it was over. We had left the town behind.

"Have something to eat," she says, tearing off a chicken leg.

I shook my head. What is wrong with her, how can she expect me to eat?

"Go on, you'll need it," she insists. "America is far."

I looked at her now, wanting to scream. Suddenly I saw: her face was tired, worn, no longer young; one large tear stood in the corner of her eye. I watched it get bigger, explode, then slide down her cheek, then another one formed and more and more came gushing from both of her eyes. Why is her sadness worse than anybody's, worse than mine, isn't she supposed to be tough? I said, "Don't, mama, don't, please." "Come sit near me," she said, "my big one, my blond one, my pretty one," and hugged me until my ribs cracked.

Whatever happens, she'll always be strong, I decided, because soon she wiped the tears with her sleeve, bit into the chicken thigh, laughed her big laugh again, and began telling stories about America as if she had been there before. Gorgeous houses, she said, with palm trees, bathrooms bigger than our kitchen. There, nobody is ever poor or sick, swimming pools in your backyard, there the wars never happen, they always make it happen somewhere else — and of course there'll be beautiful clothes for me, fortune and fame for both of her kids. She was young again, beautiful, glowing all pink, she was doing all this to have our destiny fulfilled, not hers, she said, for us.

The wheels squealed, the train rocked, Bratso slept already; soon she was asleep too. In the corridor someone sang. Through the windows carts and horses and people rushed and disappeared with the telegraph poles. The sun shimmered for awhile in the tree tops then it set bright red.

215

Nadja Tesich was born in Yugoslavia, educated in the United States and France in various fields—French Literature, Russian, mime, dance, film. She has worked in different areas of the film world—as an actress briefly, a technician, and a writer/director of her own works. She is presently an Associate Professor of Film at Brooklyn College, having also taught French Literature at Rutgers.

Ms. Tesich started writing eight years ago with a play, *After the Revolution*, and has been writing plays, screenplays, fiction since then. *Shadow Partisan* is her first novel.